A Hector Miguel Navarro Novel

From the first sentence, I was intrigued. After the first chapter, I was hooked. Hector Miguel Navarro—the Anti-Gang Enforcement Unit's new hire—took me on a tumultuous ride through New Liberty, Arizona's drug and crime-ridden streets. George Cramer is well-versed in law enforcement and gives us an insider's view that doesn't sugar-coat the violence and danger.

~Julie A. Royce, author of *Pilz* and *Traveling Michigan's Thumb*

New Liberty tells the nail-biting story of Police Officer Hector Miguel Navarro. Navarro must learn to navigate the dangerous, gang-riddled streets of suburban Phoenix and work effectively within the complex bureaucracy and relationships of the New Liberty Police Department. He makes mistakes, and he must learn from them or get out. He has doubts, and he must conquer them to stay strong. He wants to protect the vulnerable, and that's a tall order given the violent gang-bangers his unit goes up against. You'll find Navarro's journey captivating in this deeply authentic police procedural.

~Victoria Weisfeld, author of award-winning short stories and the crime novel, *Architect of Courage.*

George Cramer's police procedural novel, *New Liberty*, is the first in a new series and introduces young police officer Hector Miguel Navarro as he learns the ropes in a new gang task force unit. Along the way, he finds a dash of romance, struggles with duplicitous department brass, a questionable, PTSD-affected partner, and encounters a lot of really bad dudes. The prose is crisp, and the plot unfolds at an unrelenting pace with immediacy and a movie-like quality. This one has it all: a good mix of intriguing characters that leap off the page, plenty of complexities, and great action scenes. They all coalesce to make this one hard to put down.

~Michael A. Black, author of the Trackdown series, most recently *Devil's Vendetta, Devil's Breed,* and *Devil's Reckoning.*

The town of New Liberty, Arizona, is a dangerous place. In his latest novel *New Liberty*, author George Cramer has created a world where drugs and gangs have infiltrated a once-peaceful and orderly community, leaving behind a scarred landscape riddled with damaged lives. Cramer's protagonist, Hector Miguel Navarro, is a likable, multi-layered cop who manages to maintain both decency and hope amidst a cruel and unforgiving microverse, a world that takes an often devastating toll on its inhabitants. Navarro is on a mission to not only change the trajectory of crime that's become lodged here but to eradicate the evil that saturates the desert sands. With a solid cast of characters of good guys, bad guys, and those who fall somewhere in the middle, *New Liberty* is a riveting glimpse into a world that may seem beyond redemption. Still, it carries an unquenchable thread of hope that goodness will always be powerful enough to prevail. A good, well-researched read that will leave you eagerly anticipating the next book in the series.

~Debra Bokur, award-winning author of *The Dark Paradise Mystery series*.

In his new fiction book, *New Liberty*, George Cramer has written a gritty story that takes the reader to the seedier side of criminal gangs that prey on the citizens of the city and the New Liberty Anti-Gang Enforcement officers dedicated and determined to end their criminal empire. Once you start this book, don't plan on putting it down until the last page has been read. The tension is high, the pace is fast, and the characters are well-developed and believable. The author has managed to place the reader inside the story with his skillful writing style. I thoroughly enjoyed this book, and I promise you will, too.

~John Schembra, award-winning author of the *Vince Torelli San Francisco Homicide Detective Series*.

NEW LIBERTY

A Hector Miguel Navarro Novel

GEORGE CRAMER

A Russian Hill Press Book
United States • United Kingdom • Australia

RHP Russian Hill Press

The publisher is not responsible for websites or their content that are not owned by the publisher.

ISBN: 978-1-7378246-8-8 (softcover)
ISBN: 978-1-7378246-9-5 (eBook)
Library of Congress Control Number: 2023904376

Cover Design: Tatiana Villa, Villa Design

For the Officers of the San Leandro,
California Police Department

Past—Present—Future

"And I looked, and behold, a pale horse! And its rider's name was Death, and Hades followed him. And they were given authority . . . to kill with sword and with famine and with pestilence and by wild beasts of the earth." Rev. 6:8

1

THEY WERE ALIVE moments ago.

"I told you to use the GPS. Why'd you buy a Lexus if you aren't going to use the gadgets?" The old woman chides her even older husband.

"The map program takes too long. Besides, the boy's graduation isn't until tomorrow."

"I know, but we're not even in Phoenix. We should have been there an hour ago. Admit it. We're lost."

"Okay. I'll pull over and set the GPS. Will that make you happy?" The man was tired from the long drive. Even breaking the drive into two days from Oakland to the Arizona city was more than he should have undertaken at seventy. His wife had suggested they spend a few days in Los Angeles, maybe even visit Disneyland, but the old man had insisted. She had been right. *I should have skipped poker with the boys this time.*

"Now we're lost, exhausted, and you finally agree with me. That doesn't help much." She was younger by a decade and had offered to help with the driving. The old man was always stubborn and refused to give up the wheel. "This neighborhood looks pretty sketchy. I don't think we should stop here?"

"We'll be fine. Besides, there's no one around."

A minute later, absorbed in entering the address in the GPS, it's difficult for the old man with his arthritic hands and new trifocals. Hearing a banging on his side window, and without thinking, he hits the down switch.

"Hey, old brother, whatcha doing?" Standing next to the car door is a skinny kid, fifteen or sixteen. It's hard to see his face. He's wearing a dark hoodie with the front cinched down. His hands are jammed deep into the pockets.

"I'm checking my map. We'll be going."

"I don't think so," the kid says as his right hand appears. He's holding a small pistol, barely visible in his large hand.

"He's got a gun," screams the woman.

2

"That's right, Bro. You and the sister get out and walk away."

The man may be in his seventies, but he's not about to let a teenage punk rob him. Reaching to put the car in gear, he says, "No."

The old man doesn't hear the shot or feel the twenty-five-caliber bullet that passes through his skull and into his brain. The small lead slug comes to rest against the right side of his skull, ending his life. His wife screams as another teenager opens the passenger door and drags her out of the car. Drawing her head back exposes her neck. She sees the Ka-Bar. The blade, dull and heavy, is meant for work, not slicing throats. As the boy saws her neck open, cutting the carotid arteries, blood gurgles until she is dead.

"Don't get blood on the seat,"

"That's why I pulled her out. What about the old dude?"

"He didn't bleed much."

Now that they have killed the old couple, they aren't sure whether to run or take the Lexus. Their problem worsens when three men emerge from Ernesto's Pool Hall.

"What're you doing?" demands Jerome. "Geronimo" Dixon. The easily recognized president of the 4-Aces. Even at fifty, he is an

3

imposing figure towering over the men behind him. The man stands six feet five and carries three-hundred pounds—no fat—packed on a muscular frame.

The frightened shooter's answer is a whisper, almost apologetic. "We jacked them for the Lexus. The old man gave us shit. We had to off him and the old lady."

"Who the hell gave you permission to jack a car in 4-Aces territory?"

"No one, we didn't . . ."

"Shut up and gimme the piece. What else you got?"

The boy hands over the small pistol and the other gives up the K-Bar, "All we got."

Geronimo turns to one of the men standing behind him. "Get DeShawn."

Within minutes, DeShawn "The Knife" Galloway is at his side—Geronimo motions for the young killers to stand behind the Lexus. Out of earshot, he hands their weapons to Galloway. "This's going to bring a load of shit our way. Make the idiots disappear."

"Forever?"

"Forever." The tone of Geronimo's voice leaves no doubt.

"The old couple?"

"I ought to. If they weren't innocent civilians, I would." Geronimo lets out a sigh. "Leave them.

"Don't nobody touch da bodies, nothing. No DNA to tie the Aces to this shit."

Galloway calls the other men over and tells the first, "You drive. We gotta clean this up." To the second, "Put the fools in my Escalade. You ride with me."

Showing false bravado, the shooter speaks up. "Why?" Stepping close to Galloway, he looks down at the much older and shorter man and repeats, "Why?" adding, "I ain't no fool, old man."

Galloway raises his head and gazes into the face of the shooter. His expression is as lifeless as his eyes. The shooter does his best to maintain a defiant pose and succeeds for perhaps three seconds. His body begins to shake. The shivers betray the boy's fear; without another word, he walks to the Escalade and death.

2

SIX MONTHS EARLIER: Sergeant Robert Toliver, slim, compact, and appearing much younger than his age, completed a tour in patrol and returned to the Anti-Gang Enforcement Unit. AGE had been his wish for years. Before his promotion to sergeant seven years prior, he'd been an officer in the unit. Officer Steve Kowalski welcomed him with a handshake followed by a back-slapping man-hug. "Sergeant Toliver, welcome home.

"Thanks, Steve. It's great to be back. If you can sit your ass down, we'll get this show on the road."

"Absolutely, Sergeant Toliver, Sir." Kowalski stepped back and threw a snappy salute. Some might think his behavior disrespectful. They'd be wrong; the two men are closer than brothers.

Officer Steve Kowalski and Sergeant Robert 'Bob' Toliver's friendship goes back many years. Their history includes ten years with the New Liberty Police Department, starting the police academy together, and serving in the United States Army Reserves. Both serve with the Phoenix Area Criminal Investigation Command. During the Gulf War, Kowalski received a promotion to Warrant Officer. He was given command of their reserve unit before being called to active duty and deployed to Saudi Arabia for a year in Afghanistan. They half expect to be called up for another deployment.

Bob Toliver, and his lieutenant, Jack Delacroix, receive an afternoon summons to the Investigations Commander, Captain Mary Windsor's office, for the following day. The invitation had come via her administrative aide, Sergeant Paul Morales. The first call had been to Delacroix.

"Lieutenant Delacroix here. How may I help you?"

"Good afternoon, Lieutenant, Sergeant Morales here. I'm calling for Captain Windsor."

"Hi, Paul. What's going on?"

"Sir, Captain Windsor wants you to join her for a meeting tomorrow morning. Can you be here at oh-eight-hundred hours?"

"Yes. Is there anything I need to prepare?"

"No, sir, she wants to discuss an anti-gang program the Chief wishes to implement."

"Thanks. Tell the captain I'll be there."

Morales's next call was to Bob. "Toliver here. How may I help you?"

"Bob, Paul Morales. Queen Mary wants you at her office at eight a.m. tomorrow. Be there."

"Can you tell me why?"

"All I can tell you is the Chief has something in mind for AGE."

The line is dead before Toliver can ask another question.

Tall, statuesque, with coal-black hair, Captain Mary Windsor is often referred to—affectionately—as "Queen Mary." It's no accident. She has much in common with Queen Elizabeth II. Mary Windsor was born in London, England, on the Queen's birthday, April 21, fifty years ago. Her father, a Chief Inspector in the Metropolitan Police, died in 1986. Mary, then a Police Constable, was in an unhappy marriage to a sergeant, and her mother long since gone, had nothing to hold her in London. Divorcing her husband, she dropped his name and migrated to the United States, settling in Arizona. An experienced police officer, Windsor was among the first women hired by the New Liberty Police Department. Having worked unarmed on the mean streets of London, she had no problem holding her own in New Liberty. Her reputation as a streetwise cop grew. Windsor held up her end in every situation, earning respect, often grudgingly, of the rank-and-file. In command of the investigation division, many believe she'll be named Deputy Chief of Operations if the current D.C. ever retires.

Monday, July 8, zero-eight hundred hours, the city is a sweltering 110 degrees. Lieutenant Jack Delacroix and Sergeant Robert Toliver wait in Captain Mary Windsor's conference room buried deep within the bowels of the grimy fifty-year-old police administration building. The ancient building's air conditioning needs a long-overdue replacement. The heat is stifling. Delacroix, wearing a suit and tie, suffers the most, his white dress shirt soaked with sweat.

Wearing a lightweight polo shirt over tan chinos, Toliver is less bothered but feels prickly. Visitors often say, "at least it's a dry heat." Dry heat or not, the Arizona natives are uncomfortable. Arriving for the meeting fifteen minutes early, Bob isn't surprised to see Lieutenant Delacroix waiting. Now twenty minutes past the hour, both wonder what the captain has in mind.

Sergeant Paul Morales enters the conference room with news, "We had a double homicide outside Ernesto's Pool Hall this morning. A couple stopped for some reason. Their car was gone—probably a carjacking gone bad. The captain dropped in at the scene for a visit."

"Ernesto's is the 4-Aces hangout. Are they involved?" Toliver asks.

"Doubtless. Captain Windsor went because the media and the overzealous community activists at the Brotherhood of Mankind Church will turn the killings into a publicity nightmare for the department."

"As hot as the weather is, the violence will increase," Lieutenant Delacroix says.

"Have you guys seen the five-day forecast?" Morales asks. "If we're lucky, it might drop to a hundred on Saturday."

"It'll be back into the teens on Monday." Delacroix wipes his sweaty forehead. "Barbeque killings are going to skyrocket. We're lucky we don't work homicide."

Toliver adds, "Amen to that. A steak on the grill, a cold beer in hand, you'd think it would calm people down. It doesn't. The whole family or crew gets together, a few too many brewskis, and the old grudges come out. I heard the uniforms in District 9 have a pool going for how many will be killed this weekend. The last I heard, the smart money's on District 11 with three down by first Mass on Sunday."

"That's a good bet," Delacroix continues, "they had better hope the Chief doesn't hear. If he does, heads will roll."

Jack dozes. Toliver counts the holes in the old fiber ceiling tiles, wondering if they contain asbestos. *Damn, this is a miserable room.*

At eight-thirty, Delacroix asks Morales, "Do you think the captain will need to reschedule?"

"She called from the Chief's office. She asked that you wait another fifteen minutes. She wants to get this done today."

"I can wait. Bob?"

"No problem, L.T. I'm free until this evening. The D-Backs are playing the Dodgers. Kowalski and I have seats behind home plate."

"Thanks. Paul, can you tell us anything?"

"Sorry. The Chief had her in his office all yesterday afternoon. When she came out, the captain told me to have you here this morning. That's all I have. I'll put on a fresh pot of coffee and send out for pastries."

Toliver turns to Delacroix, "I hope the Chief doesn't expect much from my unit. We're stretched to the max. I should have twice the number of officers and another sergeant."

"We'll have to wait to see what the captain has in mind. As for personnel assignments, you're right. You know what the unit needs. She's given me the green light to submit a request for two more officers."

"What are the odds of us getting them?"

Captain Windsor arrives, cutting off Delacroix's answer. As the officers stand to attention, she raises a hand, "Sorry for the delay. Please sit. The shit has hit the fan. I had to brief the Chief."

"Yes, Ma'am."

"Is it safe to assume it's gang-related?" Delacroix asks with a slight shrug.

"Not sure. Nobody's foolish enough to pull something like this without paying tribute to the 4-Aces. I want you down there as soon as we finish. Bob, bring in four of your people—now! Tell Paul who you want. He'll call for you. Get them working the neighborhood and talking to their snitches." As Toliver stands, she adds, "Jim Collins is on the scene with his homicide detectives."

"Paul, please call Steve Kowalski, tell him to pick three officers, and get out to Ernesto's."

Captain Windsor tells Delacroix, "Jack,

you're not going to like what we have in mind. Sergeant Toliver's going to like it even less. I need your support on this." Before she finishes, Toliver returns.

"I have the entire unit on the way to Ernesto's."

"Thanks, Bob. The Chief has an idea for a new program. It's a good one, but I'm not sure we have the resources to make it happen." Jack looks like he is going to interrupt his captain.

"Please hold your comments, especially your objections, until I finish."

"Yes, Ma'am."

"The Chief has experience with gangs. At the Los Angeles FBI Field Office, he supervised a joint LAPD-FBI Gang Task Force and authored his doctoral thesis on the subject."

Sergeant Toliver groans. *This can't be good for AGE. Why does the brass always think they know best?*

"Bob, what age group's most susceptible to gang recruitment?"

"Middle school kids from eleven to fourteen. That's where we see the heaviest recruitment."

"Exactly. The Chief wants to begin a program in the city's middle schools."

Taken by surprise, Delacroix says, "Excuse me, Captain."

"Yes, Lieutenant." Her use of the formal lieutenant rank signals that she didn't appreciate the interruption.

"It can wait."

"Good. The Chief wants experienced anti-gang officers to visit every middle school monthly, if not more often. Well, Lieutenant, what'd you have to say?"

"Isn't that what the SROs are doing?"

"Yes. The School Resource Officers have advanced training in dealing with students. They play a vital role. The problem is they're not Anti-Gang experienced. Bob's people are. I'm not here to debate the issue. The Chief's orders are to begin immediately."

"My God, Captain, I can barely operate with the limited resources I have. You're asking me to give up officers for what will surely be a full-time assignment."

"Sergeant Toliver, I'm not asking. This is an order. I expect you to have a plan in place within three weeks. Do you understand?"

"Yes, Ma'am."

"Bob, I know how hard-pressed you are, and this is an enormous undertaking. We need a plan that will allow for anti-gang presentations at each middle school. Once the plan is in place, be ready to go one week later."

Delacroix asks, "Can we use the SROs to help with scheduling?"

"You can use them however you like as long as Anti-Gang Officers make the presentations. Any other questions?" Neither the lieutenant nor his sergeant has any—at least none they care to voice—at the moment.

"If your plan meets with the Chief's approval, Bob will get two more officers in three weeks."

Walking to their cars, Toliver says, "It looks like she's preoccupied.

"Yeah. Mary's got a lot on her plate. I hope this latest round of killings doesn't interfere with her chances at the Deputy Chief's slot—if he ever retires. Queen Mary would be the best Deputy Chief we've had in twenty years."

3

SERGEANT TOLIVER COMPLETES his plan in less than a week and tells his lieutenant, "Jack, if you approve the plan, I'd like to interview candidates next week."

"That makes sense. But where are we on the two dead civilians at Ernesto's? I don't want Jim Collins' wrath coming down on my shoulders."

"While I've been working on the Chief's plan, Kowalski has the unit devoted to Collins's every request."

"Thanks. Tell me about the plan."

After giving Jack a down-and-dirty overview, Toliver turns to his lieutenant for questions or comments. He has none.

"As soon as I sign my approval, I'll walk it up to Windsor, and then it goes to the deputy chief. The process usually takes weeks, but I imagine this will go much faster."

"Please ask her if I can post the openings so I can start the replacement selection process."

"Let me look this over first. I'll get back to you."

An hour later, Jack Delacroix's back in his sergeant's office. "I like it, especially having the SROs arrange and schedule the presentations. But I have a couple of suggestions. I'll hand Windsor an Operational Order for the chief to sign. The SRO supervisors will have no choice but to comply. They won't be happy, even though it's the right thing to do.

"I'm listening."

After a few editorial changes, Toliver gives the proposal to Delacroix, who takes it to Captain Windsor. Returning three hours later, he tells Toliver how his pitch fared. "After Captain Windsor signed off on the plan and the Operations Order, she called the deputy chief, who told her to send me straight to the chief's office for his signature."

"She didn't waste any time."

"No, she didn't. The Chief said to tell you it's an excellent plan and signed off with no changes. To make his intention clear to the SRO Management Team, he signed the Op Order himself."

"Wow. That was quick action. If the Chief wants something done, it gets done."

"It did this time. About your new officers."

"I have two guys in mind."

"It's not happening the way you want."

"What are you saying?"

"Not sure if the captain or the Chief made the call, but the decision's made. Starting Monday, Officers Hector Navarro and Ben Harris are on your team."

"What the hell's going on, Jack? That's not how it's done." Sergeant Toliver's face reddens. "As the unit supervisor, I'm allowed a say in who works for me."

"That's normally the case—not this time. The decision's final. We have to live with it."

"Can I at least talk to the Chief?"

"I'm sorry, Bob, but no. I already complained to him and the captain. Neither Navarro nor Harris has experience outside patrol."

"So why are they being forced on me?"

"They're good officers with excellent records, and both are high on the sergeants' list. The brass wants them to get investigative and independent initiative experience ahead of their promotions. Your request coincides with the necessity to get them the needed experience."

"Damn it. It's not right."

"No, Sergeant Toliver, it isn't. You will give these men a fair shot. Am I understood?"

"Yes, sir. I understand. I'll treat them as if I picked them myself."

"Thanks, Bob. I knew I could count on you. I'm no happier than you."

"How long will I have them?"

"Unless he steps on his dick, Navarro will be promoted in six months. Harris's one behind John Riley, and you can't forget Kowalski. You could lose them all in less than a year."

4

IT'S ALMOST OH-six-hundred hours, and Police Officer Hector Miguel Navarro has difficulty keeping his eyes open. Sunrise is the worst time of the shift for him. He has trouble staying awake with two hours remaining before turning his patrol vehicle over to the day shift. He hears the slight static buzz that always proceeds the dispatcher. It shouldn't be, but this cruiser is, without a doubt, the oldest in the fleet, and many things have long since quit working—like the heater-air conditioner. When the transmission comes, the call is for Navarro; he's to report immediately to the watch commander's office. His first thought was, "What did I screw up." The young officer acknowledges the call and heads to the precinct office. Several click-clicks on the radio from his brother and sister officers tells him they also believe he must have screwed up something.

At the station, Officer Navarro leaves his gear in the vehicle. He'll have to go back out on the street.

Hector's district commander and sergeant smile and tell him to grab a seat. *Maybe it's not an ass-chewing.* The sergeant tells him not to worry; they have good news.

"Did my request for transfer to Traffic and motors come through? Am I going to be riding?"

"No, Navarro, you're not going to motors. The results of the sergeant's exam will be posted tomorrow. You did well for someone with five years on the job. You placed third on a list of twenty."

Navarro shows his excitement with a broad smile, and "that's great news. I thought I screwed up the Assessment Center part of the exam." While deep inside, he has one regret—*Now I won't get a transfer to the Traffic Division and will never get into motors.*

"Quite the contrary, you did well. The brass thinks you need experience outside District Eight. Tomorrow's your last day here. Monday, you report to AGE."

"AGE?"

"Anti-Gang-Enforcement, street gangs.

Bob Toliver's the sergeant. Here's his number. Call him tomorrow. He'll tell you when and where to report."

"Why street gangs? Why not motors?"

"No idea. You'll learn much more in Anti-Gang than you would riding a motorcycle around like a leather god."

Both officers laugh, and the lieutenant adds, "It's a good assignment. You'll learn about the city's underbelly. District Eight is like Disneyland compared to the rest of New Liberty. Across the river, it's a war zone. Being Mexican will be an asset."

"Funny," Hector almost laughs. "I was born and raised in Connecticut. The only Mexicans I knew growing up were my parents."

Back on patrol, with an hour remaining before the end of his shift, Hector swings by Peets Coffee and picks up a latte and an apple fritter before heading to his hidey-hole behind the Safeway Store. Mulling over the pros and cons of his forthcoming transfer, he concludes that things could be worse. It is better than being stuck on The Island waiting to be promoted for who knows how long. The upside is he'll be out of uniform, no more midnight shifts, and the assignment comes with a five percent bump in pay, money to be put aside toward the down payment on a new Harley-Davidson.

Monday, July 22, fourteen-hundred hours. Hector agonizes over his choice of clothing for his first day in the anti-gang unit. He does not want to overdo it, so Hector changes out of his 75th Sturgis Motorcycle Rally T-Shirt and cargo shorts. Going through his closet, he settles on a pair of dark grey wool slacks and a pastel blue Brooks Brothers button-down collar shirt. He goes with penny loafers and tops it off with a navy-blue Armani blazer. The jacket almost covers the holstered forty-caliber Glock duty weapon. Because it's a plain-clothes assignment, Hector skips a tie. Checking himself out in a floor-length mirror, the five-nine, one-hundred-fifty-pound hunk gazing back at him looks sharp. His dark brown hair is razor cut to departmental regulation length. Even though he shaved his heavy beard twice in eight hours, his cheeks are not quite smooth—he is ready for anything. No longer working a beat in uniform, Hector leaves his ten-year-old Fat Boy chained and locked in his apartment's small garage, a space so small he can barely park his Ford Focus behind the motorcycle. Hector hopes the assignment comes with an unmarked police car that he can park on the street.

Four-fifteen finds Hector sitting with Officer Bennington Harris in unfamiliar surroundings. Neither has worked out of uniform—being in plain clothes feels strange. Line-up is at 5:00 p.m. The wall clock shows four-forty-five, which means they've been sitting in the empty room for half an hour. Much like Hector, Harris had also been called into his watch commanders' office the previous week.

New Liberty, a city of one million, is second to Phoenix in population but larger in land area. The police department's 1500 sworn officers are organized into headquarters/investigations and thirteen patrol districts, numbered one to fourteen, the thirteenth's called fourteen. The numbering system was a concession to a gullible mayor and his superstitious police chief several decades earlier.

Harris, the other replacement, hasn't given much thought to his attire. He wears dark-brown Dockers, a lightweight green and white striped polo shirt, and an Arizona Diamondbacks Jacket. His eight-inch high, zip-side uniform boots give him a modicum of comfort, and like Hector, Harris carries a Glock 40. However, he carries four additional fifteen-round magazines, handcuffs, and a Berretta Tomcat.32 in an ankle holster.

Hector can't stop bouncing a knee. "Hey, man, where's everyone?"

Harris, pacing the room, seems even less comfortable. "How would I know? I got the same message you did. Be at line-up by five." Except for the ticking of the old-style wall clock, ten minutes of silence follows.

Hector hears talking in the hallway at five to five before two men enter the room. An older guy with salt and pepper hair holds a cup in his right hand. The second man is a few inches shorter, thirty or forty-pounds lighter, with sandy brown hair. Hector reaches out to the older man. "Sergeant Toliver. I'm Hector Navarro." When the men finish shaking hands, Harris follows suit.

"It's nice to meet you gents, but I'm not the sergeant." Nodding toward the younger man, "May I present Sergeant Robert Toliver, our fearless leader."

Embarrassed, the two officers try to apologize to Sergeant Toliver, who brushes their request for forgiveness aside with a friendly, "No sweat, Steve thinks he runs the show. Grab a seat. When the rest of the crew drags in, we'll introduce you and assign you to partners."

The rest of the unit hurries in at five on the dot as if on cue. Unlike Hector, they're a mixed bag, mostly in shabby clothing. The one who looks the oldest wears a filthy Levi jacket over a grimy gray T-shirt that was once white. His khaki slacks are wrinkled and

stained. *He's slept in those many times.*
Appearing hungover, the guy sways as he
walks. Sticking out a hand as the man
approaches, Hector says, "Hi, I'm Hector
Navarro, and this is Ben Harris."

"Who gives a shit?" the man replies in a
rough and raspy voice before continuing to
the back of the small room. He doesn't
acknowledge anyone.

A red-headed female officer turns to
Hector and says, "That's Davy Jones. He's an
asshole—ignore him."

Taken aback, Hector and Harris take
seats without another word. None of the
other officers seem surprised by the older
man's conduct.

"Don't mind Jones. The prick can't help
himself. He's a total asshole," Sergeant
Toliver says before beginning the
introductions. "You've met Steve Kowalski.
He and The Preacher, also known as George
White, have the longest time in the unit—six
years."

A gigantic man raises a hand that looks
twice the average size—connected to a beefy
tattooed arm. The arm, in turn, is attached
to an enormous body that reminds Hector of
a human Godzilla. The giant grunts
something like, "God be with yah."

Harris speaks up. "How come they call
you The Preacher?"

"Call me Preacher or the Lord will come down on your head." He raises his enormous right hand above his head and says, "Meet the Lord."

Stepping back, Harris's mouth falls open, and Hector gasps as the Preacher drops his hand on a desk. They can feel the vibration in their feet. The Preacher, shaking with laughter, welcomes the new men to the unit with crushing bear hugs. The rest of the self-introductions are completed with no further shock treatments. Malik Al-Fasil, Kathryn "Katie" O'Brien, John Riley, and Jaime "The Kid" Rodriquez round out the unit.

Once finished with introductions, Sergeant Toliver explains the new Inter-vention Program. "I gave you the basics last week. The Chief's plan for activating the program is moving ahead." Looking at Hector, he continues. "Navarro and Harris are here to replace the two of you who will visit middle schools instead of fighting crime."

After their sergeant finishes explaining the plan, no one is happy. None of the officers want any part of the project. Even though this special duty would be a plus on their resumes, all express their feelings to Sergeant Toliver.

The Preacher asks, "Will these be permanent assignments?"

"Yes, at least until the school year's over."

"We'll reevaluate then. But we'll want fresh faces each year," says the lieutenant.

"To begin with, I want you to understand these assignments were decided upon by me. Lieutenant Delacroix's aware of them and has no objections."

Delacroix has one but won't overrule his sergeant. He doesn't want either of the new officers paired with Jones.

"The program begins Monday, September 10, the second week of school. Preparation begins next week. Malik, Jaime, you won the lottery."

"Why me?" No one can tell which one speaks first.

"Demographics played a big part in my decision."

Toliver points at Harris. "You and Navarro listen up. The largest group of gangbangers here in New Liberty are Black, with the 4-Aces at the top, the Hispanics, and then the Vietnamese, who are the most violent."

"Damn bangers."

"Jones, one more comment out of you, and you'll be sitting on the beach for a week. Do I make myself clear?"

"Yeah, Sarge. It's just . . . .."

"Shut the fuck up." Sergeant Toliver shocks Hector when he interrupts Jones.

He'd never heard a supervisor use that word.

Slouching down, Jones mumbles, "Semper effen Fi."

"Where was I? Oh, yes, the Vietnamese gangs, they have no fear. They're usually armed. They prefer assault weapons, and they know how to use them. Second generation, and for the most part, they lack the love their parents have for this country." Toliver says, "Malik, you have something on your mind?"

"I do, Sarge. The White man dumps on us poor Black men— again. "Malik continues, "I guess I'm lucky there are no Muslim gangs, or I'd get the double whammy."

Jaime "The Kid" Rodriquez jumps right in. "Us Hispanics are still shoveling shit for the White man."

The language and insubordination of these officers towards the sergeant surprises Hector.

"What about us women? We don't even get an honorable mention." Officer Katie O'Brien can't pass up the opportunity to take a shot. "Girls are becoming players in the gangster world."

Toliver stops her with, "If you can't deal with being left out, O'Brien, I'm sure Malik or Jaime would be happy to change places with you." He signals the end of the discussion: "Malik, Jaime, after line-up, meet me in the captain's conference room."

Kowalski had been silent during the discussion. Sensing it is time to move on; he speaks up. "Hey, Sarge."

"What?"

"What about the newbies?"

"Newbies, they ain't. Both are experienced street cops. They're here to learn gang enforcement and get plain clothes experience."

"O'Brien and I are in the middle of something with the 4-Aces. I would hate to see it messed up," Kowalski interjects.

"Not to worry, she's stuck with you" Eyeing the back of the room, Sergeant Toliver continues, "Davey. Hector is going with you."

"Geez, Sarge, I don't need a wet-nosed rookie. . .."

"Shut up, Jones. You're taking him, another word, and you'll have them both."

Jones mumbles something akin to "chicken shit."

"You have something you care to share with us, Officer Jones?"

"No, Sir, I'm as happy as a clam."

"Good. Preacher, I'm putting Officer Harris with you. Any questions?"

"Nope. I will guide him in the ways of the Lord."

"Riley, you'll partner with me unless someone's off sick or on vacation." Riley gives a nod and slumps back in his chair.

"Steve, you and Katie hit the road. Preacher, Davey, my office. Ben, Hector, relax for a few minutes."

Five minutes later, Toliver stands behind his desk, arms crossed, glaring at both officers. Bending forward, he slams his palms down—the room is immediately quiet. After a moment of silence, "Davey, I want any shit out of you, I'll squeeze your head. Preacher, you keep your homilies to yourself. None of us likes this, but we don't have a choice. I doubt they'll be here for six months. I expect you to teach them what they need to know and keep them out of trouble. Understood?"

Both men realize Sergeant Toliver is in no mood for an argument. "I don't care how, but you'll spend the shift discussing unit responsibility, policy, and procedure. Walk them through how things work and why. Unless we get a hot call, the only time you'll leave the building is for your meal break."

Toliver leaves the two officers and walks to the captain's conference room. Malik and Jaime are waiting. "Before we get started, if you have any questions, let's get them out of the way. Malik, you're senior. You go first."

"Okay, Sarge, other than my skin color, why me?"

"Fair question. Your skin color is one reason, not the sole one. You're not so old that you'll turn off the kids. You're a practicing Muslim. That alone will get their attention. They'll wonder how a Black man can be a police officer, especially a Muslim. You're a good cop. These kids need a role model if we expect to reach them. You can be that role model."

"I'm not thrilled, and as much as I hate to admit it, I have to agree."

"Thanks. You'll carry out the assignment in an excellent manner."

"What's our role? When we're not at a school?" Jaime asks.

"You remain members of AGE. You'll work out of the empty office across from Lieutenant Delacroix."

"Will the chief approve overtime?"

"Overtime is not authorized for your assignment, but if we get any in AGE, I'll call you." "Thanks, Sarge." After a brief hesitation, Jaime asks, "Why'd you choose me? I have less time here than anyone else."

"True, but your knowledge of gangs is better than anyone in the unit. You will answer questions no one else can. You were a gangbanger for what, three years?"

"Closer to four, but I was looking for a way out after less than three,"

"You managed to get out, turn your life around, and become a cop. I doubt these middle school kids can ask you anything you can't answer."

With their questions out of the way, the three spend the rest of the shift discussing how Malik and Jamie would cope with this new and unique challenge. Before their workday ends, the officers are committed to making the plan a success.

5

THE DAY DOESN'T turn out the way Hector expects. Davey Jones told him to dress like a gangbanger. He's from Connecticut. *Gangs? What do I know?* Hector's entire time on the job has been on the "Island," and he has only a vague idea of how Hispanic gangbangers dress. To be on the safe side, he takes a morning ride through the area known as Little Chihuahua. Mothers are walking kids to school; shops are open; street sweepers and delivery trucks are everywhere. No one looks like a gang member. Returning after lunch, Hector finds that the area has changed. The neighborhood looks different. Hispanic men stand or squat on street corners, and others loiter in front of convenience and liquor stores—many are young, incredibly young.

The most common form of dress is sleeveless white undershirts like those that Sylvester Stallone wore in those old *Rocky* movies. Hector thinks they're called wife-beaters. No way is he wearing one. Others wear plaid shirts. Regardless of the shirt, they wear khaki slacks or black baggy pants. Many wear green bandanas: tattoos are visible on most.

On the way out of the neighborhood, Hector stops at a clothing store. He picks out Khakis and black Dickies pants and, from a wide assortment of plaid shirts, selects five, one for each day of the workweek. Ready to check out, he asks the Latina clerk for one of the green bandanas on a shelf behind the register. She looks surprised and says something in Spanish. His vocabulary is limited to "taco" and "cerveza. *Perdón, pero no hablo Español.*"

The woman gives Hector a strange look. "You're not LSL." It's a statement, not a question.

"What's LSL?"

"You must be nuts. Why wear gang colors? LSLs are members of the Los Scorpios Locos, an extremely dangerous—violent—street gang. You want to die?"

"What?"

"If you wear green around here,

36

especially a bandana or plaid shirt, they'll kill you. If LSL doesn't, other gangs will if they think you are LSL." Shaking her head in disgust, she asks, "Who are you?"

Hector is embarrassed, but more than that, he has the strangest fluttering in his stomach. What is it, he wonders? Almost afraid to open his mouth, Hector is not sure what to say. He decides on the truth. "My name's Hector Navarro. I'm a New Liberty Police officer recently assigned to the Anti-Gang Unit. My supervisor said to get some clothes to blend in. I've been driving around the neighborhood, and this's how most of the men are dressed."

"Well, Hector Navarro, I'm Maria Elena Juarez. You need help. First off, put the red and green shirts back on the rack. Get another brown one and the tan one on the end of the rack. Never wear a bandana, any color."

Stifling an embarrassed giggle, he does as instructed. "Anything else I should know?"

"Leave the top button undone. You'll be a lot more comfortable, and more importantly, you'll look neutral, not a gang member. You might live a little longer."

Hector has the strangest sensation, his chest tingles, and he feels like he just started a new day. He decides to take a chance. "Thanks, Maria. If I need help, can I call you?"

She smiles, "Here's my card. I even might help you if I'm not busy."

Davey Jones moves listlessly. This is his first shift on the street with the new guy, Hector something. Davey isn't sure why the sergeant partnered him up with the new kid. *Anyone but Toliver, I'd think they were screwing with me. It doesn't matter, partner or not. I'm not changing.* "Hey, kid, grab your shit. Toliver wants us at Ernesto's."

"What's Ernesto's?"

"Ernesto's Pool Hall is the 4-Aces hangout. Their clubhouse's in the backroom."

"Oh," and then, "why are we meeting the sergeant there?"

"How should I know. Toliver says go, I go."

Hector doesn't ask any more questions of the red-rimmed and rheumy-eyed man.

They had spent the previous night going over unit responsibility, policy, and procedure. Jones hadn't said much. Hector hadn't said anything and was happy to let the Preacher talk. Tonight, he isn't going to say much.

At his undercover car, Jones tells Hector, "You ride shotgun and keep your mouth shut. I may have to drag you around, but that doesn't mean I have to like it."

The automobile is the oldest in the unit. By tradition, the senior officer takes their choice, usually the latest model. The newest member drives whatever's left over. It's obvious Jones takes no pride in the old car. The remains of half-eaten hamburgers and who knows what else, litter the filthy eight-year-old Ford Crown Vic. Navarro is partnered and will remain so until promoted out of the unit. He will not get the undercover car he had hoped would save him a ton of gas money.

Popping the trunk, Jones says, "Put your gear bag in here. Keep your flashlight and anything else you want to carry. I'm not opening it again."

Bending down to unzip his bag, Hector sniffs—sniffs a second time—and clenches his teeth to avoid breathing until he finds his Streamlight Stinger and notebook. Almost gagging, he steps back, "What's that? It's enough to make me puke."

"Live with it. Is that one of those fancy new flashlights? I still have the Kel-Lite they gave me in the academy."

Opening the passenger door, Hector struggles with an even more pungent stench. What is it? Rotting fish, dirty ashtrays, stale booze, and vomit come to mind. How the hell does the guy live with this? Expecting the same "Live with it" response, Hector holds his tongue.

Settling in, Jones belches, farts, stretches, and lights up a Pall Mall. The police administration banned smoking in police facilities and all vehicles years ago. Hector keeps his thoughts to himself. Rolling down the window, he's happy it's not cold or rainy. *What happens when the weather turns bad? What's next?*

What happens after that turns out to be a weapons check. Only unlike any Hector has seen since coming on the department. Davey takes his duty weapon, a Glock, from its holster, removes the magazine, racks the slide open, and collects the round as it ejects. It appears to be a departmental issue forty caliber. He lays the cartridge in an ashtray on the center console. The white ashtray sports the Marine Corps globe and anchor on the inside bottom. It is like fresh snow in comparison to the rest of the car.

"What are you doing? You wanna get us killed?"

"I check my weapons before leaving the station. Don't sweat it."

Hector knows what his new partner is doing violates at least a dozen departmental policies. *Jones will undoubtedly get fired if I report this, and I'll be labeled a snitch.* Dumbstruck, he watches. What Jones is doing is forbidden, the man knows how to handle firearms. He does it smoothly and without any unnecessary risk.

"You could get fired."

"Fuck 'em if they can't take a joke." Jones places each cartridge in the ashtray, counting as he does. Looking toward Hector, he says, "Always want to be sure you have fifteen rounds in the mag and one in the chamber." He counts as he places fifteen back into the magazine, inserts it in the butt of the pistol, snaps it in place, and slides the action back. He releases it, making sure one round is in the chamber, before removing the magazine and saying "sixteen" as he places the remaining round in the magazine and reinserts it into the weapon.

"Do you inspect your weapons every time you start a shift?"

"Yeah, every time, and when I wake up, whenever that is."

Hector finds that he has scooted forward and turned toward Jones. He's on the front edge of the seat. As he relaxes back into the car seat, Jones bends toward his left ankle, pulls the cuff away, and produces a smaller pistol, a Walther PPK .380. Jones follows the same ritual; it takes less time, only six rounds in the magazine plus one in the chamber. Finished with the second weapon, Jones takes a rag from between his seat and the console, wipes the ashtray down, and replaces the rag.

"Let's go."

As they head to Ernesto's, Hector realizes that except for the few weeks spent in training, this was the first time he'd been on the streets outside District 8, known mockingly as The Island.

Five minutes away from the station, Jones double-parks outside a low-class-looking bar. He puts the portable red light on the roof and turns on the flashers. "Wait here. I'll be back." It's close to ten minutes before Jones returns. As he pulls away, Hector smells alcohol on his breath. Jones must have read his mind. "Live with it. It doesn't concern you."

This stop-off becomes a daily occurrence; Hector's not sure if he should report Jones or with whom he can talk.

On the way to meet the rest of the unit behind a supermarket a few blocks from Ernesto's Pool Hall, Jones chain-smokes several more cigarettes, another policy violation. He throws the last one out the window a block from the meet. The AGE team stands around waiting for Kowalski and O'Brien. Within minutes, Jones lights another cigarette. The Preacher has a cigar hanging from his lips. Outside the police station, he is rarely seen without a cigar. Ben Harris, another tobacco user, spits a wad of chewing tobacco into a water bottle.

"Hey, Sarge," the Preacher asks, "How are Malik and the Kid doing?"

"They haven't started giving talks yet. Captain Windsor has them at Training, working on a PowerPoint presentation. It's still weeks until school starts."

6

"HI, THIS IS Maria. How may I help you?"

"Hi, Maria, it's Hector Navarro."

"Hector, who?"

"The cop."

"Oh, that Hector. What do you want? I'm a little busy."

"I need your help again. I did something dumb. Can I see you?"

"That depends. What'd you do?"

"I wore Converse shoes to work. They called me a fool."

"You are a fool," but she's laughing as she snorts, "you need a babysitter."

"I know. Can I see you tonight?"

"No."

"Why not?"

"School. I have night classes at Phoenix College."

"Tomorrow night?"

"Pick me up outside the store at six. You can give me a ride home."

"See you then." Hector's ecstatic. Not the first woman to interest him, Maria is the first to have the effect she does. *What is it about her?*

Maria hangs up; she isn't busy. It's the slowest day of the week, and she is delighted he called. *He might not be street-smart, but he is cute.*

Hector starts preparing for this 'date' with Maria at noon the next day. He knows it's not an actual date, but he wants to make a good impression. First, he straightens up the apartment. He doesn't expect to bring Maria home, but you never know; better ready than sorry.

How Hector dresses creates complications, but those problems led to his meeting Maria. He almost calls his mother, then decides against it. It's not as if he hasn't dated or had relationships. This time it is different. He's only talked with Maria for a few minutes. *What is about this girl? I can't keep her out of my mind.* Wearing the Converses and the Preacher calling him "Da Fool" should have upset him, but to the contrary, he views it as justification to call

Maria Juarez and ask for her help.

The first outfit he lays out looks great. He begins with a pair of Oxblood Penny Loafers, dark tan Ralph Lauren slacks, and an off-white dress shirt, finishing with a Patrick James Camel Hair sports coat. He ought to run an iron over the slacks but decides against it. His outfit decided; washing the car was next. Leaving the air-conditioned apartment brings Hector to his senses. The temperature's one-hundred-ten and will still be at least one-hundred when he picks up Maria. *Shit, I am a fool.* If his mother knew Maria, she would say, "Hector's not a fool. His infatuation with you is something he's not experienced."

Hector doesn't understand what is happening to him with this woman. Washing the car gives him time to think. He remembers something his mother told him years ago. "Son, when you meet the right woman, you'll know. I knew I would spend the rest of my life with your father after our first kiss. Believe me, you'll know." *Mom's a lot smarter than I thought.* Done with the car, he returns to the problem at hand. What to wear? His first choice won't cut it. Finished showering, he can't wear his usual day-off attire, Harley T-Shirts and shorts. Instead, Hector selects a blue Tommy Hilfiger polo shirt, long enough to cover his off-duty pistol, and a pair of faded Levi's, no rips. A glance in the mirror convinces Hector that he has made the right choice.

His cell phone rings. The caller ID shows it's Bob Toliver. *Shit, now what.*

"Hey, Hector. I hope I'm not interfering with anything on your day off."

"No problem, Sarge. What can I do for you?"

"We need you in early. . ."

He interrupts his sergeant. "Today?"

"Damn, you sound like I stabbed you. You okay?"

"I'm fine. I have a date tonight."

"Hold your horses. I'm calling about tomorrow. We have a search warrant for Ernesto's. Be at the office by six."

Hector arrives at Maria's store twenty minutes early. Not wanting to look anxious, He parks a few blocks away. He gets stares and comments from a couple of young Black men. "Hey, Bro. Fine looking ride. Yo daddy knows you gots it?" Ignoring them, Hector reads a few pages of *Perma Red*, an award-winning book by one of his favorite writers, Debra Magpie Earling. Lost in the novel, he's late for his date. He pulls to a stop in front of the store a few minutes after six. Maria comes from the store. Opening the car door, she says, "You're late. What kind of car is this?" Before she fastens her seatbelt, she asks again, "What is this thing?"

"It's a twenty-fifteen Ford Focus."

"Who are you not trying to impress? This thing looks like something my grandparents would drive. Not a cop."

"I got a good deal. Besides, I like it."

"Whatever. What kind of trouble are you in that you need my help?"

"Can we talk over dinner?"

"I said you could give me a ride home, not go on a date."

"I know. You have to eat."

"Here's my address." Maria hands him a slip of paper. "Take me home. You can visit with my parents while I shower and change."

Maria's parents take a liking to him. When Hector tells them, The only Mexican food I've ever eaten has been in restaurants," they insist he stay for dinner. The meal starts with spicy chicken and hominy soup. Somewhat of a picky eater, he's hesitant but—not wanting to embarrass Maria or himself in front of her mother and father— goes at the soup with enthusiasm and is surprised at how delicious it is. Pork carnitas follow the soup. Hector is not lying when he tells Mrs. Juarez: "This is the best Mexican food I've ever eaten."

Mr. Juarez tells Hector he was born in

Mexico and immigrated to the States as a teenager. Maria's father joined the United States Navy and did two tours in Vietnam as a Boatswain's Mate on PBRs in the Mekong Delta.

"What's a PBR?"

"Patrol Boat, Riverine. They called us the Brown Water Navy."

"How'd you meet Mrs. Juarez?"

Maria interrupts, "Dad, Hector's not interested in all that."

Mr. Juarez continues as if his daughter isn't in the room. "Between tours, I took leave and went home to Guadalajara, where I met Maria's mother. After being discharged and granted U.S. citizenship, I went back home and asked her to marry me and come to America. She said yes and made me the happiest man in Mexico."

Mr. and Mrs. Juarez express an interest in getting to know about Hector and his family. He told them he grew up in Connecticut, the son of two Yale University professors. While they are visiting, a chime sounds. Hector notices an antique mantel clock over the fireplace and comments that he can tell it's old but can't figure out if it is wood or marble.

"You'll have to ask my wife."

"It was a wedding gift to my grandparents from my great-grandparents. They bought it while on a trip to the states around 1900. It is wood and marble. It has the Seth Tomas logo on the back. My mother gave it to me on our wedding day. And I will give it to Maria on hers.

By the time he leaves, Hector is positive that he wants a relationship with Maria and her family. He forgets to ask about the Converses.

7

Sergeant Toliver calls Hector's iPhone. "We're starting at nineteen-hundred. The 4-Aces have an initiation tonight. If true, things could get nasty."

Hector is wearing the brown plaid shirt Maria suggested. He almost wore black Dickies. Instead, he decided the Khakis would be best because brown and khaki look better. Shoes? No way would he be caught wearing Converses again, so he bought two pairs of New Balance walking shoes, one black and the other gray. *No gang banger would be caught dead in these ordinary shoes.*

Arriving as the meeting begins, Hector utters a mumbled apology, drawing a humph from Davey Jones. Once Toliver finishes his briefing and turns the floor over to Kowalski and O'Brien. Katie begins, "Our informant says the 4-Aces have an initiation scheduled tonight for three wannabe members. They had a choice, shoot somebody on a drive-by or take a beat down. They decided they'd rather go with the drive-by."

"Are they gonna hit Black or Brown?" The Preacher asks.

"We haven't heard. The last the informant overheard was that the wannabes would be at Ernesto's at ten. If Geronimo approves, they get guns and a stolen car. Galloway will tail them to make sure they shoot. If they carry it off, even if no one dies, they're in the Aces. He'll take them for a ride into the desert if they lie."

Jones says, "Either way it goes down, we should have fewer assholes around town."

"Shut up. Shut the hell up, or I'll shut you up myself." O'Brien isn't happy with him. Someone's always telling Jones to 'shut up. He gives her the finger and clamps his lips together. No one in the room doubts she could beat his ass to a pulp.

O'Brien continues. "Galloway is as smart as they come. Even if we could find him, he'd make any tail we put on him. We have to hope the informant gets word to us in time to prevent anybody from getting hurt."

Toliver returns to the podium, "Any

questions for Katie or Steve before I make the assignments?"

"Who's Geronimo? Who's Galloway?" Harris asks.

Kowalski says, "I'll take this one, okay, Sarge?'

"Sure."

"New Liberty has a significant gang presence, exacerbated by Arizona's proximity to the Mexican border. Hispanics account for ten to eleven thousand gang members or affiliates throughout the state. Blacks make up the second-largest group, five or six thousand, trailed by Asians, mostly Vietnamese. The Vietnamese are the newest, only in the hundreds, but the most violent."

Harris interrupts, "Aren't there any White gangs?"

"A few. The White gangs try to keep a low profile, running guns and stealing bikes.

"Preacher, would you answer his questions about Geronimo and Galloway?"

Officer White drops the street jargon as he explains, "The 4-Aces started as a small street gang here in New Liberty twenty-odd years ago. Jerome "Geronimo" Dixon was one of the three founding members. One died in a shootout with Phoenix PD years ago, and the other disappeared after challenging Geronimo for president. When Dixon went to Florence Prison, he recruited a few lifers and arranged for a few original gang members to join him. They started a subset inside the prison. It's still going strong." After pausing to take a sip of coffee, Preacher continues. "Dixon and DeShawn Galloway have been tight since grammar school. Galloway is the gang's enforcer. They call him The Knife, but not to his face because his weapon of choice is a Japanese Tanto. That doesn't mean the man isn't proficient with firearms. He is. His appearance contrasts with Geronimo's in every aspect. Two years younger, Galloway looks every bit his forty-eight years. His hair—what's left of it—is gray and patchy. At five-seven, one-hundred-thirty pounds, the man is far from imposing. His eyes are so dark they appear black, cold, dead—his stare freezes most men. We suspect him in at least a half dozen local hits. He's a contract killer and probably has double that number of murders to his credit."

Harris stops the Preacher with another question. "You say he uses a Tanto. What's that?"

"I've seen a few. If you Google killing knives, you'll see Tanto listed among the top two or three." Preacher pauses and looks to Sergeant Toliver.

"Go on. You're doing fine."

"Originally designed for penetrating armor, it's exceptional at cutting through ribs. I understand that coming from behind, an assassin can kill the target by running the blade through the ear into the brain. It's said that the Tanto pierces bulletproof vests if the blade doesn't hit a ceramic plate." After pausing for another sip of coffee, Preacher continues. "When Dixon went to prison, an estimated thirty members existed on the outside. He pulled together a solid cadre of a half dozen or so in Florence, lifers with nothing to lose. By the time Dixon was paroled, he had solidified his position of power."

Harris interrupts. "What happened to the 4-Aces in prison?"

"Those doing time at Florence grew strong. By the time Geronimo left, they had complete control of the prison's prostitution and drug trade. Dixon was the man with the keys, the shot-caller, and the dozen or so lifers were in firm control of the yard. The 4-Aces became the go-to people for contract hits inside or outside the prison walls. Blacks coming into Florence had two choices: affiliate with the 4-Aces or get turned out to become a sex toy to be passed around."

"What happened to Geronimo after returning to New Liberty on parole?" Hector asks.

"Remember, I told you one of the founders disappeared."

"Yeah? What's the story?"

"Released from Florence, Geronimo found a weakened and shrunken gang. Unlike those in prison, the members lacked strong leadership and determination. The president enjoyed playing a gangster but avoided conflict."

Toliver stops White. "The rest of the team knows Geronimo and the gang's history, Preacher. You keep Navarro and Harris here and finish up." Turning to the others, "I want the rest of you on the streets. Davey, you wait for Navarro."

When Sergeant Toliver and the others leave, White continues the history lesson. "Geronimo was furious. He demanded that the president step down. The man refused. It was a mistake. A week later, the president disappeared and was never seen again. We figure Galloway took him out to the desert."

"Didn't the other 4-Aces suspect Geronimo had the president killed?" Harris asks.

"Sure, they did. Geronimo appointed himself president, and no one had the guts to challenge him. The 4-Aces have around three hundred members and affiliates in New Liberty. They have another hundred or so in Florence, with smaller numbers in the remaining Arizona Department of Corrections facilities. I've heard they've also taken over the privately-run prisons."

"So, who has more members, the Hispanics or the 4-Aces?" Hector asks.

"Different things."

"What do you mean?"

"Well, for one, Hispanics are a racial group. Around eleven thousand Hispanics are affiliated with twenty or so gangs in New Liberty. A few number in the thousands. Some have as little as a half dozen members. The same applies to Blacks. The 4-Aces is only one of several gangs."

"How do you keep track of them?"

"That's not possible. We do what we can to keep the gangs under control. Unless you have questions that can't wait, let's go for a ride and see if we can find those 4-Aces wannabes before someone dies."

8

ERNESTO'S IS USUALLY quiet on Wednesdays. Tonight is an exception, with every table filled; DeShawn "The Knife" Galloway plays Nine-Ball with three young men. Of all the people in the pool hall, these three stand out. Kevin, the oldest, is seventeen, and the youngest, Corky, is fifteen. They have all dressed alike—grey hoodies, black Dickies trousers, dark shoes. 4-Aces wannabes, they're waiting for Geronimo to call them into the clubhouse at the back of the pool hall. Despite trying to appear unconcerned, their faces glisten, their shirts stained with sweat. They have reason to be nervous. Tonight is their one chance to earn membership into the 4-Aces.

Galloway oversees their initiation. "When

are we gonna start?" Kevin asks. He considers himself the leader of the three.

"You start when I tell you." Galloway knows Kevin's the weakest of the three. He's sure Corky is the strongest and will kill first.

While in the storeroom, Geronimo tells the armorer, "DeShawn's going to keep the wannabes worrying for another half hour. What pieces they gonna use? I don't wanna lose anything traceable if these fools get jammed up."

"I'll give one a Mac-10 with a thirty-round mag and one spare. The other two get .38's. The numbers are gone on them all. We stole a minivan this morning, and I changed the plates."

"Where is it? It better not be round here."

"It ain't. I stashed it at da Safeway in Little Saigon."

Geronimo laces his fingers behind his shiny black skull after leaning back in his Zulu-style Chieftain's throne and staring off into a world known only to him. Lost in thought, he doesn't say anything. The armorer, nervous, starts to speak, but Geronimo stops him. "Quiet, I'm thinking." *If we drive-by on the slope heads, they'll come back on us heavy. I ain't afraid of the little people, but no sense starting a war with them.*

"Hey, boss, DeShawn's ready to bring 'em in."

"Do it."

A few minutes later, the wannabes are standing before Geronimo and the rest of the 4-Aces leadership. "Are you prepared to prove you're worthy?"

All three say, "Yes." Corky's voice is the loudest and most straightforward.

"You know what you have to do?"

This is followed by more shouts, "Waste Los Scorpios Locos."

"What happens if you don't?" Geronimo poses the question to each of the three.

"Yeah, you'll smoke our asses." Corky answers without hesitation.

The other two answer but lack the younger one's fire. *DeShawn's right: he will be a stone killer. The others are fools.*

"Corky, you take the Mac-10. Ride in the back." Geronimo tells Kevin to drive.

"Deshawn will take you out to the van. Any questions?"

Geronimo smiles: *I knew there would be none.*

Elroy "Froggy" Robinson is worried, and for a good reason. Beat-in at fifteen, Froggy prospered and now plays a significant role in the 4-Aces hierarchy. He manages human trafficking, an extremely profitable enterprise. Between the clubs, truck stops, outcalls, and streetwalkers, he operates a stable of over one hundred women and girls plus thirty boys. Froggy runs the stable well, better than any of the previous managers. So well that Geronimo leaves him and the operation free of interference or oversight. Froggy likes his job and the prestige that goes with it.

I gotta call Kowalski and O'Brien. If Galloway catches me, he'll cut off my balls before slitting my throat.

Froggy's greatest fear is going back to prison. Like most overwhelming fears, his outweigh reason. At eighteen, he did three years at a minimum-security facility in Nevada, outside the range of Geronimo's protection. *I won't be anyone's punk ever again.*

A year ago, Officer Kowalski had cornered him. "Hi, Froggy. Are you ready to go back inside? You ready to be a punk—again?"

Kowalski knew the prostitution operation from beginning to end and threatened to arrest him. Froggy tried to bluff. "The 4-Aces will protect me."

Kowalski's response was terrifying. He had enough evidence for the feds to prosecute. "You'll do time in federal prison. Where Geronimo won't be able to protect you." Froggy made the mistake of believing the detective.

"Whatcha want?"

"Not a lot, a little information, nothing that will put you in danger."

I should have known better. Talking with the cop will get me killed. Froggy has little choice. He's given Kowalski so much information that he knows Galloway would kill him without hesitation. After Galloway and the wannabes leave, Froggy waits ten minutes and then tells Geronimo, "I gotta go check on the girls working the Flying J on Tenth."

"We got a problem?"

"Not yet. I need to get the numbers up another five percent. Gas prices are up ten percent, and truck drivers want a discount. We can't let our prices get out of control."

Fifteen minutes later, halfway between Ernesto's and the Flying J, and sure he's not being followed. Froggy pulls into a 7-11 and uses the outside payphone. *They're getting harder to find.* He wonders what he'll do when all the pay phones are gone. *I'll have to get a burner.*

Kowalski answers the call like he always does with his burner cell phone. "Yeah." *It's funny how cops use banger tricks like buying burner phones so they can't be traced.* Froggy would laugh if he weren't so scared.

"Kowalski, I have something for you."

"Good. Give it to me."

"The wannabes are in a stolen minivan. They already switched the plates. They gonna pick it up at the all-night Safeway in Little Saigon."

"What color?"

"Whatcha mean color? They blood."

"No, the minivan."

"How da fuck I know?"

"They gonna hit the Vietnamese?"

"No. LSL in Little Chihuahua."

"What are they packing?

"A Mac-10 and two .38s."

"You know where the wannabes are?"

"Nope. They left Ernesto's thirty minutes ago. They should be waiting at the Safeway store. The Knife will follow to make sure they get the job done. He's in his Escalade."

"Okay. If you get anything else, you call right away."

"If I can," Froggy says while thinking—don't hold your breath.

Katie had been listening as best she could to Steve's side of the conversation. "What's wrong?"

"The little shit hung up on me. It's on—the 4-Aces have three wannabes and are on their way to Little Chihuahua to hit any Los Scorpios Locos unlucky enough to be on the streets."

"Anything else?"

"They got a Mac-10 and two .38s. Galloway is following them. If they screw up the drive-by, he'll whack them."

"That doesn't give us much to go on." O'Brien twists her long red ponytail in her left hand. "We better get moving. Is this something we can broadcast citywide?"

"Probably. It shouldn't bring any heat down on Froggy. You get the rest of the guys rolling while I call Toliver. It'll be his decision if he wants a citywide alert."

Galloway makes several passes through the Safeway parking lot before stopping fifty feet from the stolen minivan. Turning to face the three wannabes in the back of his Escalade, he asks, "You ready?" Without waiting for an answer, he points at Corky. "You know how to use that thing?"

"Yeah."

"Is it loaded and ready to go?"

"It's loaded. Safety's on."

"Good." Nodding at the two older boys, Galloway asks, "You prepared to kill some spics?"

"Yeah."

Galloway knows otherwise. Kevin's sweatshirt is soaked through with sweat. Snot dribbles from his nose; his eyes are wide and white; the young man shakes every few moments. *He'll freeze. The kid's got no heart.* The third boy, Ralphie, is in better shape. His sweatshirt's wet under the arms from the heat, not fear. His eyes look normal, and there are no shakes. *He'll take care of business.*

"Corky, sit on the floor next to the side door. When it's time, slide it open." Turning to Ralphie, "you sit in the front passenger seat." To Kevin, "you drive. Look for a group standing around on the street. Make sure there are at least five. Keep moving and go around the block. Before you turn back onto the street, have Corky slide the door open. You got it?"

"I cruise by the spics, go around the block, Corky opens da door, I go back and start shooting."

"Good. Make sure the open door faces the spics. When you start shooting, empty your guns and get out of there. Corky, don't change the magazine."

"Where we go?" Kevin asks.

"Go like hell for a few blocks, and then slow down. I'll pull in front. You follow me until I stop and get out."

"What if we get caught?" Kevin asks.

"Don't get caught." *I knew he'd be the one to ask.*

9

BOB TOLIVER IS on a personal break in the restroom. It takes a few minutes for Steve Kowalski to reach him.

"Hey, Steve. What you got?"

"The shooters are headed for Little Chihuahua. It's a drive-by. They might be there already. The rest of our guys are on the way. We need to make a citywide broadcast."

"No shit. Give me what you got. I'll have communications make the broadcast."

Five minutes later, an alert is broadcast to all New Liberty, Phoenix, Maricopa County, and surrounding police agencies. The BOLO is followed by an email to all New Liberty police department mobile computer units.

```
Attention All Units

Be on the lookout for Gang Activity -
Drive-by shooting.
Suspects: 3 Black Males - Ages Unknown
Vehicle: Minivan - No Further Description
Suspects are believed to be en route
to the Little Chihuahua area of New
Liberty for a drive-by shooting. No
specific target. It is thought they
will attack any group of Hispanics on
the streets.
Suspects should be considered armed
and dangerous - Approach with caution.
New Liberty Police Department 2211
hours Wednesday, July 24.
```

Minutes later, New Liberty Police Patrol Unit 4-L-29 makes an emergency broadcast at twenty-fourteen hours. "4-L-29 – Shots Fired."

"All units standby, 4-L-29 go ahead."

"4-L-29 I'm on Twenty-Third Avenue at Lexington. I can hear gunfire and at least one automatic weapon. It's close. Requesting additional units to this area."

"All District Four units proceed to the twenty-third and Lexington area." The police radio begins again. "We have numerous 9-1-1 calls reporting a shooting at Twenty-First and Lexington. Multiple victims. Suspects were last seen westbound on Twenty-First in a late model minivan." Within seconds, the radio comes back on the air. "Ambulances and fire department are in route."

The Watch Commander issued this broadcast within seconds, "All District Four units and all available plainclothes officers respond to the scene. Surrounding districts, establish surveillance on all routes out of District Four."

The homes in Little Chihuahua were built after World War II to accommodate the influx of veterans to the Phoenix metropolitan area. The area expanded into a dozen subdivisions with rows of identical houses competing for the dollars guaranteed by the veterans' GI Loans. The modest homes were small, with three bedrooms, one bath, and a detached garage. New Liberty grew large enough that incorporation followed in 1955. In the seventies, middle-class white inhabitants moved to newer, larger homes. One by one, they sold their homes, primarily to Mexican immigrants looking for a better life. These families worked hard and did their best to assimilate. Things began changing with the second generation. Young men who lacked a proper education and were underemployed gravitated to the emerging gangs. As the first generation died or moved away, the neighborhoods deteriorated, and gang membership grew. Homes that had sported well-kept yards fell into disrepair. Graffiti was the only paint applied to washed-out and peeling walls.

The shooting scene had been the site of a *Quinceanera* a few hours earlier.

Chucho Montemayor's cousin celebrated her fifteenth birthday at his house. After she leaves, the Vatos and homegirls stay; there is plenty of food and beer. Chucho invites the LSL Vatos and Chicas to enjoy the leftovers. The invitation went out to dozens of Los Scorpios Locos living in Little Chihuahua, "beer, food, women, at Chucho's." By 10:00 p.m., around twenty LSL remained outside the house. Chucho is a Los Scorpios Locos Teniente. He doesn't worry about the cops. No one in the neighborhood is stupid enough to call five-oh.

Chucho's got a good buzz going, but he's not quite drunk when a late model minivan comes down the street. The driver and passenger are Black. Several Vatos slide their hands under their shirts for pistols and revolvers when Chucho shouts, "Hey, blood. What are you doing? Get your Black ass outta here."

Others join in, shouting. "Yo. Stop so we can fuck you up."

Once the interlopers are gone, the LSL vatos relax. Chucho relieves his anger by shouting, "We scared them bloods off."

Minutes later, the van is back. Something is wrong; it turns the corner with the headlights out. The side door opens. Chucho knows what is happening. He shouts, "Run, run, get down." He flops to the grass behind the low brick wall in front of the house. His shouted warnings cause more confusion than alarm. Before he gets to his Glock, gunfire starts, followed by screams. Getting to his knees, Chucho hears the sound of an automatic weapon, *probably a Mac-10* and at least one handgun. Firing at the van, he sees a young Black sitting in the back, firing the Mac-10. The front passenger's firing a handgun. The driver holds a gun, but he's not firing. Chucho wonders, *out of ammo*?

Jose Maldonado, an army veteran, had taught his fellow LSL members how to hold a pistol and shoot. He showed them how those fools in gangster movies look badass but can't hit shit. Chucho has the weapon in his left hand, balanced with the right, the same shooting stance the cops use. The Mac-10 poses the greatest danger. Chucho puts a double tap through the open side door, followed by shots at the passenger with the handgun. The firing from the minivan stops. He sprays it with the last nine rounds in the magazine. The Black shooters won't return, but he runs inside the house to play it safe and grabs a loaded magazine by the front door.

Outside, a Vato yells for someone to call 9-1-1. At least six are down on the ground. Sirens are approaching from all directions. Chucho hides his pistol and orders the other LSLs to give their weapons to the girls.

Eight are hit; three are dead. Two Los Scorpios Locos and a teenage girl. A couple more look as though they might die. Chucho shouts at the others, "Get out of here." Within seconds, the dead and wounded are the only ones waiting for the cops with him.

10

RALPHIE'S DEAD, HIS body slumped over in the passenger seat. Galloway pulls his Escalade alongside the speeding minivan. The rear slider's still open. "This fool's gonna get caught." He honks several times before the wide-eyed Kevin looks his way. It takes several minutes to get him to slow down before the minivan pulls in behind the Escalade and decelerates to the speed limit. Had he not slowed and moved into a position behind Galloway, Kevin, and Corky would have been spotted, stopped, and arrested. The two-car convoy had gone but two blocks when they passed a motorcycle cop holding a radar gun in the direction of the Escalade and the minivan. Had Kevin been driving as fast and erratically as he was mere moments before, there would have been a traffic stop. But it more likely would have been a pursuit of a vehicle matching the description of the one involved in the drive-by shooting. Cops would come from all directions.

Ten minutes later, the van follows the Escalade down a narrow, pothole-filled road behind an abandoned warehouse.

"I'll get the door," Galloway's passenger shouts, jumps out of the Escalade, and slides open the warehouse door. The vehicles pull inside, and the man closes the door. Geronimo and his security detail are waiting.

Even before the minivan comes to a complete stop, Corky jumps out. Running to the front of the vehicle, he jerks the driver's door open. "You mutha, I outa kill your ass," while pulling the older and much larger Kevin from the van, throwing him to the ground, and kicking him in the stomach.

Geronimo nods for Galloway to pull Corky back. "Cool down, brother."

To DeShawn, he asks, "what happened?"

Corky interrupts, shouting, "Ralphie's dead." He kicks Kevin again and points a finger at the man, coiled up in the fetal position on the warehouse floor. "Da nigga' panicked and didn't shoot. He could' a got us all fucked up. Ralphie emptied his thirty-eight. I used up my mag."

"What you got to say?" Geronimo pulls

the whimpering Kevin to his feet.

"I was too busy driving."

"Did DeShawn tell you to shoot?"

"Yes."

"Why didn't you?" Geronimo never shows emotion when losing his temper. The disappointed tone in his voice as he talks with Kevin is as close as most will ever come to seeing his anger.

"Like I said, I couldn't. I was driving."

"Why'd you drive like a fool?"

"Whatcha mean?"

Geronimo shakes his head and then nods at Galloway. Turning to Corky, he says, "Get in the Escalade."

Once Geronimo leaves, Galloway puts his arm around the shaking driver. "It's okay, Kevin, we'll take care of everything," he whispers while sliding his Tanto under the coward's ribs and up into his heart.

The next order of business concerns the dead wannabe. "Ralphie made the initiation. He's a 4-Ace. We'll take him to the undertaker."

Galloway and Corky carry Ralphie's body to the Escalade while one of the others folds down the back seat and opens the rear doors. The body is laid in the back and covered with a blanket.

Galloway's bodyguard points at Kevin's body, "Got a five-gallon can of gas in the back of the minivan. Put this piece of garbage inside. Douse him and the van. I'll move my Escalade outside, and then you light them on fire and close the door."

11

DINNER WITH MARIA'S parents was fun but not what Hector had hoped. He figured since he had showered and changed, she owed him a real date.

"Hi, it's me, Hector."

"Hector, who?"

"Ha, Ha. I had a good time with you and your folks. Will I ever get to finish that date you promised me?"

"I never promised you anything. But I'll take pity on you."

"How's that?"

"You may take me to dinner, but not this week. Next week, I'm off Friday and Saturday, I have plans for Saturday, so it'll have to be Friday."

"Okay, I'll get reservations at Cocina

Madrigal. It's one of the best Mexican restaurants in Phoenix."

"No, you won't. I eat the best Mexican food in Arizona every day. I want seafood. Surprise me, and it better be good."

Maria is amazed and pleased with Hector's choice of restaurants. Chula Seafood in Scottsdale has a fine reputation. She has long wanted to eat there. It is far out of her price range but not so extravagant that she suspects Hector of spending more than he can afford to impress her. But she has to admit she is impressed by his choice.

"I hope this is up to your standards."

"It is. Thanks for bringing me here," Maria says as she opens the menu. "Do you mind if I order for both of us?" Hector has no objection. As far as he's concerned, she can order anything, and he would tell her it was delicious. Hector is smitten with this woman.

The server took Hector's drink order, a bottle of La Crema Monterey Chardonnay. Maria chided him for spending fifty dollars on a wine she could buy at Costco for fifteen. "You'll have to learn to be a bit more frugal if you want to date me," she said with a laugh.

"Please bring us a half-dozen of the Kumiai Oysters," Maria requested. After the server moves away, she tells Hector, "This will satisfy your need for Mexican food. Kumiai Oysters come from the Guerrero Negro Lagoon in Baja California.

"Guerrero Negro Lagoon sounds familiar."

"It should be. It's where gray whales go to calve every year."

The couple spent the better part of an hour learning about each other while enjoying Maria's choice of dishes. She had the house special, fresh halibut, which went well with the California Chardonnay.

It was evident to anyone passing their table that this young couple was interested in each other.

"I enjoyed dinner, and I even enjoyed you. I'd invite you in, but my folks are already in bed."

"Can I see you again?"

"That would be nice." As Hector leans in to give her a good night peck, she meets his mouth with hers. A long, heady kiss leaves him weak, as if his knees will fail him. Maria's response was nothing like Hector had expected. When Maria pulled away, she smiled, turned, and hurried into the house.

Starting up in his Ford Focus, Hector looked back as the porch light went out. "Holy Shit!" flew from his lips.

Hector waited a day and a half. He couldn't hold off any longer before calling Maria.

"It took you long enough." When Hector stammers, Maria tells him, "The answer to your question is yes."

"What question?"

"Yes, I will go out with you again."

After that, they go out at least once a week and meet for lunch and coffee when their schedules allow. After a few months, Hector was a regular guest at the Juarez home.

Maria, her father, and Mrs. Juarez began to speak more Spanish. Hector slowly picked up the language that should have been his first.

12

EVEN THOUGH HE'S stuck working with Davey Jones, Hector is learning. Jones isn't a teacher; he's not even a real partner but knows the streets and recognizes most of the Los Scorpios Locos and many other gangbangers by sight. He doesn't like to talk with anyone, especially the bangers. Hector gets to chat with many more than if he had partnered with any other AGE investigator.

With the Spanish Maria is forcing him to learn, Hector begins to understand some of the gangbangers' conversations when the young men are jammed up on the street. At first, they laugh at his feeble attempts at the language, but they cut him a little slack as Hector becomes somewhat conversant.

One evening at the line-up, Sergeant

Toliver tells Hector to partner with Katie O'Brien for the night. He sends Jones out with Steve Kowalski. Afterward, telling O'Brien and Hector to wait.

"Katie, patrol has a twenty-two-year-old Chicana in custody on a shaky shoplift. The arresting officer thinks the girl is a potential informant."

"Sarge, I have more CIs than I can manage."

"I know. Let me finish."

"Sorry."

"No problem. I want you to help Navarro with her. It's time he had his own CIs. Hector, you up for it?"

"Sure, sarge."

"Good. I'll tell the jail to hold on to the girl until you talk with her."

Davey Jones and Hector had never discussed Confidential Informants, let alone how to turn one. He and Katie spend an hour going over departmental policy and procedure. "The big thing with CIs is they're either on the books or off. Departmental policy forbids having any off-the-books informants."

"What's that mean?" Hector had read about the prohibition but hadn't given it any thought.

"You list on-the-books CIs in a confidential record available to Lieutenant

Delacroix, Captain Windsor, and of course, the Chief. You will fill out forms and sign protocols, which you must follow. Off-the-book informants are not registered with the department. The Chief fired the last guy caught trying it."

"If that's the case, why would anyone use an off-the-book informant?"

"Who knows? A thousand reasons, none of them good. I'm telling you, never use an off-the-books CI."

Arriving at the jail, Katie tells Hector, "We'll watch the young woman for a few minutes before talking to her." The interview rooms are four-by-six, with a table and two chairs with the backs to the door. The suspect sits in a chair anchored to the floor behind the table. He sits with his back to the wall while handcuffed by one wrist to a ring on the tabletop. The rooms have one-way mirrored windows allowing other officers and prosecutors to watch and listen to the interviews. Making the interrogation room even more depressing, an otherwise long-forgotten Criminal Justice study suggested that walls painted gray with pink and yellow splatters tend to calm violent or upset people. The paint job reminds Hector of vomit, a belief held by most cops and prisoners alike.

The arresting officer is waiting for them in the adjacent observation room. "I haven't finished my report yet. I'll wait until you talk to Ontiveros. Teresa Ontiveros, that's her name. I can release her with a warning or book her. Whatever you want. The drug store owner doesn't care as long as she stays out of his store."

"What'd she boost?"

"Enfamil. She claims it's for her baby."

"Do you believe her?"

"I'm not sure. She speaks street Spanglish and appears uneducated. But my gut tells me it's an act. I'm positive Ontiveros is educated."

Katie tells him, "We'll talk to her. Where'll we find you when we're done?"

"I'm off in an hour. I'll wait in the break room until you tell me how to finish the report."

"Thanks, we shouldn't be any longer than that."

Hector starts to follow the officer out. Katie takes his arm, "Not yet. We need to talk." He knows he is not going to talk—just listen. "Tell me everything you can about Teresa."

"I didn't pay much attention to her. I was listening to the officer."

"Wrong answer, Navarro."

Calling him Navarro sends a message *I've screwed up*. Hector tries again. "Well, she's Hispanic. She looks to be in her early twenties. She's dressed like a street girl, not a whore, and is pretty. That's it."

Already angry because she has to work with him instead of her partner, Katie looks at Hector with disdain. "Pretty. Just like a man. Didn't anyone ever teach you how to describe a person?"

He avoids her icy glare. The Irish in Katie comes to the surface as her face turns red, redder than her hair; her anger is palpable. Both are silent for a good minute. Finally, unable to take her ire any longer, Hector says, "I'm sorry. I'm ready to learn."

"I guess it's not your fault. Working on The Island, you probably never made an arrest or had to describe a suspect."

Hector can't contradict Katie. More than a few times working in District 8, he might go an entire shift without a call and days, weeks even, where he never made an arrest.

She takes a deep breath and lets it out. "Get out your notebook and write as I describe her." Before beginning, she turns away from the viewing window, her back to the girl.

"Start at the head and work your way down to the subject's feet. She has black hair, not dark brown—black. It's in a ponytail, long, waist length, clean, and cared for. What does that tell you?" Katie asks.

"She cares about her hair?" It's more a question than an answer.

"Now I know why the Preacher calls you Da Fool. She spends time on her hair. It's well-groomed—she isn't a street girl. Describe her face."

Hesitant to answer for fear of her wrath, Hector stares at a pink splatter on the wall.

"Describe her face."

Trying to see the girl's face in his mind, he finds it blank. Hector is more concerned about not answering than giving the wrong answer. "She has a pretty face."

"Can you describe your girlfriend's face?"

"Yes, but that's different."

"Yes. It's different. Do you know why? No. You don't have a clue. You look at your girlfriend, and you see her. The girl in the interview room is less than nothing to you. You looked at her and wrote her off. From here on out, look at people and see who they are, not what you think they are."

"Yes, Ma'am."

Giving him a frosty look, "Call me Ma'am again, and I'll kick your puny ass. This girl is a woman, a beautiful woman. She's wearing a set of inexpensive silver with turquoise earrings that complement her dark hair and features. Her makeup's subtle, not flashy.

Her face and skin are blemish-free—clean. She takes pride in her appearance." Katie's tone softens before continuing. "At least you were right about her being Hispanic. Did you notice the small chain around her neck?"

"No. Why?"

"She's a good Catholic. Unless I miss my guess, there'll be a crucifix or patron saint on that chain. I doubt she uses drugs or smokes. Describe her dress."

"Shabby."

"Wrong! She doesn't have much money, the dress is frayed, not shabby, and her shoes are worn but well-maintained. It's a summer dress with a light green floral pattern, another sign she isn't a street girl. Someone in Los Scorpios Locos victimized her."

"What makes you say that?" Hector asks in wonder.

"Did you see her tattoo?"

"No."

"Turn around and look at her. Study her as someone you're interested in—someone you want to know. Believe me, if you do, she will be your informant. You must know everything there is to know about your informants."

Hector stares at the girl momentarily before he realizes what Katie has been trying to tell him. She isn't a street girl. She's a person with a past, a present, and a future. She's no longer a girl—she's a woman—Theresa Ontiveros. She'll be part of his life. It takes him the better part of five minutes to spot the small bluish mark on the outside web of her left hand. Hector points at the tattoo and asks, "What does it mean?"

In a gentle voice, Katie answers, "We'll let her tell you. It's why I know she'll be your CI."

"Teresa, I'm Officer O'Brien. This is Officer Navarro. We want to talk to you."

"Why should I talk to you? I want out of here. My baby needs me."

"Where is your baby?

"*Mi Madre is* watching her."

"Where's the baby's father?"

The only response is a slight shrug of the young woman's shoulders.

Katie lets it slide. "Why are you here?"

"You know. I boosted stuff." Ontiveros tries to act tough.

She can't carry it off. Hector realizes it's all she can do to keep from crying. He's supposed to follow Katie's lead, but something forces him to speak up. "Ms. Ontiveros, you were arrested for shoplifting, but that's not why you're here." Tears run down her cheeks. She holds her eyes wide in a futile attempt to stem the flow. All pretense of defiance disappears. Her shoulders lose any semblance of control as they buckle. Her head sags until her chin rests on her chest. Her tears begin in earnest.

Hector lacks experience with crying women but senses this isn't an act. Looking at Katie, he mouths, "What?"

"Give her a minute, and then continue. You're doing fine."

Following Katie's suggestion to give the girl some time, Hector makes a few comments in his notebook, writing what he knows about her and a few questions he doesn't want to miss asking. Seeing that Ontiveros has regained her composure, he speaks up. "Ms. Ontiveros, we need to talk. Please look at me."

She stops crying and looks up at Hector.

"Tell us why you were shoplifting."

"Why should I tell you?" Grimacing, she adds, "you don't care what happens to me."

"That's bullshit. You're smarter than you pretend. Most people steal Enfamil to make money, but you didn't. You need food for your daughter."

Katie nods her approval.

With a sniffle, Ontiveros looks him in the eye. "If you know that, you know why I was shoplifting."

Katie was right. Her English is flawless. She is educated. She is not a street girl. "I need to feed my baby. Another one of the girls is watching her."

"So, who's the father?" Hector loses any small amount of rapport he'd built up.

Ontiveros looks up; her brown eyes darken and narrow with hatred. Her next words freeze him. "Sanchez and his pigs raped me so many times, who knows who the father is."

Hector gapes at her. *What can I say? What should I do?*

He turns to Katie in confusion. She gestures for him to sit back as she bends forward and takes the girl's left hand into hers.

Katie whispers as she touches the small tattoo on the web of Teresa's left hand. "Because of this?"

Ontiveros's response is barely perceptible, the slightest nod.

"Can I explain? He's unfamiliar with the ways of Los Scorpios Locos." Ontiveros nods in understanding.

"Hector, they kidnapped Teresa. First, they gave her a beat-down. Then she was tattooed, imprisoned, and raped by members of Los Scorpios Locos. The only escape is death."

"What do you mean? How can Sanchez get away with that?"

Ontiveros looks up and whispers, "Yes.

Yes, they can. They did it to me." She lowers her gaze to the grimy tabletop and adds, "and to many other girls and women."

Stunned into silence, Hector wonders, *how can this be?*

"Teresa. I can tell him later."

"No. He should know my world, a world of missing, taken, and murdered women. Go ahead."

"If I miss something, stop me."

The young detective had never seen Katie treat anyone with such tenderness.

"Hector, they'll never teach you this in the academy. The powers that be can't acknowledge this happens in New Liberty— anywhere. If they did, they would be bounced out of office in a heartbeat."

Hector hesitates for a moment before asking what powers.

"Jesus, Hector, the mayor, council members, the Governor, and even the President."

He decides to let that sink in and ask his Professor of Political Science father what he knows to be true.

"Teresa was probably in school when taken."

"Yes. I was attending Phoenix Community College when he spotted me."

Shit, that's the same college Maria attends.

"Once Sanchez marked her, she was doomed. He's the Comandante of the Los Scorpios Locos."

"I know who Sanchez is. What do you mean doomed?" Hector snaps and immediately regrets it.

"Once Sanchez fancied her, he made a play for her. Is that right, Teresa?"

"Yes, he stopped me at the bus stop in front of the college. Sanchez told me I should be his woman. He was so crude." She says with a visible shudder before continuing. "I told him there was no way I'd be his woman—his anything—ever."

"What'd he do?"

"He called me a *puta apestosa*, a smelly whore, and drove off."

"That wasn't the end of it, was it?"

"No. It was the beginning."

Turning to Hector, Katie says, "He told a trusted LSL woman he wanted Teresa." After a pause, she continues. "Show Hector."

Ontiveros puts her left hand on the table with the web face up, revealing a small, crude bluish tattoo. Three letters, LSL, are visible. Hector looks into her eyes with an unspoken question.

"Sanchez wanted me as a sex slave, not his woman. I remained his exclusive property until he was tired of me. Then, I became the gangs' plaything."

"The woman and one or two others found and kidnapped Teresa, then beat her unconscious. They used a needle and a regular ink pen to tattoo her. Inked-in, she became enslaved. If she tries to escape, they'll kill her. Right, Teresa?"

"Yes, they'll give me to Diablo."

"Once inked-in, they took Teresa to a house and forced her to stay with other women belonging to Los Scorpios Locos. Because Sanchez chose her, she had her own room where he had sex with her whenever the bastard felt like it. If he brought Teresa to his home, it would disrespect his wife—his family." After an audible sigh, "How long before Sanchez tired of you?"

"I lost track of time. It was three or four months before he replaced me."

Confused, Hector winces, "Replaced?"

"Men like Sanchez aren't interested in long-term relationships, except for the women they marry." Ontiveros sobs and continues. "We quit struggling, and the men lose interest. Three months was longer than usual."

Not knowing how to respond, Hector asks if she wants anything.

"Some water and Kleenex, please."

"I'll be right back." He leaves the women alone.

When Hector returns with the water and

tissue, Katie has her ponytail wrapped around her left hand. Ontiveros thanks him and continues explaining the hell her life has become.

"I didn't quit fighting him. When Sanchez tired of beating me, he gave me to the gang. Any LSL can screw me—anytime. When I got pregnant, they lost interest in me. I live with eight other pregnant girls. They give us nothing. We do whatever it takes to eat—to survive. Once our babies are six months old, they sell them and put us back where they can screw us. Olivia's four months old."

Aghast, Hector exclaims, "How can this be? How long will you be a slave?"

"Until I die, or they decide to kill me. As long as I look good and follow the gang rules, I belong to LSL. After they tire of me, I'll be put in a brothel or forced to walk the streets as a prostitute." Hector realizes it's like a horror story, only worse. He can't imagine a happy ending.

"You could run away or go to the police."

"They'll find me and feed me to Diablo."

"What's Diablo?"

"Diablo is a giant Rottweiler trained to kill," Katie says. "I planned to tell you later, but let's get it out of the way. We have no proof, but we've heard enough stories to be certain it's real."

Shaking like a leaf in a windstorm,

Ontiveros declares, "It's true."

The idea of a vicious dog killing people is sickening. Hector asks, "What makes you think it's true?"

"One of the girls tried to get away. She took her baby and left on a Greyhound Bus for her hometown, McAllen, Texas. When she arrived, she found her mama and papa tied to chairs. First, two Los Scorpios Locos raped her in front of her parents and then stabbed them to death. They put her and the baby in the trunk of her parents' car and drove back here. The baby died on the trip."

The more she says, the more Hector's hatred for Sanchez and Los Scorpios Locos grows. "What happened to her?"

The young woman shivers as she cries.

"Tell me if I'm wrong. Sanchez took all the girls out to the ranch. He keeps Diablo in a pit and makes you watch. Am I right so far?" Katie asks.

"Yes. Then Sanchez laughed. It wasn't funny. It scared me. When he saw how frightened we were, he laughed even more and pointed at two of his *tenientes*, lieutenants. They picked the girl up and held her over the pit. Diablo barked and jumped at her. It was terrible." Ontiveros is crying. She pauses to blow her nose before continuing. "As they lowered her inch-by-inch, Diablo jumped and bit her foot. It was beyond torture as the dog began eating her alive. Her screams were horrible."

Katie asks, "You want to stop?" The girl cries and lays her head on the table. "Get her a glass of water."

Hector goes down the hall to the bathroom, his face clammy, almost overcome with nausea; he can't remember ever feeling so ill. He washes his face before going to the break room for a glass of water. The uniformed officer is waiting. "Are you guys done yet?"

"No, but we want her to walk on this. Can you make it happen?"

"I figured you might. The report is written and ready to submit. As soon as you want, I'll walk Ontiveros out. I already closed the case."

"Thanks, I owe you one."

Back in the interview room, Ontiveros has regained her composure. Katie says, "Teresa's willing to call you from time to time. She knows the risk." Katie hands him a CIR, a Confidential Informant Registration File.

"What's this?"

"Open it."

Hector finds a checklist on the left and a stack of forms on the right.

"Teresa must sign the one that states she will not break the law. If she does, and we find out, we'll prosecute her."

The forms are simple, a warning form and a questionnaire asking for details on how the CI came to the officer's attention. It asked what, if anything, he had done anything for the woman. Hector looks at Katie, "Can we step out for a minute?"

"The officer dropped the charges. Do I write that down?"

"No. The arresting officer determined there was insufficient evidence to prosecute her. He called us because he thought Ontiveros would talk to us. She's a voluntary CI."

"What do I write?"

"Fill out the background information. Get as much as you can without jacking Ontiveros up too much. Don't forget to ask about her life before LSL. Have her read the admonishment to behave and sign it. We'll write down everything she told us after she's released."

The two spend another half hour getting the paperwork out of the way. Hector gives her a slip of paper with his name and cell phone number. "I always answer it hello, nothing more. Call me tomorrow and tell me what's going on."

"I want Katie's number too. In case I can't reach you."

Katie sends for a jailer to release Ontiveros.

"Shouldn't we give her a ride?"

"Think. You've been on the streets long enough that you'll be recognized. Most gangbangers in New Liberty know me by sight. What happens to her if some LSL Vato sees her getting dropped off by AGE officers?"

"I guess I didn't think."

"You must never forget every move you make affects others. You're responsible for Teresa until they kill her—they will one day. Maybe because of you or because she looks at Sanchez the wrong way, and he decides to make an example of her. What she does wrong or doesn't do, makes little difference. Eventually, they will kill her. Never treat a CI differently. It's a dead-bang giveaway. Don't get emotionally involved with her or any CI. And for God's sake, don't even imagine sleeping with her."

Anxious to change the subject, Hector asks, "What happened to the girl who ran away?"

"They dangled her for a few minutes. Sanchez nodded. They dropped her in the pit."

"What happened then?"

"What do you think happened?" An exasperated Katie shakes her head.

"The fucking dog ate her!"

13

WITH THREE DEAD bodies, the investigation falls to the Homicide Squad.

Sergeant Toliver and the AGE officers are positive the shooters are 4-Aces. He's confident Kowalski will have the shooters' names within days, if not hours. However, knowledge does not always equal arrest or prosecution.

Even before Kowalski gets the names, he tells Toliver, "Geronimo ordered the killings as part of a 4-Aces initiation. Galloway picked the time and place, provided weapons, and guided the shooters to and from the killing zone."

"How soon can you call your informant?"

"I already tried. No answer. He's at Ernesto's, celebrating the initiation. I doubt we'll hear from him before tomorrow morning."

"Should we pay a visit to Ernesto's? We might get an idea of who the new members are?"

Kowalski says, "We could. It might backfire."

"How do you figure?"

"If we get inside, Geronimo will figure out that someone gave us the information."

"What if we visit four or five gangs?"

Kowalski thinks a moment before saying, "It's up to you, Bob. But I agree, it is the smart way to go. Everyone knows this was a drive-by. Besides, it never hurts to show the gangs we're pissed. Keep the pressure on. And with luck, some will see a chance to put some hurt on the 4-Aces and drop a dime."

"You're right. I'll call homicide and the watch commander. You take the 4-Aces. I want Harris and Navarro to ride with you or O'Brien."

"O'Brien's my partner."

"I want them to see you and Katie in action. Humor me. Your choice, Harris or Navarro?"

Thursday, July 25, at zero-one-hundred hours. The homicide lieutenant and the watch commander are skeptical, but considering they have three dead, they agree preemptive action might help keep a lid on open warfare. New Liberty Police Officers hit the clubhouses of five gangs. Each team comprises two AGE officers, one homicide investigator, and six uniformed officers.

As expected, Katie is upset. "Damn it, Steve. Why's Toliver splitting us up?"

"I don't like it any more than you, but he's the boss. He wants the rookies with us."

"Yeah, yeah, why'd I get stuck with Harris? He's such a tight ass."

"Okay, partner. I'll take him if you want."

"Forget it. This way, I have something else to bitch about for a change. Good luck with Geronimo. You'll need it."

DeShawn Galloway interrupts Geronimo's welcoming of Corky into the 4-Aces by tapping him on the shoulder. "We have company. That cop, Kowalski, he's out front with five or six other cops."

"They here about the spics?"

"What else?"

"A snitch?"

"Sure, they got snitches. We knew they would be around sooner or later."

"Take Corky with you. I don't want the cops to see him."

Galloway and Corky go out the back door

and find uniformed cops waiting. Galloway tells Corky, "Don't sweat it. It's the gang cops we have to avoid."

Kowalski isn't surprised at Galloway's absence. Kowalski knows he's hiding the shooters. "Hector, keep the camera handy. If I point someone out, take their picture before they have time to hide their faces."

The room is silent for a moment before Geronimo's voice booms, "Officer Kowalski, what brings you to our humble abode?"

Geronimo sits on his Zulu Chieftain's throne as Kowalski walks across the room with Hector and Jim Collins at his sides. "You know why we're here. A Black crew paid a visit to Little Chihuahua a few hours ago. Any chance they were 4-Aces?"

"Why, Officer Kowalski, the 4-Aces are a peaceful neighborhood group."

"Right."

Geronimo isn't sure how successful the drive-by was. The best way to find out, ask *The Man*. "What happened in spic town?"

"You likely know better than I do. So far, two LSLs and a civilian are dead. We don't know for sure how many are wounded."

"You talk to Sanchez. Give him our condolences."

"Sure. I'll let him know how upset you are. Where's The Knife?"

"What knife?"

Kowalski lets that slide. "Who'd you initiate tonight?"

Geronimo gives him a look that suggests he thinks the cop is crazy and does not answer.

Kowalski introduces the large man to his left. "This's Detective Sergeant Collins. He has some questions for you."

"Good evening, Detective Collins. What's a brother doing with AGE?"

"I'm homicide, investigating a shooting on the Los Scorpios Locos turf earlier tonight. You know anything about that?"

"Are you the one who played football for the Cardinals?"

"I played a little football, but that's not why I'm here. I want to know about the shootings. Where were you at ten?"

"I've been here since yesterday afternoon, even had dinner here." Geronimo gestures with a finger and indicates the twenty or so people in the hall. "All these brothers and sisters will testify to that."

The detective lowers his head shaking it before straightening up and saying, "Oh, I'm sure they will."

"I'm a peaceful man. Violence on the streets hurts me deeply. How many of those poor souls were hurt in the drive-by?"

"I didn't say there was a drive-by."

"Why, Detective Collins, you sound

suspicious. You must have missed the ABC15 Eleven O'clock news. They say Blacks did the shooting, but I bet it was those Vietnamese. How can we help you?"

"I need a list of witnesses who can corroborate your alibi."

Detective Collins and the uniformed officers begin collecting names. The confusion caused by the women and older men shuffling around and hiding the younger men makes the process difficult. In frustration, Collins turns to Geronimo. "Can't you get your people to stand still? I wanna get this over with."

"You barge into my house uninvited, you accuse me of murder, and you want my help. Unless you got a warrant, get your Uncle Tom ass and your White masters out of here." Geronimo speaks loud enough for all to hear.

The crowd, which has remained silent, begins chanting, "Fuck you, Uncle Tom," and "Get out."

Kowalski whispers in Collins's ear. "We have photographs of everyone, and our people can ID them. Galloway and the shooters are nowhere around. I suggest we walk away."

Collins agrees and signals the uniformed officers to follow, taking his time as he walks out through the front door of Ernesto's. On the sidewalk, he asks Kowalski, "What gives?"

"Geronimo's playing the role. We put up with this crap all the time. He knows we know his crew did the shooting. He also knows we can't prove anything," Kowalski adds, "for now."

14

LOS SCORPIOS LOCOS JOSE Maldonado, Jr. is buried. Maldonado served honorably in the U.S. Army but not for the love of his country. He was jumped-in into Los Scorpios Locos at the old age of seventeen. The LSL commander ordered him to refrain from tattooing. "Yo, little brother. You join the army, keep clean, and learn to use automatic weapons." Maldonado's parents believed he had joined the army to escape the gangs.

His years of military service complete, Maldonado returned to New Liberty and Los Scorpios Locos. His parents were proud of their son—for a few days. After reporting to Sanchez, Maldonado visited an LSL tattoo artist and soon sported gang tattoos from head to foot. His parents were devastated.

Today, a few months later, they're over-whelmed with sorrow as they lay their one child to rest. The army provides an honor guard and a twenty-one-gun salute. Nothing makes up for the ghastly demonstration by the hundred or so Los Scorpios Locos who show up drunk and rowdy at the funeral home. Even the women sport gang colors— green shirts or bandanas.

Sanchez interrupts the service as he speaks to the parents. "Jose was a good soldier. I promise we'll revenge him and the other Vatos."

"Leave us alone." Outraged, Mr. Maldonado shouts as he rises from the pew. "You and your filthy gang killed him."

"Watch your mouth, old man."

Mrs. Maldonado, fearing for her husband, pulls him back. "Jose, please."

Sinking back, Mr. Maldonado sobs, "Leave us alone."

"Let us pray." The priest begins.

Before the church service started, Sanchez passed the word to his lieutenants, "War council at my house after they take Jose away." The comandante is so focused on revenge; that he can't hold off for one minute—his thirst for revenge clouds all reason.

A dozen Los Scorpios Locos lieutenants gather at their comandante's home. The customary Tequila shots are offered to the memory of Maldonado and the other Los Scorpios Locos killed in the drive-by. "I called you here to plan payback on the 4-Aces. Chucho, this happened on your ground. What you got?"

Chucho Montemayor knew his boss, furious and wanting revenge, would blame him. Within an hour of the shooting, he began plotting a hit on the 4-Aces that would meet Sanchez's demand for blood or at least appease him for the time being. If it isn't enough to quench the LSL leader's bloodlust, Chucho will be sacrificed to Diablo. He would rather kill himself than suffer that fate.

"I want to hit 'em at Ernesto's," the psychopathic gang leader screams. "So, what's your plan?" as he sneers at his youngest lieutenant.

Chucho explains his proposal over the next hour, and Sanchez and the other lieutenants like the plan. They accept the proposal; it's up to the comandante to approve the hit and set a date. Chucho wants to go tonight. Sanchez won't allow it.

"Geronimo will expect something on the one-month anniversary, the twenty-fourth. You go on August twenty-third."

15

CORKY'S INITIATION IS the talk of all the Black gangs, not just the 4-Aces. The youngster earned the respect of many older original gang members, or OGMs as they're called. Galloway says, "The kid has a bright future with the Aces," and takes the newest gang member under his wing.

James "Li'l Mo" Morris is unhappy. *I was in line to apprentice to Galloway until Corky came along. Now I'm sitting on the sidelines. If it weren't for the little prick, I'd be DeShawn's boy. It ain't right.*

Ralphie and Kevin died during the initiation. "Ralphie acted like an Ace and was killed. Kevin didn't perform for shit." Even though a small handful know how Kevin died, most suspect Galloway dealt with him.

After all, he left Kevin's body in the minivan for the cops to find while Ralphie had a 4-Aces funeral.

Chucho Montemayor is far from happy. The Blacks killed Los Scorpios Locos Vatos at his house, and the shooters are still walking around.

Chucho isn't surprised that Sanchez gives him the assignment. As a lieutenant, he must punish the wrongdoers. He wants to kill those who dishonored his home and shot down his friends. What bothers him are the terms, "Two weeks, or you take the niggas place."

"Whatcha mean?"

"You kill them, or you dance with Diablo."

As he feared, Sanchez is pitiless. "You'd put me in the pit?"

"*Si Ese, comprende?*"

Chucho does what the cops do—he offers a reward. Calling the brothers and sisters he knows, offering a thousand dollars for the names of the 4-Aces who did the drive-by. Then Chucho calls the Blacks he knows from high school and county jail. Within an hour, Li'l Mo Morris calls. "Yo, Chucho, how's your spic ass hanging?"

"Cut the shit, Li'l Mo. The drive-by."

"Yo. I heard there's money for da names. That for real?"

"If I say it, it's real. What you got?"

"I'll give you the names, but not until I see the money."

Meeting Li'l Mo out in the desert at midnight, Chucho shows him the cash.

The little Black man can't wait to rat out his brothers. "It was an initiation."

"No shit, *Ese*. Run it down."

"Galloway ran it. He ordered a drive-by in Little Chihuahua. He followed the wannabes but kept back. A young brother sat in the back with a Mac-10. Two were in front with thirty-eights."

"What're their names? Where do they live?"

"Don't matter. Kevin and Ralphie dead."

"Did we kill 'em?"

"You spics shot Ralphie, but Galloway took care of Kevin."

"Whatcha mean?"

"He died in the van. Kevin was a punk, so Galloway put a blade in the kid's heart."

"Who was the one with the Mac-10?"

"That be Corky, he fifteen. He live on Thirty-Eight with his moms."

"What's the number?"

"Who knows, never been there?"

"Here's five hundred. You get the other

half when I get the address. What's Corky drive?"

"Shit, you wanna get me killed? I told you, he's a kid. He doesn't drive."

After telling Li'l Mo he wants the number before sunup, Chucho leaves. An hour later, the turncoat calls. "I got his address and the license for his mom's car. I'll meet you at the same place."

"I'll be there at five, don't be late."

Chucho likes the place. It's a mile off the highway on a dirt road and up a canyon to an abandoned mine. Li'l Mo can't be trusted. He'll rat anyone out and set them up if he thinks he can get away with it. With that in mind, Chucho knows he must plan for a double-cross, one that would leave him dead. He'll be ready for anything Li'l Mo tries.

Chucho beats Li'l Mo by an hour and parks behind an old building fifty yards from where they had met earlier. It's eerie—as quiet as a cemetery. The moon is full, but the canyon walls are so high they block the light. He can't remember a spot so dark. Even with a flashlight, it's hard to see, and the night swallows the light. Walking back to the meeting place, the gravel grates underfoot, breaking the silence. It is so quiet the sound echoes off the canyon walls. Finding a crack in the canyon wall, he hides within feet of the spot where the two had talked earlier. Unless

Li'l Mo shines a light into the gap, he'll never see his killer. The rocks are still warm from the heat of the day. It relaxes Chucho. Leaning against the rock wall, he dozes off. What seems like seconds pass before he's startled awake by the sound of a car. It could be around the corner or a mile down the road. That's how echoes carry over the silent desert. Within minutes, lights reflect off the canyon walls.

Li'l Mo parks less than ten feet from Chucho and turns off the motor. For another minute, he leaves the headlights on, illuminating the roadway leading back to the entrance to the canyon. The silence is deafening. The car windows are open. The smell of marijuana wafts through the cold night air. *What an idiot—driving up this narrow canyon smoking dope.*

Chucho hears voices; the snitch is not alone. It's a setup—*never could trust that blood.* He recognizes Li'l Mo's voice. "Chucho will be here at five. You grab the shotgun and get behind the car when you see his headlights. After he stops, I'll get out and walk to the front of the car."

"Where's the sawed-off?" A second male voice asks.

"In the trunk. Chucho gets here, you wait until I light a cigarette. You stand up and blow his spic ass away when he gets between the cars. Don't give him a chance."

"What'll I get?"

"You get half the money, two-fifty. Get the sawed-off."

They get out, and Li'l Mo opens the trunk. The other man bends in to retrieve the weapon.

Chucho steps behind them, and the gravel crunches. It is loud—deafening. Startled, the second one straightens up so fast he hits his head on the trunk lid.

"Li'l Mo was gonna cheat you."

The man swivels to the sound in the darkness, "Whatcha mean?"

"It was a thousand, not five hundred." Chucho shoots him in the face.

"Li'l Mo, shame on you, *Ese*. Did you even get the address?"

"No, man, but I can take you there. Please don't shoot me."

"How can I trust you? You were going to have your friend off me."

Li'l Mo begs. "Please, I'll do anything."

They all say that when they realize they're going to die.

"No problem *Ese*. I promise I won't shoot you. Tell me how to get to the kid's house."

Li'l Mo can't wait to offer up Corky. The frightened man's directions are so detailed that Chucho knows how to find the young killer.

Chucho puts his pistol inside his pants belt and extends his right hand. "No hard feelings." Li'l Mo lets out a sigh of relief and takes his hand. Chucho pulls him in and stabs him in the stomach. He's left-handed. As Li'l Mo dies, he looks up with a silent question.

Lifting his shoulder in a shrug, "I didn't shoot you. A promise is a promise."

Corky has been under Galloway's protection since the drive-by. A week after the last Los Scorpios Locos funeral, he decides Corky can go home. The kid has been bugging him to go. Besides, Galloway needs some private time with a woman.

Chucho follows another piece of advice Jose Maldonado brought home from the army. Blend in—stay motionless, and eventually, you will be ignored. Ignored is invisible. In a matter of days, the kid comes home. An Escalade pulls up to the house as darkness falls. The driver does not get out: a kid who looks to be fifteen or sixteen climbs out and runs up the porch. He has a small duffle bag with him. A porch light comes on. A heavyset Black woman wearing a nightgown opens the door and yells, "Corky."

"I got you. You little shit," Chucho whispers to himself. He calls two Vatos and has them meet him. "Bring three burners and heat." When they arrive, he rides by the kid's house with them. Taking one of the burners, he has them drop him at his car.

"You watch the house tonight. If the kid moves, I want to know. I'll be back in the morning. You got heat?" They do.

Chucho enjoys his first good night's sleep in a week. Only four days are left until he has to go into the pit with Diablo. *I'll make it—this time. Someday I'll have to kill Sanchez.*

The next morning, Chucho calls the two vatos at six. "I'm a block away. Did the kid do anything?"

"No. The lights went out around eleven. It's been quiet ever since."

"Go eat, take a piss, and be back in an hour."

The kid's mom works in the front yard for an hour before Corky comes out. He's wearing baggy pants hanging below red underpants and a red headband, 4-Aces. Chucho hits redial. "He's getting ready to move. Be ready. An old blue Ford's in the driveway." The two are talking; both seem agitated. After some arm gesturing, the kid goes back into the house. He comes out a few minutes later, waves at his mother, and gets into the Ford.

Corky pulls out of the driveway.

Chucho tells the others which way the youngster is headed. The kid stays on 38th; there are stop signs every three blocks. "Pull on to Thirty-eighth in front of him and slow down. Stop and wait at the next stop sign. He'll be behind you. I'll box him in."

If Chucho's vatos had been looking forward instead of fastening all their attention on Corky, they might have seen the marked police car slowing, crossing thirty-eighth at the stop. Had they been, Chucho would have postponed the hit for one more cross street or another time.

Corky pulls up and stops behind the Los Scorpios Locos car at the intersection. Playing on his car's radio is *Fuckin' with B.I.G. It ain't safe* from the rapper's song, "Who Shot Ya."

Chucho stops a foot behind the blue Ford, eases out, leaves the car door ajar, and walks up to Corky's driver's side door. To his right is a rundown liquor store. Event flyers and 4-Aces graffiti cover the walls and windows. Several old men sit on a bench next to the entrance. Each of them holds a brown paper bag, alkies with forties. Across the intersection, an old Black woman in a crossing guard uniform seems to be shielding a group of little kids on their way to school.

At the old Ford's driver's side, Chucho is happy that the window is down, making the target much easier to execute. The kid's attention is on the Vatos in front of him.

"Yo, Corky?"

"Yeah." The kid doesn't even look up.

Chucho puts the forty against the teenager's left temple and pulls the trigger. Blood splatters across the passenger side of the car.

The two officers in the car might have heard the shot if the vehicle's windows had been open and the radio was not pounding out Queen's "Bohemian Rhapsody" as loud as they could stand.

Swinging his arms wide as he takes the few steps back to his car, Chucho gives it his best imitation of Notorious B.I.G. as he raps, *Fuckin' with LSL ain't safe.* Laughing, he yells, "Go," gets in his car, and drives away at the speed limit. The kid isn't his first kill, but this one feels good—delicious. He hopes it will be enough to satisfy Sanchez. It won't be. Chucho knows he'll have to appease the monster's ego, or Sanchez will keep his promise and feed Chucho to Diablo.

A Valley Metro bus stops at the cross street. The driver, a young White man, stares as Chucho drives through the intersection. How many passengers saw him shoot the kid? With any luck, they'll tell the cops, "A

Mexican-looking guy. That's all I can tell you."

Sanchez is not satisfied. He demands more "I want Geronimo and the 4-Aces humiliated.

16

INSIDE THE OLD warehouse, the air is cool. Outside, the temperature is well over one hundred. Chucho paces. He thinks something smells funny, like gas and fire, and something he can't quite place. He can't know it's the same warehouse where the 4-Aces wannabes, Ralphie, and Kevin died. The floor under the mini-van is scorched, and the warehouse floor is covered with the residue of many fires. Chucho accepts the odors as like dozens of other abandoned buildings. The scent that eludes him is that of burnt flesh.

Three of Chucho's soldiers lean against a Yukon stolen earlier in the day. All around the SUV, the floor is burnt black. Where are the others? He told them to be here at eight.

Mexicans, you can't ever count on them. Before he decides to call them, a car pulls up outside. A minute later, the roll-up rises, and two vehicles pull inside. They were stolen earlier in Phoenix, and both have cold license plates. Chucho has twelve soldiers, four to a car—handpicked fighters. Not one will let him down, but he knows he can't ease up on them.

"Make sure you have a full tank of gas."

Chucho gets his M-16 from the car, racks a cartridge into the chamber, and adds another to the magazine. Next, he examines the four spare mags; each contains thirty rounds. He makes sure all his men have weapons and ammunition. Some carry Glock .40 Caliber pistols; others have M-16s or AK-47s. Chucho wishes everyone carried the same caliber.

"Let's go over this again. We gotta figure the aces will have at least one guy on lookout." The others agree. "You stay on my tail until we get a few blocks from Ernesto's, then stay back five or six car lengths." The drivers nod assent.

Chucho takes a hand grenade from the trunk of his car as he asks, "Any questions?"

"Yo, Chucho. You going to dump that grenade through the window?"

"No, I'm gonna open the front door and throw it in."

"Man, you got balls, *Ese.*"

Chucho doesn't tell them he doesn't want to take a chance; the grenade might bounce back if he tries throwing it through the bar window. "When I stop, you come into the driveway." He tells the drivers to pull into the driveway and stop the same distance from the entrance. "Get out and stand behind the cars." His soldiers will do as told. Chucho gives them ten minutes to take a leak and have a last smoke.

When they're all back, "We don't stop for anything except cops. If anyone gets stopped, we block the pigs and kill them. If that happens, we hit the 4-Aces another day."

At 10:00 p.m., Chucho has his driver stop next to Ernesto's. He's pumped—scared.

No one is in front of the pool hall as Chucho walks with an exaggerated swagger to the front door with the grenade. He pulls the pin and holds down the release. The door opens, and a Black man stares out.

Without a word, the man steps back inside and screams, "Spics."

Chucho opens the door and throws the grenade over the heads of those at the first table. As soon as the grenade explodes, the Yukon moves, giving them a clear shot of the parking lot. Holding their weapons the way

Jose Maldonado taught them, they're ready. A few of the 4-Aces reach the lot. Chucho screams, "This is for Jose." After emptying his second mag, he shouts, "Go, Vatos, Go."

Back at the warehouse, one driver collects the weapons and takes them to a safe house. The other drivers drop the soldiers off at the clubs they had come from before the shooting. "Make sure you talk to a lot of Vatos and sisters. Make sure they know you never left the club." After the drivers drop the shooters off, they drive to remote desert locations. Others drive them home in cold cars. Another crew douses the vehicles with gas and burns them. Chucho picks up a girl, Teresa Ontiveros, and takes her to a club.

Sanchez is pleased.

The news on the radio is sketchy at best.

> Shooting at Ernesto's in New Liberty.

> Eight dead and at least a dozen wounded, several not expected to survive the night.

The next day, the *Arizona Republic* covers the shooting in more detail.

> Eight people killed and eight injured in what police believe was gang-related retaliation for a drive-by shooting last

month in the area of New Liberty known as Little Chihuahua. In that incident, four men believed to be members of the Los Scorpios Locos gang were gunned down.

Police responded to reports of an explosion and gunfire at Ernesto's Pool Hall around 9:50 p.m. Hundreds of shots were fired. At least one military -style hand grenade was allegedly used.

According to police spokesperson Captain Mary Windsor, the street gang unit was called upon to investigate because the area is known for gang activity, prostitution, and narcotics trafficking.

Four men and a woman died at the scene, and two more died at local hospitals. All the men are believed to be members of the 4-Aces gang. Mr. Jerome Dixon, interviewed at the scene, told this reporter, "We're not a gang. Most of us grew up in New Liberty. We went to school together, and yes, a few of us have been to prison. We like to socialize."

Sources within law enforcement who spoke on condition of anonymity confirmed Ernesto's Pool Hall is the home of an African American gang, the 4-Aces. Sources dispute what Mr. Dixon claims. "They're a gang, and Geronimo Dixon is their leader."

Detective James Collins is the lead investigator on this shooting and the incident in Little Chihuahua last month. Detective Collins declined an interview for this story.

James Kennemore, Staff Writer.

Sanchez sends Chucho out of town. "Geronimo figures out you the one. He'll be coming for your ass. Get to Tucson and stay at my Tia Juanita's place. Tell your soldiers to get out of town. I'll tell you when it's safe to come back."

17

DEPUTY MEDICAL EXAMINER Liz Bannister will conduct all the autopsies on the LSL shooting victims. She is new to the Maricopa County Medical Examiner's Office but not to pathology. After earning her M.D. from John Hopkins, she completed a residency at Stanford, followed by a prestigious fellowship at the office of the Los Angeles Medical Examiner-Coroner. Her next stop was the Office of Chief Medical Examiner, City of New York. Two years later, wanting to be nearer her family, she took a step down and accepted a position with Maricopa County. Athletic, she's an attractive six-foot-tall Eurasian with deep red hair and green eyes.

She met Officer Steve Kowalski when he arrived at her first New Liberty homicide scene. She was greeted by a plain-clothes officer who unabashedly looked her over from head to foot. Never one to avoid a challenge, Liz says, "So, you like what you see?" While thinking, my, aren't you one handsome man?

The officer, taken off guard, stammered, "Yes, Ma'am, I mean no, Doctor, please excuse me." His face turned a bright red as he hurried away.

The detective in charge of the scene introduced himself. "Afternoon, Doctor. I'm Detective Sergeant Jim Collins. I have to say I've never seen Kowalski blush before, let alone turn tail and skedaddle like that."

"Kowalski? Who is he?"

"Steve Kowalski, he's the officer who put the bad guy down."

"Okay, detective, let's take a look at the deceased."

The next time Liz Bannister sees Kowalski is a year later, shortly before her sister Joyce marries Bob Toliver. Joyce, a few years younger, fashions herself a matchmaker. With her and Bob getting married, she does her best to find the right man for her older sister. "Come on, Sis. It's not a blind date. He's Bob's best man, and you're my maid of honor. It's dinner. It'll give us a chance to talk about the wedding. Besides, you'll like him."

"You win, I'll be there? Do I bring anything?"

"No. *La Azul Noche* at seven-thirty, be there."

"*La Azul Noche,* I've never been there. Isn't that a little expensive for a cop?"

"It's a special occasion. Liz, promise me you'll be there?"

"Yes, I'll be there."

Liz arrives late, quite late. What she assumed would be the routine autopsy of an unattended death took longer than anticipated after she found the decedent, who weighed 450 pounds, had slipped off the gurney. Moreover, the fall exposed a heretofore unseen gunshot wound to the back. "I'm sorry, we had a problem at work," she says, sliding into the empty chair across from Joyce. She gives Bob Toliver a peck on his cheek. Turning to the other man, she freezes. The officer who had checked her out stands within arm's length. She remembers how he flushed and ran when she confronted him.

Before Liz or Steve can speak, Joyce senses something from her sister's reaction. "Steve, this is my sister, Liz. Liz, meet Bob's best friend and best man, Steve Kowalski."

Liz does not intend to help this guy. "We have met. Isn't that correct, Mr. Kowalski?"

Much to her surprise, he doesn't seem to

be in the least bit embarrassed. Kowalski laughs. "Joyce, I haven't met your sister, not officially."

"What's that mean?" Joyce looks baffled.

"I did what any healthy red-blooded man would do. I checked her out. Your sister's the hottest M.E. I've ever seen."

Now it's Liz's turn to blush. Joyce is enjoying her sister's reaction. "Oh, Steve, you must tell us the whole story."

Toliver looks from face to face in amusement. "Yes. We have to hear the story."

"It's not fair. You've had time for drinks. You'll have to wait until I catch up." Liz orders a Manhattan. Waiting for her drink to arrive, she notices that the restaurant is all she has heard and more. The walls are a deep blue, highlighted by lighter colors that bring out the subtle sense of a warm spring night. The mellow sound of Spanish love songs sung so softly that Liz feels rather than hears the music. The décor enhances the feeling of relaxation in an elegant hacienda. Joyce couldn't have picked a better place to practice her matchmaking. *This guy doesn't seem the same.* She decides she doesn't want to embarrass either of them, whoever he is. "Steve, we were both tired and more than a little on edge. Can we forget it? Start over?"

Kowalski saves the moment. "My best friend's marrying the woman of his dreams.

Let's get this show on the road."

Dinner lives up to expectations. Liz can see that her sister and Bob are anxious to get away for some pre-nuptial sex. "You guys take off. Steve and I'll be fine."

As Toliver reaches for his wallet, Steve puts up a hand to stop him. "I have this. You kids get out of here."

Moving to the bar, Steve surprises her by taking an arm and helping her into a booth: *Humm, a gentleman. Be careful. Remember the way he looked at you.* As they settle in, drinks arrive, surprising Liz. "I didn't see you order. I'm not sure I should have another."

"Don't worry. I'm not going to try to seduce you."

Liz can't decide whether to be mad or flattered. They spend an hour getting to know one another. Neither is what the other imagined.

18

THE INCESSANT RINGING of his departmental cell phone forces Bob Toliver out of a deep sleep. "Toliver here."

"Bob, Jim Collins, sorry to call at this hour."

"You wouldn't be calling if it weren't important. Did you get any sleep? I got three hours."

"No. I'm still running with the shooting. A New Liberty Fire Battalion Chief called; he says they have a burnt-out minivan with a crispy critter inside. Can you meet me there?"

"Give me the address. I'll be there in thirty minutes."

"Thanks, Bob. This case is a homicide, but I need your help."

"I'll grab Steve. You want us to pick up coffee?"

"Yeah, black, very black, very hot."

"What, no cream, no sweetener?"

"Funny. I need as much caffeine as I can get."

"I'll hurry."

Toliver stretches as his wife sits up with a sigh. "I guess I won't see you until breakfast or later?"

"I'm sorry, honey. The fire department found a dead body that might be one of last night's shooters." Collins didn't say anything about the connection, but Toliver assumes Collins wouldn't have called if he didn't suspect a link.

Without another word, Joyce Toliver lies back, instantly asleep. She is used to the middle-of-the-night calls that require her husband to leave their bed.

"Thanks for the coffee, Bob. I needed it. Before we go in, you must put on safety gear. The Battalion Chief and Fire Inspector are cooperative. The fire was short-lived but intense."

Toliver shakes his head as he takes a swallow of coffee. "Do they have any idea of the victim's race, age, gender, time, or cause of death?"

"The Medical Examiner's sure it's a male based on the physique. She'll have to run lab tests to confirm it. The body is in the back of the van, burned beyond recognition. The victim, and the van, were doused with an accelerant—gasoline—then torched. The odor is strong in there. The Fire Inspector said that inside the van, they got a strong response on the meter."

Kowalski says, "My guess would be one of the shooters was hit and died. Galloway intended to burn the minivan from the get-go. With the kid dead, he figured to clean up the entire mess in one move."

Detective Collins is already geared up. "Let's look at the scene before the M.E. moves the body?"

The AGE officers gear up, and the three detectives follow the Battalion Chief inside to the scene. The Chief tells them, "This building's part of a complex used in World War II and then again during the Korean War. They made landing craft." He explains that the cavernous building has stood idle since 1952. Every piece of equipment, anything of value, has long since been looted, leaving a hollow shell. "The blaze vented up through hundreds of broken skylights. The fire itself was quite intense due to an accelerant but brief. Once the contents of the minivan were consumed, there was no other fuel to feed the fire. After the fire was extinguished, during overhaul, the firefighters found the body in the back of the van. They called this a crime scene and released the site to the Fire Inspector."

A group of geared-up people waits near the van. Deputy Medical Examiner Liz Bannister appears to be the center of attention. As the official representative of the M. E's Office, she has charge of the body until she releases the remains to a funeral home. No doubt exists that death was not the result of natural causes. Her office will take the body and turn the scene over to Detective Collins after talking with the Fire Inspector, a uniformed officer, and three Crime Scene Investigators. Dr. Bannister's accustomed to being the center of attention. She's six feet tall, with deep red hair and green eyes. It's common knowledge that she has become the heart and soul of the Maricopa County Medical Examiner's Office.

"Why are the famous AGE officers here with you, Detective Collins?"

"We're always on the lookout for an opportunity to watch the M.E.s preeminent witch doctor in action," Bob Toliver says as he embraces his sister-in-law.

Kowalski mumbles a quiet, "Hi, Doctor Bannister." He's been in love with her since that night at *La Azul Noche*.

"Hi, yourself, Kowalski." She knows how he feels. Like him, Dr. Bannister's career demands rule out time for a serious relationship. *Not yet anyway*, she keeps telling herself.

Turning to Detective Sergeant Collins, "Jim, I'm sure it's a male. I can't give you the exact time of death. The fire alarm came in at midnight. It was out by the time the Fire Department arrived."

"Thanks, Doc. How soon can you move the body? We want to examine the van?"

"I've been discussing that with the Fire Inspector and the CSI guys. They're done with the exterior and almost done inside the van. Once they finish up, I can move the body. After they finish with any photos you need, we'll take the corpse to the morgue."

Detective Collins thanks her. "That works for me."

He asks the fire investigator, "Inspector, what can we handle for you? How soon can you release the scene?" Collins's anxious to get started on his investigation.

"I have what I need from outside the van. Once Doc Bannister removes the body, I'll collect a few samples. They used an accelerant, and we need a few other photos. I should finish in ten to fifteen minutes. Then you guys can have it."

The lead CSI Investigator tells Detective

Collins, "We'll need at least an hour before we can tow the van and complete our work."

Dr. Bannister moves the body revealing no evidentiary surprises. She helps her assistant load the remains in the M.E.s van and leaves for the morgue. The Fire Inspector finishes in less time than estimated. He and CSI work together and share the evidence. An inspection of the van confirms what they all expected. CSI finds no weapons in it.

Back outside, the investigators start to go over what they know. Collins begins, "Well, we have five dead."

Toliver and Kowalski lookup. Toliver asks, "Five?"

"The fourth victim died on the operating table. That makes three bangers, a civilian, and with the body in the van, the total is five."

19

HECTOR RETURNS TO the AGE office with the photographs he took of as many of the 4-Aces and their women as possible. Sure, that he'd gotten them all, the young officer went to a one-hour photo shop and ordered four sets of prints. Hector gives the photos to Sergeant Toliver.

"What the hell? Are you out of your mind?" Hector is stunned by his sergeant's unexpected outburst.

Hector steps back, palms up. "I knew you wanted these A-S-A-P, so I had them printed." Pausing, he adds, "I paid for them out of pocket. What's wrong?"

"And you're going to be a sergeant." Shaking his head, Toliver stamps out of the squad room.

Turning to Kowalski, Hector asks, "What's wrong? What'd I do?"

"When you went to the photoshop, did you give the flash drive to the person behind the counter?"

"Yes."

"And then what?"

"She said the prints would be ready in a half-hour. So, I went next door to Dean's Beans and had a latte."

"You had a latte, a fucking latte."

"Officer Hector-Fucking-Miguel Navarro, do you know why I had you take those photos?"

"Yes, so we could identify everyone there and, with any luck, get a lead on the shooters."

"That's right, Navarro. If the shooter's in one of the photos, what then?"

"Detective Collins can use them to identify a suspect and help build his case."

"Before, but not after your fuckup. The photos are good for intelligence, nothing else."

"What do you mean?" Hector asks, confused.

"Sit down." He sits, and Kowalski hands him a departmental form. "What's this?"

"It's a Photograph Record Control form. It's to list photographic evidence." With a start, he realizes why the sergeant's mad.

"Oh, Shit, I blew it."

"You had better hope we don't need those photographs. If we do, a good prosecutor might get them into evidence. But I doubt it. The defense attorneys will rip you a new asshole. Not to mention how everything in this investigation could be subject to a misconduct charge."

"I'm sorry, Steve. I screwed up. Is there anything I can do to fix this?"

"No. Stay out of Toliver's way for a day or two, then throw yourself on his mercy."

Hector lucks out because none of the shooters are in the photographs. The AGE officers identify a few 4-Aces not previously known as associates. Even more important, Toliver does not write him up.

Hector realizes he has to think before acting, something he should have learned when Katie helped him with Teresa Ontiveros. He owes her and the sergeant an apology.

20

"SARGE, WHY ME? I've never even been in a massage parlor." Hector whines, Officer John Riley snickers. He thinks it's funny.

"Hey, Navarro, what's wrong?" Someone chimes in, "You still a virgin?"

"The Chief ordered every plain-clothes unit in the department to assign officers to assist the vice cops in a prostitution crackdown. You drew the short straw for Friday. You all have to work the detail one night. Saturday, it's Harris. Sunday is Riley's turn in the barrel."

Harris responds with, "Son of a bitch." Everyone except Hector and Sergeant Toliver joins in the laughter.

Harris can't share his most private thoughts. *This ought to be interesting. Still in*

*the closet, I'm supposed to get a prostitute to
proposition me. Why Me?*

Harris and Riley join Hector in
chorusing, "Why me, Sarge?"

"Aside from the fact that I say you're
doing it, there's the sergeant's list. You three
have never worked a day in the vice unit. This
detail should give you some idea of what their
job entails."

Friday, August 30, nineteen-forty-seven
hours. Hector is in the vice squad room. "I'm
Officer Navarro from AGE. I'm here for
massage parlor duty."

The sergeant, the only woman in a room
full of male officers, a petite thirty-something
blonde, is barely visible over the podium. She
smiles, "Grab a seat. Anywhere's fine."

At precisely eight, she introduces herself.
"I'm Sergeant Deborah Jordan. You can call
me Sergeant. Thank you all for volunteering
and showing up tonight." Her comment
meets with a chorus of expletives.

An hour later, Hector's sitting in a ten-
year-old Honda with a vice officer outside
Golden Joy Massage. The location is in a
rundown strip mall in a part of town called
Little Saigon. Three of the seven storefronts
are boarded up, and the panels are covered
with graffiti. Most inhabitants are of Asian
descent, and—as the name implies—many

are first and second-generation Vietnamese.

"This is gang territory. What if someone recognizes me?"

The vice officer slumps forward, his chin almost touching his chest, laughing, and shaking his head from side to side.

"Look, Navarro. It's simple. If anyone recognizes you, leave. Otherwise, you talk with the girl and get her to offer you sex for money."

"How do I do that without mentioning sex or money?"

"Jesus, Navarro, haven't you ever propositioned a woman?"

"Yes, but never a prostitute. What am I supposed to say if she makes an offer?"

"Have a change of heart, make up a story, and get out. We won't make any arrests tonight."

Hector's surprise shows. "I thought our job is to bust as many hookers as possible— slow down the trade—at least enough to get the mayor and city council off the Chief's back."

"Look, if we arrest one girl, within minutes, every parlor in town will shut down faster than you can say pussy. We send officers into every parlor. Some we visit three or four times a night. If you get a clean solicitation, come out, and we'll write a crime report."

"Okay, what happens next?"

"Sergeant Jordan will review every report. If she thinks an incident justifies an arrest, we'll get an identification on the parlor and the girl. When all that's finished, she'll take the package to the County Attorney's Office."

"What will she take to the prosecutor?"

"We prepare a separate file for each girl with rap sheets, photographs, and the officer's report. It helps if the girls have priors. Once the complaints are issued, the Deputy County Attorney and the sergeant will meet with a judge. That way, if there are any questions, they can take care of them. The judge signs all the arrest and search warrants."

"Who serves the warrants?"

"We do. We coordinate the arrests so that we hit every massage parlor simultaneously. Like I said before, one arrest and half these girls will be on their way to a parlor in another town within the hour."

"So, if I get a solicitation, I make an excuse and leave. What else do I need to know?"

"Get a name if you can. It'll be a street name, but at least we'll have the girl's working name. When you come out, I'll pick you up around the corner. We'll park somewhere quiet. You write your statement with as much detail as possible. While you're doing that, I'll write the crime report. You'll probably have to re-write your statement the first few times. That's all right, it's expected. If I'm satisfied with the report, we notify the sergeant and move to another massage parlor. Get going."

Inside, Hector is surprised to find the anteroom is neat and clean, reminding him of a doctor's waiting room. They even have a rack with travel magazines. The walls are covered in a blue wallpaper so pale it's almost white, decorated with delicate images of seascapes. To the left is the receptionist's station. Seated behind the modernistic counter is an Asian woman of indeterminable age. She could be anywhere from forty to sixty. Wearing a modest summer dress, she greets him in unaccented English. "Good evening. How may I help you?"

He can't remember ever being this nervous. Hector's mind tells him it's irrational. After all, it's just a woman. At most, the crime is a misdemeanor. *I can do this.* He soon relearns the old cliché: *it's easier said than done* is true.

He stammers out an awkward and high-pitched, "Ah . . . ah, I want a massage."

The woman smiles. "You've come to the right place. What do you have in mind?"

Standing there like a twelve-year-old at

his first boy-girl party, the woman takes pity on him. "This is your first time, isn't it?"

Another clumsy answer, "Yes, what am I supposed to do?"

"The massage is forty for the first half-hour. You pay me before I take you back. If you want anything beyond the basic, that's between you and the girl."

The vice cop had given Hector two hundred dollars in twenties and said, "Make sure the gal in charge sees that you have a roll. You want her to know you have enough for extras." Hector takes the roll of bills out of his pants pocket and gives the woman two twenties. She deposits the cash in her bra.

She says from behind the counter, "Come on, honey, let's get you fixed up." She offers Hector her hand. He accepts, and she gives him a squeeze as she pulls it to her bosom.

"This way," she says, opening the door to a hallway with three doors along each side. The walls are painted a shade darker than those in the waiting room. The carpet is beige plush with vacuum lines. Muffled voices come from one of the rooms.

She knocks at the last door on the left. From inside comes a female voice. "Yes."

"Julie, I have a gentleman for you. May we come in?" Without waiting for an answer, she opens the door and leads Hector into a neat, clean room, all blue with pale painted walls and a dark red carpet. Besides an oversized massage table, the room has two easy chairs, a freestanding cabinet, the same color as the walls, and a small table with a lamp. A book, *Perma Red,* by Debra Magpie Earling, lays open on a chair.

"This is Julie. She'll take good care of you. Julie, this gentleman tells me he's never visited a massage parlor." The older woman lets go of his hand and steps out. The masseuse is Caucasian, not Asian, as he'd assumed she would be. She's in her thirties and looks more like a soccer mom than Hector had imagined for a prostitute—as if he had a clue.

"You know my name. What's yours?" she asks in a friendly tone.

"Hector." The sergeant hadn't told the officers what to say if a girl asked for a name. He figures the less he lies, the better.

"Well, Hector, what can I do for you."

"Don't know, all new to me."

Julie is quiet for a moment. It's as though she is sizing him up before deciding what she will do. Looking at her, Hector remembers when Katie O'Brien taught him what to look for when describing a woman as a person. Hector starts at the top and works his way down. In his mind, he fills out a Field Identification Card.

- Female – Caucasian
- Light brown hair, long
- Blue eyes
- 5'6" – 5'8"
- 130 pounds
- Dark blue jacket
- Light blue blouse
- Nice boobs – *Oops, scratch that*
- Dark blue pants
- Black open-toe shoes

"Like what you see?"

His eyes locked on her breasts, Hector feels the red flush on his cheeks as he looks away, saying, "Sorry, I was thinking."

With a smile and a slight laugh, she says, "My boobs? That a subject for later." She pauses while he considers that statement. "Do you want anything special? You need to strip and get on the table."

His discomfort evident; she smiles as she opens the cabinet. It contains a stack of folded towels and sheets and several bottles of rubbing oil. She takes out a large towel and hands it to him.

"I'll step outside. You get out of your clothes, wrap this around your waist and get up on the table."

Julie leaves the room. Hector searches for an escape route. *Shit, I can't get out of here.* Taking his clothes off, he feels exposed—vulnerable. *I'm undressing for a woman I know nothing about, except she's a hooker.* He's glad to see there are no skid marks on his skivvies. Wrapping his tidy whities inside his shirt, along with his socks, he rolls it all inside his chinos. Hector puts the bundle on a chair. No sooner does he have the towel around himself and lying on the table, as if by magic, the door opens, and Julie comes back into the room. *How'd she know? Am I on camera?* Embarrassed, Hector blushes again.

He finds himself struggling with what he's supposed to do. *I'm almost naked with a woman I'm sure is a prostitute, and I gotta get her to proposition me. Why me?* His confusion shows.

"You want a straight massage or something special?"

What'd the sergeant say? Special? Does that qualify as sex?

"What's the difference between a straight massage and something special?"

I don't know much about massage parlor sex, but hey, let the games begin. This woman is no one's fool. She won't blurt out something as simple as "I'll fuck you for fifty bucks."

He's a welterweight up against a heavyweight.

Julie looks at him with a twinkle in her

eye. "What do you think a massage is?"

"I roll on my stomach. You rub oil on my back."

"I do more. I massage your neck, shoulders, legs, and feet. Is that all you want?"

"I guess. What's a special?" Hector's lying on his back with his hands behind his head. It's uncomfortable. Standing at the foot of the table, Julie does nothing to help. He stares at the ceiling, trying to gather his thoughts and plan his next move. *Like I have a move. Who am I kidding?* Glancing down, Hector is sure she's looking under the towel at his junk. Squeezing his legs together, it's Hector's turn to say, "Like what you see?"

She doesn't blush. She shrugs and makes one of those faces that tells the person she's thinking, "I've seen better."

"Come on. What's a special?" This time his face doesn't redden.

"Whatever you say. What kind of work do you do?"

"I'm a truck driver."

"I doubt it."

"Why?"

Julie crosses her arms across her chest, squints, and then points, "Your hands. They're too delicate for a truck driver, too smooth, and have no callouses. You want to give me a massage with those soft hands?"

Hector settles in for the duration. He is competitive, and this is a challenge. Getting her to solicit him isn't going to be easy. He's sure she's figured him for a cop and is playing him. *I might not get you, lady, but I'll give you my best shot.*

They go back and forth for ten minutes as she massages his back. Finally, "Why are you here? You say you've never been to a massage parlor. Why today? Why here?"

"I've had a hard day. I'm beat. The stress is getting to me, and I was heading home when I saw your sign."

She gives him one of those "I doubt that" looks followed by, "And?"

"I thought, why not give it a try."

"You don't look stressed out."

Hector has no idea where it came from; certainly not something he had planned or ever heard of. "I wish I had a joint. Maybe if I had one to smoke, I'd relax enough to tell you what I want?" Julie gets a weird look on her face; her mouth opens, and she takes a step back.

"You want a joint?" Julie says as she turns to the right, and her eyebrows arch.

"Yeah, that would be great."

Julie smiles and relaxes, the tension going out of her. Hector's request takes her off her game. She's ready and armed for the sex-for-money dance but not this. "I have a couple." She moves to the side of the table, kneels, pulls out a purse, stands up, and hesitates. After a moment, she's decided. She opens the bag and takes out a Marlboro Cigarette hard-pack. Flipping the lid open, she bends toward him, revealing her breasts. He can see that the box contains several small hand-rolled cigarettes and some regular ones. She gives him a hand-rolled cigarette. "You can't smoke here. I'll get fired. Your time's up. If you figure out what you want, come back, and I'll make it happen." With that, Julie wipes her hands on a clean towel, turns, and is out the door before he can think of anything to say.

As soon as Hector gets his clothes on, he's gone like Superman—*faster than a speeding bullet*.

Back in the car, the vice officer can't believe it. "She did what? You gotta be shitting me."

"Honest. I couldn't get a proposition, so I asked the gal for a joint, and she gave me one." Hector shows him the small hand-rolled marijuana cigarette.

The vice cop convulses with laughter. Hector's afraid the man's going to wet himself.

"We're done here. We gotta go to the station. Sergeant Jordan is never going to believe this shit." The vice cop says once he gets his laughter under control.

The sergeant is upset when they show up hours early.

Hearing her detective recount Hector's story, she starts laughing and tells Hector she wants to hear it from him. Hector describes the details for her, "'I swear, one second she's looking at me as if I'm the biggest liar since Clinton said, 'I did not have sexual relations with that woman.'"

"Nobody'll believe this. I can't wait to tell the lieutenant." She picks up her phone. "Lieutenant, you got a minute? Can you come down to the vice office? We have something you're never going to believe." She pauses and adds, "serious as a heart attack, boss. You gotta see this report."

When the lieutenant and sergeant finish laughing at the "hooker gives cop weed instead of blow-job" story, Hector suggests, "Should we check to make sure it is marijuana." A simple field test confirms that it is.

It doesn't take long to identify Julie. She is a soccer mom. A single parent with three girls, she's an insurance adjuster by day. She supplements her income a few nights a week by working a shift at the Golden Joy Massage Parlor.

Officers take fifteen women into custody for sex-related crimes on the day the arrest warrants are served. Julie, the sixteenth, is brought in on a misdemeanor charge of providing marijuana. She didn't solicit a single undercover officer. Hector persuades the sergeant and the prosecutor that justice would be better served by not charging her with a felony; *what she did is not even a crime in several adjoining states.*

He's sure Julie is asking herself, "Why me?"

21

GOLDEN JOY MASSAGE belongs to a network of parlors that pay extortion money for protection to Vietnamese street gangs. The protection comes with criminal defense. The attorney they have on retainer, Robert Muncie, represents Julie. After reading Officer Navarro's report and talking with her, he convinces her to accept a plea bargain. Julie pleads guilty and enrolls in a first-offender diversion program.

Hector learns of the deal at the Fire Chief's Office. A few weeks after his night in Vice, Hector meets with the Fire Chief and Attorney Muncie. The meeting occurs because Davey Jones and Hector had been surveilling a 4-Ace's corner where a pair of lightweight drug dealers sell various drugs.

Neither officer routinely make drug arrests, but these two street dealers work for Geronimo Dixon. A late-model BMW rolls by their corner. After the second pass, it pulls up to the dealers. Davey grabs his binoculars and sees a transaction go down. Jones is not what you can call proactive, but he looks at Hector and says, "You see that?"

"I did."

"Let's roust 'em."

They stop the BMW and get the driver out of the car. He has a vial of crack cocaine in his hand. "Give me the vial,"

"What vial?"

Jones is tired of this guy. "Give me the crack before I pop your fuckin head open."

The guy doesn't take kindly to Jones' request and tells him to go fuck himself.

Hector tries a more reasonable approach. "Come on, sir. Give us the vial." The man doesn't care for Hector's request any more than Davey's. His hand goes up. He throws the vial on the ground and stomps on it, spreading the contents into the blacktop. Hector's no happier than Jones. "Okay, asshole. You're under arrest."

Davey reaches for the guy's left arm, only to have his hand slapped away—and the fight is on. They arrest him for obstructing and resisting a police officer.

At the station, his shoes are taken and

sent to the lab for testing. No surprise, the narcotics field test results come back positive for cocaine. Still, it's clear to both detectives that there is not enough for a usable quantity. During booking, he's asked, "Where do you work?" His answer comes as a surprise.

"I'm a lieutenant at NLFD." He's on the New Liberty Fire Department.

Many options are open to the firefighter as a first-time offender, including diversion and dismissal of all charges. The Fire Chief isn't sure what he wants to do when it comes to disciplining or terminating this outstanding employee who tried to kick the asses of two cops.

Sergeant Toliver calls Hector in for a chat. *A chat? Something's up.*

"Hector, you remember that fire lieutenant you and Jones busted for resisting?"

"Yes, I remember the asshole."

"He may be one, but the Fire Chief isn't sure he wants to fire him. The lone charge is resisting. He claims you jumped him for no reason."

"That's bullshit."

"The Fire Chief wants to hear your story firsthand. In one hour, you report to him at

Fire Headquarters. You'll meet with the Chief, the lieutenant, and his attorney. Any questions?" Toliver doesn't wait for an answer. "Good, I didn't think you did."

Hector goes to the meeting, the attorney who represented Julie from the massage parlor case, Ralph Muncie is there. When Hector arrives, the meeting is in progress. The Chief's secretary takes him in. The asshole's talking. When he sees Hector, he shuts up. The Chief comes from behind his desk and shakes hands. "Thank you for coming, Officer Navarro. I appreciate it." The Fire Chief is a decent chap, but Hector wonders, "How can he consider keeping this guy on the Fire Department."

"No problem Chief. I'm happy to help." While thinking, "I'm here because Sergeant Toliver ordered me to come to this bullshit meeting. I have no doubt that everyone in the room knows what I'm thinking."

The Chief tells him the lieutenant has given his side of the story. "Now, if you would, please give us your perspective?"

Hector wants to say, "Your lieutenant is a crackhead, and when we caught him, he resisted. I wish I'd used a nightstick on his head." Instead, he repeats the bullshit line, "No problem Chief. I'm happy to help."

Finished with his story, the Chief thanks Hector and turns to his subordinate. "Is there anything you wish to add? "The lieutenant shakes his head in the negative. "Your Battalion Chief will be in contact. Stay available. That will be all."

Before the guy gets out the door, the attorney says, "I have some questions for Officer Navarro."

"Lieutenant, I said that would be all." The Chief looks unhappy.

As soon as the door closes behind the lieutenant, he turns to the attorney. "Mr. Muncie, this is not a hearing. I asked Officer Navarro here as a courtesy to you. Not so you could question him in hopes of finding something for the lieutenant's criminal case. Do I make myself clear?"

The attorney takes it well. "Yes, sir. That was not my intention. If that's what you think, I apologize to you and Officer Navarro."

"Hector. Do you mind if I call you Hector?" the Chief asks.

"No, sir, that's fine."

"Mr. Muncie and I have matters to discuss in private. But, before you leave, there's something that you might find interesting." He turns his head toward the attorney. "Ralph, do you want to tell him about that other case of yours?" The Chief turns back to Hector. "So that you know, Mr. Muncie and I have been friends since grammar school. The difference between us is that I have an honest job."

"Officer Navarro, please call me Bob. I represent a massage parlor employee you arrested. It seems you couldn't get her to solicit you."

"If you mean the gal at the Golden Joy, that's right."

"Yeah, that's the one. I'm used to cops lying about solicitations. These are working girls; they know the game and how to handle undercover cops."

"I figured that out real quick. No way in hell was she going to solicit me. It was not going to happen."

"When I read your police report, I knew it had to be true. Nobody could ever make up such a cockamamie story, so I pled her out, and she got a diversion program. I mentioned to Julie I'd be meeting you today. She said to give you a message."

"What's that? I imagine she's not happy with me."

"'Actually, Hector, far from it. She said, 'Tell him no hard feelings. I was positive he was a cop, but asking for a joint threw me. No cop ever did that. So, I thought, maybe the guy isn't a cop, so, no harm in giving him a joint.'"

After a good laugh, the Chief thanks Hector and tells him he can go. As he reaches the door, "You didn't ask, but I can tell you that Mr. Muncie is not going to be happy with my decision. Have a good day."

22

HECTOR'S CELL PHONE rings. "Hi, Hector. It's me, Teresa. I have something."

"Where've you been, Ontiveros?" A pause, and then, "how's your daughter?"

"Olivas's fine. I don't have much time."

"Whatcha got?"

"You hear about some Black kid getting shot in a car? They called him Porky, Cory, or something like that."

Sitting at his desk, he grabs a notepad and begins to write. Listening carefully, Hector tries to sound nonchalant, "Could be. Tell me what you heard."

"Sanchez had a party a couple of days ago for the sub-comandante and *tenientes*. They were celebrating getting revenge for the drive-by last July."

"Go ahead. I'm listening."

"The pigs were doing shots and before long were drunk. After Sanchez left, they started saying what a great man Chucho was. It was as if we weren't even there. Chucho drank less than the rest of them. He wanted me. The pig screwing me was happy to share."

"What does this have to do with some kid getting shot?"

"'The pig said to Chucho, 'anything for the Vato who popped that fucking drive-by blood.'"

"Did they say where the shooting occurred?"

"Chucho didn't talk to me. He sent me back after he finished with me. The pig was talking to another Vato. I lay down near them and pretended to sleep. They said Chucho shot that Black punk, Porky, or something. He walked up to the kid's car window and asked him his name. When the kid answered, Chucho shot him in the head."

"Do you know Chucho's real name?"

"Jesus Montemayor. Chucho is the youngest *Teniente*, twenty. That's all I got."

"Was that Teresa Ontiveros?" Katie seemed to hear every word said in the unit.

"Yes. She has info on the 4-Aces kid that got popped."

"Why do you call her Ontiveros? Why not Teresa?"

"I'm trying to keep her at a distance. Then maybe it won't be so bad when, as you say, she gets killed."

"It'll be bad, regardless. What'd Teresa have to say about the killing?"

After filling her in on what Ontiveros said, Katie smiled. "Chucho is one vicious bastard. Let's go see the boss."

Toliver understands immediately, picks up the phone, and calls Detective Collins. "Jim, Bob Toliver here. Two of my investigators have the name of the shooter on that 4-Aces kid." A pause, then, "Yeah, come on over. They'll be waiting for you." After hanging up, he says, "Excellent work O'Brien."

"It wasn't my CI, Sarge. Hector turned her, and she called him."

"Okay, good work, Hector. I see O'Brien's hand in there somewhere. When Jim Collins gets here, you tell him everything except who the CI is. She is on the books?"

"Yes, she is."

"Good to hear. I wouldn't want to see Katie's bad habits rub off on you."

"Jeez, Sarge, that's mean. Besides, he's partners with Jones, not me."

Jim Collins's hulk fills the doorway. The man is still built like the linebacker he was when he played for the Arizona Cardinals twenty years ago. After Hector tells Sergeant Collins what he heard from the CI, the detective asks for the CIs name. Hector takes the opportunity to throw a curve. "Sorry, Sergeant, I can't give you *his* name."

"You might have to divulge him later in a judge's chambers during an *In-Camera* hearing."

"I'll cross that bridge when I come to it. Besides, I heard you have at least a dozen witnesses to the shooting. With all those, an ID should be easy."

"It should be, but most will clam up and forget everything they saw. They're frightened. This killing is gang-related, and no one wants to get involved. Who can blame them?"

Sergeant Toliver joins the conversation. "Jim, when you get a warrant for Montemayor, I'd appreciate it if you let me and my unit help serve it."

"No sweat, I want you there. The medical examiner said the shot was a through-and-through. The techs found a forty-caliber slug on the seat next to the body. It's circumstantial, but I'm sure it's the round that killed Corky. That's his street name. His real name was Charles Rogers."

"Is there anything I can ask my informant for you?"

"Yeah, Hector. Ask him if Chucho has a pistol, and if so, what can he tell us?" Hector nods assent, and Collins continues. "Another car stopped in front of Corky and blocked him in. Two guys were in that car. Who are they, and what're their names? We can lay a felony murder charge on them. With three birds, we have a better chance of turning one."

Sergeant Toliver asks a question. "Jim, you get anywhere with that case back in July, the one involving the elderly couple found outside Ernesto's? The ones headed for their grandson's graduation in Phoenix."

"No. We have nothing. I thought sure the victim's Lexus would show up. It hasn't."

Hector had read about the case in *The Arizona Republic*. "Detective, do you think the 4-Aces killed them?"

"I'm sure they did, but we have nothing to tie them to the murders. For all we know, it was a carjacking gone bad that happened to go down in front of Ernesto's."

Detective Collins has better luck with the witnesses than he could have hoped. Five agree to view a photo line-up. They all say they'll testify if necessary. Jesus Carlos Montemayor, also known as Chucho, is identified as the shooter by three witnesses.

It's as if Collins hit the Super Lotto.

Hector has no way to contact Ontiveros. Los Scorpios Locos doesn't allow inked-in girls to have cell phones. He waits three days for her call. "Hi, Hector."

"Hi, Teresa."

"Teresa? What happened to calling me Ontiveros?"

Hector has no answer for her, so he ignores the question. "What's going on? You have something for me?"

"No. I figured you'd have enough information about that kid who was shot you'd want to talk to me again. I heard the other girls talking. His name was Corky."

"I do have a few questions for you."

When he finishes, Ontiveros says, "I'll call you from work tonight."

"Work? You have a job?"

"They want my baby healthy when they sell her, so they let me get a job at McDonald's. I make enough to keep her fed."

"I have a question. If you can't have a cell phone, how do you call me?"

"I have a burner hidden where I can get it when grocery shopping for Olivia."

It's almost midnight before Ontiveros calls back.

"Chucho lives with his mother, the same place the drive-by happened in July. He drives a green Monte Carlo."

"Good, good. What about the gun and the other guys?"

"You sure are impatient, Officer Navarro. When Chucho screwed me at the party, he had a big square-looking gun. I know nothing about guns. Does that help?"

"It might. The other guys?" She gives him the names. Hector recognizes them as LSL bangers. Thanking her, he tells her to call in a day or two.

Detective Collins has a surveillance team set up on Chucho's house. Parked on the street, the Monte Carlo matches the witnesses' description down to the gray primer-painted left front fender. The license plate is registered to a salvaged Chrysler.

After showing the witnesses photos of the Monte Carlo, he has enough for a search warrant for the car.

"Thanks for the information, Hector. The Monte Carlo is a winner. We can't do much about the gun, we need more before we can search for a .40 caliber pistol. By the way, two witnesses identified the driver of the other car. We have enough for an arrest warrant. The passenger has a parole violation. We'll pick all three up at the same time."

23

NINE IN THE morning, Chucho gets a call from Sanchez. "Hey, Chucho. How you doing, *Ese*? You bangin' my *Tia Juanita*?"

"Hell, no, man, she's old enough to be my mother. But her next-door neighbor sure likes my brown meat."

"Cool. It's time to make a move. Geronimo's people are looking for you. They might find you. The word on the street is that you're in Tucson."

Chucho had known it wouldn't be long before the 4-Aces looked at Tucson. "What do you want me to do?"

"Nuthin. I'm sending a girl to pick you up, a civilian who doesn't know anything. She'll drop you off at a safe house. Don't talk to her."

The girl shows up an hour later, "You Chucho?"

"Si."

Nothing more is said during the three-hour drive to New Liberty. In late September, the weather should be changing. It's not; it should be in the eighties when they leave Tucson. Chucho doesn't need the voice on the radio to tell him it's hot with an excessive heat warning. 105 degrees, it's fucking hot. The woman's car is at least twenty years old, and the air conditioning isn't strong enough to move air. He tries to sleep but is too worried about what's waiting for him in New Liberty. He can't even check his email or play *Candy Crush*; the burner phone Sanchez gave him doesn't have Wi-Fi. After what seems more like six hours, the girl stops in front of a neat home in an upper-middle-class Anglo neighborhood. She points toward the front door without looking at her passenger. As expected, it's hotter in New Liberty.

"Thank you, sister." She doesn't answer him.

The house, built in the sixties, is single-story with an old, shingled roof, the walls painted light green with dark green shutters and trim. The attractive front yard sports manicured grass, complete with a white picket fence and two calla lilies planted on either side of the steps. The safe house is as vanilla as anything he had ever seen. An elderly Caucasian woman opens the front door a few inches. "*Que es su nombre?*"

Chucho barely speaks Spanish but understands her question. "*Mi nombre es Chucho.*" She gives him an inquisitive look. "Jesus Carlos Montemayor." Without another word, she opens the door. The second he steps through the door, he feels it—air conditioning—*thank God.*

She leads him to the back of the house, pointing out the bathroom and opening the door to a bedroom. "Stay here, except to use the bathroom. I'll bring your meals. Someone will come tonight with word from Sanchez."

It is a long wait, even with a television in the room. Sometime after dinner, Chucho falls asleep.

"Chucho, wake up." Someone is shaking him. Opening his eyes, it's Sanchez. "Get up. We don't have a lot of time."

"What's going on?"

"You're hot, too hot. Geronimo's on the warpath. The 4-Aces won't quit until they get you, plus the cops have warrants out for you."

"Warrants? How'd they get me?" Chucho's not surprised that Geronimo is after him, but the cops and the warrants catch him off-guard.

"Some snitch called that nigga cop, Collins. He found witnesses who identified you as the Vato who threw the grenade. The other warrant is for that kid you popped, Corky."

"What happens to me?" *Not much we can do about any warrants. If the cops get me, Geronimo will have me shanked in lockup.* Chucho understands he's screwed, whoever gets him.

"I'm going to get you out of town. You wanna go to Mexico or L.A.?"

"I don't speak Spanish. The cartels won't have any use for me. I'll go to L.A."

"Makes sense. Stay here until we move you. One of your crew's in the other bedroom. He'll be going with you."

"How do we get to L.A.?"

"Vatos from *La Eme* will be here sometime Saturday to drive you. You'll be under their protection as long as you're in L.A." Sanchez picks up a duffle bag and throws it on the bed. "For you."

Chucho's not surprised when he opens the bag and finds an M-16, a half dozen loaded magazines, a couple boxes of ammo, and a bundle of cash. He has no idea how much trouble he'll be facing but expects plenty.

Saturday, September 14, it's noon. The guys from L.A. haven't shown up; all he can do is sit, wait, and worry. What if they don't show? What if La Eme decides not to get involved? Chucho is beyond anxious.

After a trip to the bathroom, he hears sounds coming from a closed door. Curious, he knocks, waits then opens the door surprising a Vato watching television. Chucho recognizes him, a soldier from his crew. "Hey *Ese*, why are you here?"

"I got warrants for that Corky hit, waiting for a ride to Los Angeles."

"I guess we'll be riding together," Chuco says, returning to his room. *At least I won't be alone in L.A.*

A little after one, there's a knock at the door. The old woman comes in without waiting. "They're here." She leaves the door open and delivers the same message to the other guy.

At the front door, the old woman stops him before opening it. "I've been watching an unfamiliar car parked a block away, doesn't seem to be anyone in it, but I've never seen it before. Your ride drove right by it. If they had seen anyone, they wouldn't have stopped. Be careful, *Vaya Con Dios*.

Chucho thanks her and looks out between the curtains. The car is a light brown Toyota Camry. It doesn't look like a cop car, but to be on the safe side, he looks down the street in the other direction. The road seems clear for three or four blocks. Stepping outside, Chucho sees the front doors of a dark green GMC Yukon open and waiting. Two Vatos get out, open the passenger doors, and stand by. Chucho takes another look at the Camry—something's wrong. Even though he should have run, he walks across the lawn to the Yukon. After one last look, Chucho puts the duffle bag on the seat and slides in next to it. "Let's go. That damn Camry makes me nervous. It could be cops."

The driver looks at the front passenger, who says, "I didn't see anyone in it."

Chucho watches the Camry as the driver backs the Yukon out.

"Shit, they're coming." Turning forward, he says, "Drive normally. Let's see what happens."

A block away, the driver says, "cop." He gestures at a marked police car driven by a female cop. The cruiser is white, with green stripes and lettering. It is pulling from a side street, and the car pulls in behind the Yukon—within seconds—she turns on her lights and siren.

"Somebody snitched." Chucho doesn't need to say it but does.

The driver, a long way from L.A., says, "I got no idea where we are. Suggestions?"

"No. Keep driving. I gotta think." A minute later, Chucho changes his mind, "Screw it. Try to lose them. It's the only chance we got."

The *La Eme* guy is good at fast, evasive driving. If he'd had any idea where he was, the Vato would have lost the cops. After several turns, he slides the Yukon into a school parking lot and pulls between a row of buildings. He's got nowhere to go with the Camry right behind. At the back of the schoolyard, he rams a chain-link fence. It doesn't give, and the Yukon comes to a sudden stop.

A Chicano guy gets out of the Camry, points a gun, and yells to turn off the motor and throw out the keys. The driver asks Chucho what he wants to do.

"I don't want to get arrested." Chucho knows that would be a death sentence. "Wait a minute."

"Roll down the window and throw out the keys," the cop yells again—much louder.

"Do what he says." The Vato does as ordered. The cop starts yelling to get out and lie on the ground.

"Are you carrying?"

The La Eme Vatos say no and that the car is clean.

"All they have on you is reckless and running. Get out and do what the cop says.

We're going to run while they arrest you."

Turning to his friend, Chucho says, "Vato, as soon as they're on the ground, open your door and run." The man starts running as soon as the two get out, and one of the detectives goes after him. The cop in the marked car stays fixed on the Yukon; the plainclothes guys start after the runner. Chucho knew that the runner would draw attention. That's why he remained in the Yukon for a few seconds longer than his LSL Vato.

Chucho knows other cops will arrive any minute. He grabs the duffle bag and runs toward the school buildings. For a few seconds, he thinks he might have pulled it off, but then he realizes he's being followed. From the direction of the Yukon, a male voice shouts, "Freeze motherfucker, stop, or I'll shoot." Chucho runs faster.

Taking a chance, he glances back. The cop chasing him is old and carries a pistol. Chucho knows he can outrun this guy, and sprints through an open gate in the chain-link fence, onto the school grounds, and runs around several buildings. He wishes there were kids playing in the field so he could use one of the brats as a shield to slow the pig down. *I can't let them box me in. I won't die running.*

Jose Maldonado had taught him that a

man sitting presents a smaller target, can support a rifle, and shoot much more accurately. Chucho's far enough ahead of the pig that he can get set up and kill him when he comes around the corner. Sitting down, Chucho experiences several sensations. *The sun's hot on his back, and the grass burns his ass through his chinos. I'm gonna die. That old saying, 'it's a good day to die," is bullshit.* Chucho feels all this while catching his breath and loading a fresh magazine into the M-16. After feeding a round into the firing chamber, he lays the other magazines next to his leg. From the time Chucho sits until he is ready takes but seconds.

Where's that cop? Chucho figures he'll ease around the corner of the last building. The cop surprises him. Movement catches his eye a dozen yards away from the corner of the building. Before he can change position to fire, the cop backs out of sight. In frustration, Chucho puts a few rounds into the building, followed by a second burst in the direction he saw the cop move behind the wall. If the old guy doesn't show in a few seconds, Chucho figures he'll get off his ass and circle out and around and have the old cop cold.

Sensing movement more than seeing it, Chucho glances across the field and sees another cop coming his way. He turns and fires off the first mag in his direction. The cop fires—doesn't miss. Hit in the leg, Chucho hurts but manages to stay seated upright. Blood covers his pants from his thigh to his knee. *Man, this shit burns like a mutha.*

The cop emerges from behind the building, fires, and ducks back as Chucho returns fire. Chucho has one thought: *I'll kill some of them fuckers before I die.* Getting up off the grass hurts like hell with a bullet in his leg. Chucho thinks he has a few seconds while the cop who shot him reloads; he moves out around the corner. Every step hurts. Another burst of shots comes from the direction of the cop on the ground. *How'd he miss?* Chucho's almost in position to shoot when the firing starts again—from several guns.

Chucho wakes up several days later with a tube in his throat; the doctors tell him he was fortunate to have survived with three bullet wounds.

He doesn't feel lucky. Geronimo is out there somewhere—waiting

24

HECTOR IS DELIGHTED Maria Juarez finally agreed to stay over, but not until he asks her—in Spanish. After making love, they talk long into the night. Moments after falling asleep, his cell rings. *Maybe if I ignore it, it'll stop ringing.*

"Hector, answer the damn thing."

Reaching across Maria, he snatches it off the nightstand. "Hector."

"Navarro, it's Bob Toliver. Get your ass out of bed. Be here in an hour." The phone goes dead.

"I've gotta go to work. Please stay."

Hector can see that Maria isn't keen on getting up and driving home in the middle of the night. "I'm going back to sleep. I doubt I'll be here when you get back."

An hour later, he's in Toliver's office. His

sergeant's first words are, "Aren't those the same clothes you wore yesterday?" Before Hector can think of an answer, Toliver asks, "Where's your partner? I called him first."

"How would I know? All you said was to get my ass in here."

"Go get some coffee. You look like you need it, and bring me a cup, black. I'll call Jones again."

Davey Jones shows up twenty minutes later.

"Where the hell have you been? I told you to be here twenty minutes ago."

"Why are we here, Sarge?" Hector dares to ask before Davey has a chance to reply.

"Remember Jim Collins supervised the homicide investigation after the drive-by shooting of the Los Scorpios Locos in July."

Jones interrupts, "What's that got to do with us?"

"How many times do I have to tell you to shut up? The 4-Aces did the shooting, but there's no usable evidence. When LSL retaliated, Chucho Montemayor was the shooter. Well, Collins found five witnesses willing to talk, and three positively identified Montemayor in a photo line-up."

"We know." Jones says, "Collins got a warrant weeks ago."

"Katie, fill everyone in on what the informant told you."

"Chucho will be at a safe house today. She didn't have the house number but gave me the street name and a detailed description of the place, down to a white picket fence."

Sergeant Tolliver gives instructions. "Jim and his partner are standing by with a patrol unit a few blocks away. You and Hector will replace them on point while they grab a bite. Here's what Jim figures is the address." Adding, "It's the only one on the block with a white picket fence."

Hector wonders why Ontiveros didn't call him. *Why'd she call O'Brien?* He calls Katie, who tells him, "Teresa tried to call you. It went straight to voice mail. She didn't want to leave a message." He checks two missed calls. He'd put the phone on vibrate at dinner with Maria, forgot to check for calls, and didn't turn it back on until he got up to take a leak. "Damn it."

The temperature is expected to reach one hundred degrees in New Liberty. *No way am I going to suffer with the smell of Jones and his pigsty of a car in this heat.*

"I'm driving." Hector knows Davey is hungover because he smells of stale booze oozing out of his pores as he walks alongside the younger man to Hector's temporary undercover car. Before they're out of the lot, Jones is snoring.

Using the clean Camry helps a little. *But boy, does Collins stink. He looks and smells like he spent the night in a bar.* "Now my car's gonna smell," Hector says aloud.

Hector flips the switch that shuts off the brake and headlights as they roll to a stop behind Collins's gray undercover Crown Victoria. The detective sergeant comes to the driver's window, "Thanks, we've been here since before midnight. We'll grab a bite, clean up, and be back in a couple of hours. It's been quiet since the lights went out around midnight."

Jones is still sound asleep when the sun comes up; Hector is almost asleep himself when the radio crackles to life. "Hector, you out there?" Before answering, he shakes Jones awake.

"Yeah, Sarge, we've been here since five, nothing going on."

"Jaime and Malik will relieve you at fourteen hundred. Call me if you see anything."

By seven, the temperature is eighty. Jones squirms. "I gotta pee."

"Davey, we can't leave. Collins will be back soon, and we can hit a gas station."

Ten minutes later, he whines, "I can't wait any longer,"

"Wait a minute." Hector retrieves two bottles of water from the trunk and guzzles one. He hands Davey the empty, "Use this and put the lid on when you're done peeing."

"Nothing with a mouth smaller than a Gatorade top will fit my dick. Davey pretends to shoot himself in the head, "Whatever," and takes the bottle.

After another twenty minutes, and with nothing happening, Hector asks Davey about his assignment in Anti-Gang. "Davey, there's something I'm curious about."

"I bet. What is it this time?"

"You don't like working AGE, so why don't you transfer out."

"I'm going to retire at the end of the year, so why make waves? Besides, the brass doesn't trust me in uniform. They don't think I can get along with the nice people."

Jim Collins radios at eight. "I'm a block away. I'll wait here until you have movement."

The following five hours drag as the temperature climbs well past the one-hundred mark. Jones's irritability, together with his odor, becomes unbearable. Hector tires of the man's complaints. "Davey, shut up, Malik will be here in an hour, and we'll be out of here."

"It won't be soon enough." Just then, a shiny dark green Yukon passes the unmarked car before pulling up and parking in the driveway of the safe house.

Hector grabs the radio, "Jim."

"I saw it. When you see the occupants, give us a description, and let Toliver know." He comes back.

Toliver comes on the radio. "Jim, Bob here. I copy. I'll head your way with Malik and Jaime after I notify the watch commander. This could be it."

The SUV is a dark green late model GMC Yukon, almost Los Scorpios Locos colors. It remains parked with the occupants not moving. The windows are blacked out. In the rearview window, Hector sees two men in the front seat before he and Jones duck out of sight. Nothing happens for five long minutes, and then the house's front door opens. A man comes out to the porch. He looks up and down the street. Satisfied, he nods in the direction of the Yukon. The occupants get out and open the back doors. A second man appears on the porch. As the two walk to the Yukon, Hector gets on the radio. "Jim, two men are exiting the house and walking to the Yukon."

"Montemayor?" asks Collins.

"I don't recognize the first man. The second's wearing a hoodie and bent over. I can't see his face. It's a little guy carrying a duffle bag. Could be him." In seconds, he's back on the radio. "The guy with the duffle bag is in the right rear passenger seat. They're starting up. Wait. They backed out and are headed your way. We'll follow."

Jim Collins orders them to stay back a safe distance until the Yukon is out of the area. "When I tell you, light 'em up along with the patrol officer, we'll make a high-risk stop."

A few blocks out of the area, Collins calls for the stop. The patrol car pulls in behind the Yukon. Jones and Hector are behind the marked vehicle when the uniformed officer turns on her lights and siren. The Yukon continues without increasing speed or evasive action for four or five blocks. The officers settle in for what looks to be an O.J. Simpson car chase. The watch commander calls for radio silence except for the lead chase car. The officer is calm and professional as she calls off the intersections.

Suddenly the Yukon accelerates and turns down an alley. At the next street, the driver turns right. Approaching sixty, the driver jams on the brakes and makes another right. The patrol car overshoots the intersection. Hector assumes the lead position. "Davey, call the chase." Jones surprises him as he does an excellent job—hung over.

"West on Beatty Street approaching Wells Middle School." No sooner has Davey made this broadcast than the Yukon brakes hard and pulls into the school parking lot, stopping at the fence. No one gets out.

Pulling to a stop behind the Yukon, Hector and Davey get out and squat behind the Camry. Davey shouts, "Turn off the motor and throw the keys out the window." Nothing. He yells again—louder. The driver's window comes down, and the keys are tossed out. "Get out of the vehicle and get down on the ground."

Hector repeats the same command as he looks around for cover officers—where are they? The front doors open, and two men get out. "Lie on the ground, hands on your head." They comply. "Interlace your fingers."

Hector repeats the command to exit the vehicle. Nothing happens for a few seconds, then the left passenger door opens, and a man takes off running. The right rear door opens as Hector goes after the first man. The one with the duffle bag runs towards the school buildings with Jones in pursuit. Hector runs a hundred yards before he hears gunfire—automatic weapon gunfire—coming from the direction Jones went. *Davey's more important than this asshole.*

Hector runs toward the gunfire; he spots Chucho sitting on the ground, firing toward the school building. Hector can't see Davey. Chucho isn't looking in his direction, so

Hector runs straight at him, thinking you stupid shit, you're going to get yourself killed. When he's forty yards away, Chucho sees him and turns in his direction. On the open school field without cover, Hector dives to the ground and dumps all sixteen rounds in Chucho's direction.

Before this moment, he had never fired his Glock except at the police range and never from more than twenty-five yards. Chucho slumps. *I might have hit him.* Hector recognizes the weapon Chucho is firing as an M-16. Jones comes around the corner and empties his Glock before Chucho's firing drives him back behind the building. As Hector reloads with his second magazine, Chucho stands up. As if completely ignoring him, Chucho begins a wide circle around the building, moving into a firing position that gives him a clear shot at Jones. Davey doesn't stand a chance. Hector empties his second magazine at Chucho without any visible effect. He hears a shout, and a uniformed officer flops down by his side. "I'm out of ammo." Without hesitation, the officer hands him a magazine.

They run forward as other officers arrive. At twenty yards, both drop prone and empty their weapons at Chucho. Several officers began firing as he falls to the ground. Walking up on Chucho, Hector hears firing from where the other man had run. He later learns that the man was shot twice. Chucho took three hits.

Bob Toliver, Malik, and Jaime watch Hector turn toward the sound of gunfire. Hector isn't aware, but uniformed officers follow him. One uniformed officer stayed with the two on the ground while the three AGE officers followed the other passenger. When cornered, the man opened fire. Toliver put two slugs into him. Malik and Jaime both missed.

Lieutenant Fugett arrives ahead of Lieutenant Delacroix, secures the scene, and turns it over to Homicide Detective Sergeant Collins. Internal Affairs separates all the officers and takes weapons from all those involved in the shootings before the departmental shooting team interviews begin. No one died, so the investigation remains in-house.

Lieutenant Fugett's Internal Affairs Investigators place the officers on Administrative Leave. After five days, IA and the Shooting Board ruled the shooting justified.

Lieutenant Delacroix calls Hector into his office. "Tell me, Navarro, do you have an M-4 or a shotgun in your trunk?"

Hector hadn't thought of the long guns when he ran past the Camry chasing Davey and the shooter. All he can say is, "Oh, shit."

Delacroix softens the officer's embarrassment: "If you had stopped long enough to get a long gun, you might have been too late to save Jones. You did good."

A few days later, a nurse finds Montemayor dead—strangled in his hospital bed. Four playing cards, all aces on his chest, says it all.

The police officer guarding Chucho's door swears that no one entered the room during his watch. He passes a polygraph.

A homicide investigation is started, and all the investigators know who ordered the hit. But there is no evidence linking Geronimo, Galloway, or any of the 4-Aces to the crime.

25

AS THE AGE team shuffles to their feet, Captain Windsor waves her hands for all the officers to remain seated, "Relax, keep your seats. Bob, you have any coffee?" Toliver pours the captain her coffee as she takes a seat next to Lieutenant Delacroix. "Good evening, Jack." She takes a quick swallow of coffee and continues. "I won't take up much of your time. The Chief and I are proud of your unit's work in helping solve the Los Scorpios Locos homicides. Without your effort, homicide might still be looking for suspects. Thank you." Turning to Jack Delacroix, she finishes with, "Unless you mind, I'll stay for the briefing."

"Please do." To the AGE officers, Delacroix says, "You've earned the right to take point tonight. SWAT will make entry, followed by your officers, with Homicide providing backup. You make the arrests and then turn the suspects over to Homicide. As soon as the scene's secure, SWAT will stand down. Detective Sergeant Collins will arrange to have Dixon and Galloway transported to headquarters, where he will coordinate the questioning. These thugs are dangerous, so be careful. I don't want anyone hurt. Sergeant Toliver will be in tactical command. Bob, it's all yours."

"Thanks, Lieutenant. Malik, Jamie, it's good to have you back, even if it's only for tonight. I'm sure the overtime pay helps." Everyone in the room laughs. After thanking the Homicide Lieutenant and SWAT Commander, Lieutenant Claudia Foss, Toliver continues. "The judge authorized night service. Here's how we'll set up. . .."

The plan calls for Toliver and the three lieutenants to observe from the undercover mobile command post at eleven p.m. Lieutenant Foss is not thrilled. She would have preferred to make an entry with her SWAT team. Her two sergeants are grinning like a pair of Cheshire cats. Their boss is rarely stuck on the sidelines.

"Steve, I want to hit Ernesto's the second we confirm that Dixon and Galloway are inside. Regardless, we go in no later than zero-one-hundred hours before they start leaving the clubhouse." Glancing around the room, Toliver asks, "Any questions?"

Malik Al-Fasil has one question. "The parking lots are going to be pretty full. How do we come in?"

"Good question." Addressing the packed room, Toliver continues, "you'll all rendez-vous at Firehouse 18. It's close, and the back lot's out of sight of the road. Once I give Steve Kowalski the signal, you saddle up, four to a car, and drive to Ernesto's. Don't rush. I want you all to arrive at the same time. When you're in sight, I'll leave the command post and walk to the front of the pool hall. Park wherever you can and hustle to your assigned positions. Once we are all, and I mean all set, I'll do the knock-and-announce at the front entrance. Inside, I'll do another at the interior door to the 4-Aces clubhouse."

"Homicide, your team will follow and park at the command post. Who's in tactical command of your unit?" Toliver continues.

Sergeant Collins answers. "I'll have command of the detectives, and the lieutenant will be in the Command Center."

After making the entry team assign-ments, Toliver releases them with these orders: "Review your assignment, get a bite, and be at Firehouse 18 ready to go no later than twenty-three hundred hours."

Jack Delacroix adds, "Remember, these assholes, all the 4-Aces, and their women are considered armed and dangerous. Make sure you check your weapons and have on your body armor. Maintain radio silence, and don't forget, all communication will be by cell phone until we make entry."

"Good luck, be careful, and stay safe," Captain Windsor adds as the officers leave.

26

DRIVING TO THE station to pick up Officer Navarro, Jones detours. He needs a little something to take the edge off, nothing serious, a shot or two. A regular the bartender greets him, "Hey, Davey. How goes it? The usual?" Without waiting for an answer, she pours a double shot of Jack Daniels and slides a beer bottle across the counter. Jones downs the whiskey in one gulp. After another double, he finishes the beer, leaves a twenty on the bar, and returns to his undercover car.

Hector should have told Sergeant Toliver about his partner's drinking. He wasn't positive, and Davey hides his condition reasonably well.

Hector lied to himself. Has his partner been drinking tonight? Maria had warned him, "You have to tell your sergeant. Davey could get someone killed." He resisted, not wanting to get a reputation as a rat. Maria gave him a second option. "If you won't tell Bob, talk to Steve. He'll know what to do." Hector didn't take her advice. Now it's too late, and he thinks it'll screw up the operation if he says something. Jones had promised to keep his drinking under control. Jones makes many promises, but his promises are worthless when it comes to alcohol.

There's no sense in asking Jones why he's late. Hector can tell he's been drinking by the empty mint wrappers on the front seat of his car. Jones doesn't say anything, nor does Hector, but passing a McDonald's a few blocks from Firehouse 18, he commands, "Pull in here."

"Why?"

"You need coffee. Get the fucking coffee."

Sergeant Toliver joins the others in the mobile command post and calls Kowalski. "Steve, we're ready, is everything set at the firehouse?"

"We're good to go." Kowalski doesn't mention that Jones and Navarro are late arriving.

"Give your informant a call. We go as

soon as we confirm Geronimo and Galloway are inside."

Toliver's wait for the call back from Kowalski seems like an eternity. In reality, it's less than ten minutes. "Bob. They're inside with about ten 4-Aces plus four or five women."

"Get saddled up. I'll start walking. When you approach Ernesto's, flash your lights. I should be at the front door by the time you park."

"Be careful, Bob. Give me five minutes to get everyone moving, Kowalski tells his friend and sergeant.

Hector can tell that Jones is in no shape to drive and tells him, "We're riding with Malik and Jamie." Davey doesn't object because it makes sense; the four of them are to enter the rear door of the clubhouse together.

Jones says, "Chuck, you do the knock and announce. I'll get the door."

"How many times I gotta tell you, never call me Chuck, you racist prick. My name is Malik."

"Yeah, whatever. I knew you long before you changed your name."

Malik suppresses his anger as he parks ten feet from the back door.

The radio crackles to life with Bob

Toliver's voice. "They're inside. Let's move it."

As he reaches the door, Malik shouts, "Police. Search warrant. Open up." Before Malik finishes, Jones grabs the doorknob. The door flies open, and several women burst out, fleeing the chaos.

"Police. No one move," Sergeant Toliver yells seconds before Malik and the others reach the back door.

Hector can see little between Jones and Malik; they block most of the doorway. Toliver is grappling with Geronimo, and the next instant, Hector hears the report of a large caliber gun from close in front. Jones is on the ground but gets back up and runs with Hector at his heels. The gunshot silences the crowd.

"I'm hit," Bob Toliver looks as though he's in a daze, slumping to the ground.

Geronimo is standing next to Toliver. His head tilted to the side, eyes wide, mouth wide open, a pistol on the floor at his feet.

The first to Toliver, Hector checks for signs of life.

"He's gone. He's dead," Hector gasps, holding his sergeant in his arms. The shot got him on the side where there was a gap in the protection given by the body armor. Bob Toliver's bulletproof vest is on the inside of his raid jacket. Looking down, he sees blood on Toliver's left side, equaled by a widening stain on Hector's shirt.

"It's okay, son. It's okay." Hector looks up into the face of Sergeant Collins. "He's gone. You can let go."

"You killed him, you mother fucker," Jones yells at Geronimo Dixon in his alcohol-fueled rage.

Jones raises his gun. Hector tries to stop him with a swing at the officer's pistol.

"No, Davey," Hector shouts.

In what appears as a calm, deliberate act, Officer David Jones brings his .40 Caliber Glock up. He steps to the gang leader's side, jams the muzzle against the man's head, and shoots Geronimo Dixon in the right temple.

Within seconds of the second shot, the SWAT Team has the room under control. The men and women are handcuffed and secured. Homicide detectives take DeShawn "The Knife" Galloway away. SWAT takes everyone out of the clubhouse and lines them up against the parking lot wall. The scene of a double homicide, the bar, and the clubhouse fall under the authority of the Homicide Lieutenant.

Lieutenant Delacroix orders Sergeant Collins to take Officer Jones' pistol from him. He assigns Malik and Jaime to watch Jones.

Sergeant Collins sits Hector in a booth

and tells him to wait. Twenty minutes later, either ignored or forgotten, he hears Collins whispering to his lieutenant and Jack Delacroix.

"We've scoured the area." Sergeant Collins tells the lieutenants, "We found two casings, one by the rear door and the other five feet from Geronimo's body. They both appear to be departmental issue forty-caliber."

"All that were present during the shooting agree they heard two shots," Delacroix says. After shaking his head and taking a deep breath, he adds, "Everyone in the clubhouse has confirmed that. Have you checked all our people's weapons?"

"Yes, Sir. We have examined every weapon carried by every officer here on the scene of the killings, except for Officer Jones' duty weapon, none show evidence of recent use. His has been fired." Looking around, before continuing, "When I examined his weapon, there was one in the chamber and thirteen in the magazine. That leaves two rounds unaccounted for."

The homicide lieutenant is next. "My God, Jim, are you saying Jones killed Bob Toliver?"

The hesitation and the look on Collins's face tell him all he needs to know.

"Jesus Christ."

"Look, Boss, I'm not saying Jones killed them both. The Medical Examiner will have to remove the bullets, and the lab will have to compare the slugs."

Delacroix interrupts. "Jim, we know. Please tell us what you think happened. We won't hold you to it. We need to understand. We need to know how to manage this."

"I have no doubt Jones was drinking before coming on duty tonight. I have no doubt that his accidental discharge killed Bob Toliver." Collins pauses, taking a long breath and exhaling before continuing, "I have no doubt it was an accident. Jones fell as he came through the door discharging his weapon, and the round ricocheted off the floor before hitting Sergeant Toliver."

The lieutenants exchange looks. Jim Collins is rarely wrong.

Hector goes to the car where Malik and Jamie are guarding Jones. He has a nagging feeling that he's missing something.

"I want to talk to Davey."

"Go ahead." Malik says, "we're not stopping you."

"In private."

Malik and Jamie exchange glances, shrug and walk a short distance away.

Davey is sobbing. "Hector, I killed him."

His face glistens with tears. Snot is running down and over his mouth. His goatee gleams with the sheen of the thick mucus.

Hector hands him a handkerchief. "Here, wipe your face." Jones does and then stretches his hand out with the wet cloth. "Keep it."

"I killed him. I killed Bob." Davey sobs.

"And Geronimo, you shot him. Why?"

Jones looks up. Hector can see the hate and anger as his partner clenches his teeth. "Fuck him. He deserved to die."

"Davey, be careful what you say. If they charge you with murder, people will remember what you said."

"Who cares what happened to that bastard? It's Bob. I killed Bob. They're all saying I was the one who killed him. I fell. My gun went off. I'm so sorry." Jones is weeping. "Gimme a little privacy, please. Leave me alone."

Hector turns and steps toward Malik and Jamie. Malik shakes his head, and tears glisten on his face. Hector can tell from how the officer moves and breathes that he's troubled. Jamie doesn't look much better. Hector asks the officers. "What's going to happen to Davey?"

Before Jamie can answer, there's a gunshot—remarkably close. Followed by a thump as a small pistol falls to the car floor.

Hector spins as Davey slumps forward. In the glare of the parking lot lights, he can see the back of Davey's head gapes open with gore, hair, and brain matter. The back window is dark with blood splatter.

Officer David Jones is dead—suicide.

Hector's mind shrieks. *Davey's drinking killed three men—I could have prevented it—it's my fault.*

Bending into the back of the car, Hector recognizes the pistol as the PPK Jones carried in an ankle holster. He forgot it when he came to talk to Davey. As other officers rush up, Hector roars, "No one thought to take his backup?" as much to himself as the others.

Lieutenant Delacroix calls Captain Windsor. "Bob Toliver's dead, shot, and yes, he had on his vest. The bullet entered through a gap on the left side and likely took out his heart. How soon can you get here?"

After the briefest pause, Captain Windsor answers, "I'll be there as soon as I call the Chief. How's Kowalski?"

"Not good. He wants to be the one to tell Bob's wife."

"Once we get the scene under control, you and Steve go see her."

"Captain, there's more."

"What?" She knows it's going to be a long night.

"After Toliver went down, Davey Jones killed Geronimo Dixon."

"Is there a problem? Was it a clean shoot?"

"No, Ma'am. Dixon was unarmed, and Officer Jones executed him."

"Jesus, Jack. It can't get much worse than that."

"I'm afraid it does.—two shots—Jim Collins believes they both came from Davey Jones' pistol."

"Are you telling me that Jones killed Bob Toliver?"

"Most likely. We recovered two departmental issue forty caliber casings. Jones has the standard fifteen-round magazine; counting the round in the chamber, we should have sixteen rounds— two missing." Delacroix hesitates.

"Jack. What is it? Tell me."

"It gets worse." He looks around; there's no one else within earshot. "I'm quite sure he's been drinking. Collins agrees."

"Is there anything else I should know before I call the Chief?"

"No, Ma'am, that's it."

"I'll call the Chief. You call Internal Affairs. I want Bill Fugett to manage this. Have Jones confined until Fugett gets here and takes him into custody."

"Lieutenant Delacroix starts to question his captain. "Ma'am, what . . .""

Captain Windsor cuts him off. "Yes, you heard me, in custody—in cuffs. He'll need his union representative and a lawyer. We're going to do this by the book. Something the two of us should have done long ago."

"I have officers sitting on him. When Fugett gets here, I'll have him stay with Jones unless the IA investigators are here by then."

Twenty-eight minutes later, Captain Windsor arrives at Ernesto's, and per departmental protocol, she assumes command of the incident scene. Detective Sergeant James Collins records the date and time in his notebook. A few minutes later, Lieutenant Fugett arrives. Clustered at Captain Windsor's car, they discuss the route the investigation will take with Jack Delacroix and the homicide lieutenant. They're interrupted by the unmistakable sound of a single gunshot coming from the back of the parking lot. Taking defensive positions, they pull their weapons. Hearing no other gunshots, the four rush to the back of the building. An undercover car is parked ten feet from the back door of the building. The right rear door of the sedan is open, with half a dozen police officers standing in a half-circle a few feet away.

Her first thought is for the safety of her officers. Captain Windsor asks, "What happened?' Is anyone hurt?" For a moment, no one speaks. "I said—what happened!"

Several officers, visibly shaken, back away from the car. Looking from face to face, she sees tears. After what seems an eternity, a young Hispanic officer turns to her.

"He killed himself."

"Who? What?" The officer looks at her with a face imprinted with sadness and anguish. He appears near collapse. After a second or two, she recognizes him. "You're Officer Navarro."

"Yes, Ma'am, I'm Hector Navarro. He's my partner, Davey Jones—he had a backup gun. When he found out he killed Sergeant Toliver, Davey started crying and asked for privacy. He shot himself. He's dead. It's my fault."

Sergeant Collins pulls Hector aside and puts him in the back of his car. "Hector, what was going on with Officer Jones? You were his partner. If you knew Davey had been drinking, you had a duty to report it. Do you understand?"

"Yes, I do."

Sergeant Collins stands up, looking left, right, and behind. The nearest officer is twenty feet away. Hector sits sideways with his feet on the rough parking lot pavement and can see what the detective is doing. Collins puts his hands on Hector's shoulders, leans in, and whispers, "Before I have you transported to the station for a formal statement, do you have anything to say to me?"

"Huh . . . what . . . what do you mean?"

Collins tightens his grip, "Look at me." Hector looks into his eyes. "Officer Navarro, did I hear you say you want your union representative and an attorney present before you say anything else?"

What's he trying to tell me?

Sergeant Collins is nodding his head. "Say it," he whispers so low Hector has to lean close to hear.

"You mean . . . ?"

Again, the sergeant nods.

Hector can't help it. He has trouble breathing. Tears flow: his chest feels like a medicine ball is bouncing on it. In a strange and strangled voice, Officer Navarro says, "Sir. I want—I want to talk to my union rep," Hector expels a loud breath and curls forward.

Sergeant Collins softly says, "Hector, you have to finish. Tell me about the attorney.

"I want an attorney before I answer any questions."

I must be a criminal. I'm hiding behind the Fifth Amendment.

Sergeant Collins gives him a gentle squeeze, "That's good. That's good." As his hands recede, his demeanor changes—his voice rises. "Well, if you refuse to give me a statement until you meet with your union representative and an attorney, that's your prerogative. Nothing more we can do here. Give me your badge and your weapon."

Hector gives up the badge that means so much to him, more even than the pistol. "What happens to me? What do I do?"

"You go home and wait for a call from your commanding officer. He'll make the investigation official. You're suspended, with pay, until further notice. Do you understand?"

"Yes, sir."

"I'll notify Lieutenant Delacroix." The detective calls to a uniformed officer. "Give Officer Navarro a ride to the station so he can pick up his car. He rides up front— understand?" It's evident to anyone within hearing range it is not a request. It's an order. The officer gives Hector a ride to the station. Besides asking him for directions to his parked car, the driver never says a word.

27

INSTEAD OF HIS apartment, Hector goes to Maria's. He can't face the night alone.

"Hector, what's going on? I have to get up in a few hours."

After telling her what happened, Maria calls her boss and leaves a message that she won't be at work. Hector takes a long hot shower: but it doesn't help. He feels dirty—filthy. It's as if he'll never be able to cleanse himself of the events of the night.

Maria sees the blood on his clothes; and throws them in the washer. She would throw them away, except that would leave Hector without any clothes. The blood on his body washes off; in his mind, it remains. Try as he might, it won't go away. As Hector cries, Maria joins him in the shower.

"It's okay. I'm here. I won't leave you alone." She holds him until the tears stop and the hot water's exhausted. She dries him off as the crying begins again. In bed, she holds Hector until he falls asleep.

That's when the nightmares start. Bob Toliver is the first—sitting naked on the edge of an autopsy table. *Hector can see the wound.*

"Hector, why didn't you tell me Davey was drinking on the job? If you had, he and I would still be alive." Bob shakes him. *"Answer me. Why didn't you tell me?"*

Hector must have screamed because Maria's rocking him in her arms. "It's okay. You had a nightmare." She doesn't ask about his dream while holding him as one would a frightened child.

After falling back into a fitful sleep, his next visitor is Davey Jones. Hector tries arguing with Davey, but it does no good.

"Hey, Hector, why didn't you stop me from drinking? It's your fault that Bob and I are dead."

"Hector. Hector. Wake up. Steve Kowalski's on the phone." He looks at the clock. It's almost noon.

"Hi, Steve. How'd you find me?"

"Easy. When you didn't answer your cell phone, I knew you would be with Maria."

"Whatcha want? I'm not supposed to

218

talk with anyone until I talk with my union rep."

"This isn't an official call. I want to make sure you're okay and see if you need anything."

"I got your best friend killed. You must hate me."

"The first thing you must understand is that you didn't get Bob Toliver killed. Until you realize that, you better avoid Internal Affairs or any other investigator. You'll say something that will get you fired. Don't say or do anything stupid."

"If I didn't get him killed, who did?"

"It wasn't your fault. Believe me."

"I'm trying."

"Good. Keep trying, or you'll wind up like Davey. Do you need anything?"

"No. I'll stay with Maria for a few days. What happens next?"

"Jack Delacroix will make your suspension official. Can I give him this number? If not, turn on your cell phone. Turn it off after you talk to him. Or you will be getting calls from people you shouldn't talk to. You can check your messages and call back those you want."

"Tell the lieutenant to call me here but tell him not to give Maria's number to anyone else."

"Got it."

"What about Davey?"

"His autopsy's finished, so's Bob's. Their bodies will be released to their families tomorrow."

"What happens next?"

"Bob will have a departmental funeral. Davey won't. I'm the liaison officer for Joyce. Have you met Bob's wife?"

"No. I doubt she'll ever want to meet me."

"You're wrong, Hector. Anyway, his funeral is Saturday. When I have more, I'll call."

Hector can't speak. Maria takes the phone. "Hi, Steve, it's Maria. He can't talk."

"I know. Hector has to accept the fact that this wasn't entirely his fault. Call me if either of you needs anything."

"Thanks, Steve."

"No sweat. Make sure he doesn't talk to anyone, and I mean anyone other than Jack Delacroix and his union rep."

28

WITH GERONIMO DEAD, Galloway assumes leadership of the 4-Aces. All agree he is the best man for the job until a new leader is selected; he knows more about the gang's organization and membership than anyone else. He's feared enough that under his leadership, none of the aces will try to break off any part of the gang's business enterprises for themselves.

Calling a meeting of the leaders at the clubhouse, Galloway stands in front of Geronimo's oversize chair. He stands silent with his right hand over his left elbow until the room quiets before beginning, "We have to make sure that all the brothers, inside and out of prison, know what happened. The cop that killed Geronimo is dead, so we don't have to off the pig. Do any of you have a problem with me running things?" After considering what Galloway says, they all pledge their allegiance and agree he is the man for the job—for the time being—maybe.

"Froggy, I want you to make sure that the whores behave. They might try to leave. Nothing changes. You still manage them. Make sure no one tries to move in on our territory or steal any of them."

"I can do that, Knife, but I'm gonna need a few soldiers."

Moving so that he's nose-to-nose with Froggy, Galloway snarls, "Don't ever call me Knife." When he turns to face the others, his displeasure is visible enough that several men step back. Never again will Galloway be called *Knife*—to his face.

"Sorry, DeShawn, it won't happen again."

"Good. Why do you need soldiers?"

"Several spic gangs, including the LSLs, will see this as an opportunity to take over our turf. We have to convince them that's a bad idea. We'll have to beat down, maybe even smoke a couple to make an example. We'll have brothers out there stopping any move on our girls or territory."

Several, including those running the street dealers, realize the gang's business interests are at risk. "Froggy, you'll get your soldiers. Does anyone else need extra men?"

They will have to call in brothers from other chapters to handle the requests.

Froggy's concerns are justified. Sanchez and the Los Scorpios Locos are smarting from the loss of Chucho at the hands of the 4-Aces. Sanchez is ready. He knows with Geronimo dead; the 4-Aces are weakened, but not for long. *I'll have to move fast.*

Always a step ahead of his opponents, Galloway's aware of several who will want to become the president. He will speak to each chapter leader and make sure all the leaders are loyal to him during the chaos that will follow. "I'll get you the extra help."

After assigning soldiers, Galloway turns to the business of Geronimo's funeral. Many times smaller, but in several ways, his sendoff will be like what the police have planned for Bob Toliver.

29

MARIA AND HECTOR attend the first of the two
police officer funerals they'll attend the week
before his Internal Affairs hearing. This one
is for David Jones. Jones was Catholic,
something Hector hadn't known. Because he
committed suicide, there's no church service,
and he isn't buried in a Catholic cemetery.
His is a graveside service at Chapel of Angels
Cemetery. His sole survivor, a daughter, sits
at the graveside. Having a daughter is
something else Hector had not known. He
and Maria are surprised to see a Marine
Honor Guard. One of the Marines plays taps;
seven others give Davey a twenty-one-gun
salute. A dozen veterans are wearing VFW
caps. The department chaplain and twenty or
so New Liberty officers are in uniform, while

the Anti-Gang Unit and Jack Delacroix are in civilian attire. After a brief service, most offer their condolences to Davey's daughter and leave. Except for the older veterans, Maria and Hector are the last to leave.

Two of the local television stations are set up at a discrete distance. One of the reporters tries to interview Jack Delacroix. He tells the reporter, "I have nothing to say. Please leave us alone. We're here to pay our respects and say goodbye to our friend and colleague."

Steve Kowalski invites Hector to join the others at a local watering hole. He declines. It doesn't seem appropriate, considering Bob Toliver's death.

Three veterans, one Hispanic and two Black, stop Hector. All wear the United States Marine Corps crossed flags pins on their lapels. One of them asks, "Aren't you Officer Navarro?"

"Yes, Sir, I am."

"You were Corporal Jones's partner, weren't you?"

"I was."

Nodding at the men with him, the man says, "We served with him. Corporal Jones was one hell of a Marine. Did you know he picked up two purple hearts and the Navy Cross in Iraq? He saved our lives and should have gotten the Medal of Honor." Maria and Hector talk with the Marines for a good half hour. One is a Gunnery Sergeant, and the other two are Lance Corporals. Their Marine Corps reserve unit had been called up for Desert Storm.

"Jones was a lance corporal the day our unit came under heavy fire while occupying a compound north of Baghdad. The four of us, including Jones, had been wounded earlier in the fight. Insurgent fighters tossed two grenades over a wall into a room where we were holed up. Jones grabbed one of the grenades and pitched it back out a window before it exploded. He threw himself on top of the second one," Gunny tells the couple.

Hector is dumbfounded. Jones had never mentioned being a Marine, let alone a decorated combat veteran. "How'd he survive the second grenade?"

"It didn't explode. God knows why not. After a few seconds, he realized it wasn't going to detonate. Jones stood and threw it out the window."

"What happened then?" Maria asks.

"Jesus here was tending to our wounds. Jones grabbed his M4, charged into the compound, engaged the enemy, and killed three. Thus forcing the rest to withdraw, the corporal was seriously wounded. We didn't think he would make it, but he surprised us.

"Sir, Davey never told me any of this."

The three veterans exchange glances.

The gunny continues. "He was never the same after that. We returned to the states shortly after, and Corporal Jones began drinking seriously. The shrinks at the Veterans Administration said he had Post-Traumatic Stress Disorder, but, by then, he was back at the police department."

During the ride back to her apartment, Maria asks, "I thought you said Officer Jones was a racist?"

"He was."

"If Davey was such a racist, how come those three Marines loved him?"

"I don't have an answer."

Wednesday, Bob Toliver's funeral is different. The crowd is estimated at four thousand; most are in a uniform of one sort or another. The Army sends an Honor Guard. Toliver's entire Army Criminal Investigation unit is there in uniform. Police officers from throughout the U.S. and Canada have come to pay their respects. Mexico even sent a contingent of Federal Police. Every local and national television network news team showed up at the service.

Hector was not invited to join the AGE unit; all wore uniforms. Without a badge or gun, he would have looked out of place. Bob Toliver was also Catholic. The Saints Simon and Jude Cathedral in Phoenix is filled to overflowing. Large screen monitors are set up for those unable to get inside. He and Maria join a group of civilians near one of the screens and watch as Steve Kowalski gives the eulogy. The service lasts two hours; more hours pass as the procession forms up and clears the cathedral.

"Are we going to the cemetery?" Maria asks.

Hector tells her, "We can't get to the cemetery in time for the graveside service," as they wait to get to his car. An hour passes, and police, fire, and military vehicles continue to form up and move away. "It's seventeen miles from here to the National Memorial Cemetery. Bob's family is already there. The bishop won't wait two or three hours for everyone to get there before holding the graveside service."

"Do you think we can get into the cathedral? I want to pray and light candles for Bob and Officer Jones."

"You want to light a candle for Davey Jones? What are you thinking?" Hector can't believe his ears.

"He was sick. God's forgiven him. You need to forgive him. Only then will you be able to forgive yourself."

30

PRESIDENT OF THE 4-Aces is a position of power DeShawn Galloway finds to his liking. The club has not decided who will become the permanent president. Galloway has. He will be as soon as he deals with the other two senior lieutenants who want the title. Galloway decides to kill both in a manner that discourages any other candidates from stepping forward while decrying the killings as the result of an unknown assailant. Galloway has known the two men for ten to fifteen years and accepts that either could be a successful and popular leader. Although people fear Galloway, he would never be popular. *I will not give up the leadership of the 4-Aces no matter what I have to do.*

"I have something that needs doing." The

call is on a burner to a burner.

"Anything," replies a calm voice.

"I'll be sending a man to El Paso for a meeting. I don't want him coming back—ever."

"It's not a long flight, and I can be there and set tomorrow."

"Good. Do you have a burner passport ready? Otherwise, you gotta drive."

"Yes, Sir, I do. Where's he staying?"

"I'll put him in a suite near the airport, at the Wyndham Hotel. But it doesn't matter. The day after tomorrow, you pick him up at a bar near the airport between seven and eight. Pick out one that works best for you. You need anything, money?"

"No. Text me a picture on this burner. I'll dump it and pick up another."

Galloway's next call was to Big Joe, the man he figured had the best chance of beating him for the chief's chair. The biggest lieutenant—Big Joe feared no man—except Galloway. He was called Big Joe by everyone in the club but Galloway. Big Joe was a boastful bully who loved one-upmanship. What Galloway planned included a surprise his competitor would be unable to pass up.

"Joe, I have something I need you to handle. Meet me at Ernesto's in an hour."

"I'll be there." The man was more curious

than suspicious. He knew Galloway had decided to remain the shot caller. Until the club decided otherwise, he was still running the organization. It was not unusual for Galloway to be abrupt on the telephone. He didn't ever risk a wiretap by the feds or the locals.

Galloway chose Ernesto's because he wanted to be seen meeting with Big Joe and wanted him to brag about his mission. Every member of the 4-Aces would know by tomorrow that Big Joe was the odds-on favorite to replace Geronimo. Why else would Galloway trust him with such an important assignment?

"What you need, DeShawn?"

"I got a message from a brother doing ten at Rogelio Sanchez State. That's in El Paso."

"I know where it is."

"You got a clean ID you can use to fly?"

"Yeah. Why you sending me there."

"The brothers at Rogelio Sanchez want to affiliate with the 4-Aces and take over the prison." Galloway leans forward and whispers, "they have a good chance if we act right away and throw our support behind them."

"Why now?"

"The White supremacists have a void at the top. The man with the keys died, and there's a fight for shot caller."

"Okay, what am I doing?"

"You meet with their outside man and explain the facts of life to him. I want you to decide if we will bring ten or twelve new brothers into the club. If you do, make the same arrangements we have with our brothers in Florence. If you think we can win, give them the go-ahead and let me know."

"Who do I meet?"

"I don't know. You'll be contacted not far from the airport."

"Okay."

"You'll get a text telling you when and where. The brothers at Rogelio Sanchez are paranoid and worried there could be a leak before we take over. Word gets out, and they'll all be dead within a week."

"Yeah, we'd do the same at one of our prisons. What about a guard?"

"If they can't bring one in, take a pass, but I'm guessing they already have one."

"How do we get word in and out of the prison while I'm in El Paso? I know the cons only get one visitor each weekend."

"That's why you are going up on Wednesday. It'll give you time to meet with this relative and work out the details. Before you ask, I don't know who the contact is."

"How will he know me?"

"That's a good question. Get a new burner from the bar."

"What?"

"Do it." Even Big Joe knew better than to argue with Galloway. When he returned, Galloway pulled a slip of paper out of his shirt pocket, took a photo of Big Joe, punched in a number, and sent a text with the photograph." He smashed the burner on the tabletop before dropping it on the floor, stomping on it, breaking it beyond repair, picking it up, and putting it in his jacket pocket. Galloway wasn't taking any chances. "The number I used was a one-time burner for the contact."

"He better smash it up. I don't need my picture showing up where it doesn't belong."

"Don't worry. I can guarantee it won't." Galloway had found a way to identify the assassin's target. The killer would take one look at the image and memorize it before destroying the burner.

Big Joe was as proud as a peacock. When Galloway left the table and said his goodbyes to the other Aces, Big Joe had one thought: Galloway's made a big mistake. When I bring Rogelio Sanchez and El Paso into the 4-Aces, there's no way he can stop me from taking over as president. The first thing I'm doing is killing that ugly old bastard.

"The next round's on me," he shouted for all to hear. Big Joe was off and running—running off the mouth—just as Galloway had planned.

31

LATE IN THE afternoon, Hector gets a call from his union representative. "Hector, Internal Affairs has scheduled an appointment for you to be interviewed by Jim Collins before our meeting at the IA office."

"Okay." His voice quivers.

"You meet me there tomorrow at ten. We'll get your story straight before we meet with Collins."

"Will you be with me during the interview?"

"Yes, unless you want me to wait outside."

"I want you there. After I talk to Sergeant Collins, what happens?"

"Things are going to get sticky."

"Sticky? Whatcha mean, sticky?"

"You'll have to decide if you want to talk with IA or to refuse. If you don't, you'll be fired for insubordination. If you talk, you might say something that can be used against you in a criminal case."

"Criminal case, I haven't committed any crime."

"Look, Hector, you haven't violated any law, but you sure as hell used bad judgment. But you never know. What if they're looking for a scapegoat?"

"What are you going to tell Collins, Hector?" Maria asks the moment he tells her what the department has scheduled.

"The truth. I have to. I don't have a choice."

"You always have a choice."

"What choice? All I can do is tell the truth. Do you want me to lie?"

"No, you can refuse to talk."

"If I do that, I lose my job. I'll talk, and I'll tell the truth."

"*Te Amo* Hector." Maria wraps her arms around him.

"I have to call my mom."

"Are you going to tell her what happened to Officer Jones and Sergeant Toliver? You said you didn't want to bother your parents until this is settled."

Hector smiles, his heart filled with joy as he pulls Maria to his chest. "*Te Amo,* Maria. I promised mom I'd call her the second I found the woman I'm going to marry."

"What makes you think I'll marry you?"

"You will."

Friday, October 18, zero-nine-fifty hours. His union representative, a twenty-year veteran, is waiting; he's been a union rep for half those years. "Before we begin, I must inform you that I'm not an attorney. Any advice I give you deals solely with your rights as an employee of the New Liberty Police Department, nothing more. Do you understand that?"

"Yes, I do."

"Today, you'll be interviewed about the incident that occurred during the morning hours of Saturday, October twelfth. You may invoke your right to remain silent. If you do, Collins will then order you to answer his questions. If you refuse, you will be subject to disciplinary action and will be fired."

"I understand, I intend to answer all his questions."

"Once Collins is finished with you, Internal Affairs will question you. The same applies there. You answer or risk firing for insubordination."

"All I can do is tell the truth."

"I'll talk with Collins. We'll establish the ground rules, I'll get you, and we'll get started."

Once his representative is in with Sergeant Collins, Hector has an overwhelming urge to vomit. It's a good ten minutes before the officer comes out.

"Come with me. We have to talk." Finding an empty office, he begins, "I have no idea what's going on. Something strange is happening."

"What do you mean?"

"Like I said, I don't know. Here's what you're going to do. Collins will ask you ten questions, no more. You'll answer them all with a yes or no."

"Yes, or no?"

"Yeah, yes or no. Nothing more. You will not elaborate. You will not volunteer anything. Let's go."

Sergeant Collins is formal. "Officer Navarro, I've called you here today to obtain your formal statement about an incident that occurred during the early morning hours of Saturday, October twelfth. The incident occurred within the City Limits of New Liberty, Arizona, at an establishment known as Ernesto's Pool Hall." Sergeant Collins isn't the same man who sent Hector home that awful morning at Ernesto's. "Were you at

Ernesto's on the date and time in question?"

"Yes, I was on . . .. "

Sergeant Collins holds up a hand as if signaling a stop. Turning to the union rep, "Doesn't he know how to answer a question with a simple yes or no?"

After a whispered admonishment from his union rep, Hector says, "Yes."

Sergeant Collins waves a yellow legal pad in his face. "I've written down what we will be discussing today. I'll record all your answers on this tablet. We will not tape-record the interview."

Hector nods at the sergeant, turns to his union rep, and gives him a questioning look as if saying, "what's this about."

"Answer his questions."

"Are you a New Liberty police officer?"

"Yes."

"Did you assist in the service of a search warrant at Ernesto's on October 12th?"

"Yes."

"Did you see Officer David Jones fall?"

"Yes."

"Did you hear a gunshot?"

"Yes."

"Did you see Sergeant Robert Toliver fall to the ground?"

Hector begins to explain what happened. Sergeant Collins shakes his head. "A yes or no will suffice."

"Yes."

"Did you see Officer David Jones shoot a man you knew as Jerome "Geronimo" Dixon?"

"Yes."

"Did you try to stop him?"

"Yes."

It goes on for a few minutes before Sergeant Collins hands Hector the tablet. "Read this over."

After Hector finishes, the sergeant asks, "Is this your statement?"

"Yes."

"Sign it." Hector signs at the bottom of the page.

The union rep asks, "Is there anything else you need from Officer Navarro?"

"No, but I have something to tell him."

"Officer Navarro and I are interested in anything you have to say."

"Officer Navarro, thank you for coming in today and giving me your statement. Your conduct during the incident was within departmental policy and procedure. Your suspension is rescinded and will not appear on your permanent record. Internal Affairs has closed its investigation, and you won't give them a statement or meet with them. You'll report to your commanding officer on Monday. That will be all." Sergeant Collins stands, shakes hands with the two men, opens the office door, and directs them to leave. In the hallway, Hector asks the union rep, "what happened in there?"

"Hell, if I know, I've never seen anything like this. Be glad and get out of here before they change their minds."

32

BIG JOE FLEW first class to El Paso knowing Galloway would be pissed, but, *What the hell? He'll be gone soon enough.* After landing, he rented a Shelby Mustang—thinking the hell with his soon-to-be-dead boss.

After checking in at the hotel, he went to the pool. Four mojitos later, the burner buzzed. "Iron Horse Saloon Hondo Pass Drive. 8:00 pm."

Big Joe wrote the message on a napkin, put the burner in his shorts pocket, and walked to the pool. Not a swimmer, he jumped in at the four-foot depth and sat on the bottom long enough to leave the burner, making it worthless. Getting out, he dried off and had one more mojito.

When Big Joe left, the assassin waited

five minutes before entering the pool and retrieving the burner phone.

The hooded assassin took an Uber to a health spa a mile from the Iron Horse Saloon. The tip was generous but not large enough to draw attention. Walking to the door, going inside, and waiting until the Uber was out of sight, the assassin returned and began a circuitous walk to the Iron Horse Saloon. A block from the saloon, the hoody was cinched tight around the face. After spending ten minutes looking for anything out of the ordinary, Hoody entered the bar and stood left of the door until everything came into focus. The establishment was as advertised. The parking lot and the street in front were packed with motorcycles, all some form of a Harley-Davidson. The bar top was at least thirty feet long. The side room, packed with bikers and rough-looking women, contained four pool tables. The noise was over-whelming. The restaurant reminded Hoody of the Hideaway Grill in Cave Creek, Arizona. Hoody took a small booth near the back, in a dark corner, of the crowded bar that was well over fire standards and ordered a tonic and lime. The wait began. At eight-fifteen, the target wandered in, took a stool away from the pool tables, and ordered a mojito.

"You Big Joe?"

"Yeah, you're late," lying he added.

"You're not what I expected. What'll I call you?"

"Hoody."

"Uh?"

"Hoody is all you need." Sitting across from Big Joe, Hoody gripped an elbow and sat straight as an arrow.

"Shit name," Big Joe said as he felt there was something about the contact that struck him as familiar. He couldn't put his finger on it but had no time to mull it over.

"No matter. Our Black asses are out of place in here with all these bikers." Hoody had chosen the Iron Horse Saloon for that reason, intending to place Big Joe in an uncomfortable position and reluctant to talk over how to kill White supremacist inmates and take control of a prison.

"Shit, ain't no bikers scare me." His comment was all bravado, and they both knew it.

"Maybe, but we don't want to draw any attention. You got a room?"

The first thing that crossed Big Joe's mind was that this could work out well. The second was that his room was a safe haven, "You got a car?"

"No, I took a cab. If you got one, I'll ride with you."

This statement, plus a half dozen mojitos, put Big Joe at ease.

"Yo, let's go."

"Nice car. Must be expensive."

"Don't worry. It ain't costing you anything."

The following morning the burnt-out shell of the Shelby Mustang was found in Juarez, Mexico. Big Joe was never seen again.

33

MARIA AND HECTOR are enjoying dinner at her parent's house when he receives a terse telephone call. "Officer Navarro, this is Lieutenant Delacroix. You're to report to Sergeant Kowalski at the AGE office tomorrow at nine a.m. Do you understand?"

"Yes, sir, I ...." The line's dead. *Shit. Half the calls I get end with a hang-up.*

Maria has an enquiring look that says, why'd you answer your cell phone during dinner, and what was that about? Before he can think of an answer, Mr. Juarez says, "Leave the man alone, Maria. Can't you see it was important?"

"Papa," and then thinking better of it, she drops the matter. Hector knows she won't drop it for long. He's right. After dinner, he thanks Mr. and Mrs. Juarez before they leave. As they back out of her parent's driveway, Maria asks—demands is a better word, "Well, are you going to tell me what that was about?"

Hector tries to deflect with an off-the-wall question. "You know our first date when you had me drive you to your parents' house? You said that was your home. Why'd you do that?"

"I said I want to know about that call."

Although it crosses his mind, Hector is not foolish enough to ask her what she means by *that call.*

"It was Jack Delacroix. He ordered me to report to Steve Kowalski at nine tomorrow. Funny, he called him Sergeant Kowalski."

"Weren't you expecting his call?"

"Yes, I was. I didn't expect the lieutenant to be so formal. He didn't even let me talk."

"They told you your record's clear. It can't be all that bad." Maria sounds positive.

"If that's the case, why do I feel guilty? Officially I'm off the hook. Does that mean there's a coverup? I don't know. Unofficially who knows what could happen? They'll pass me over for a promotion, at the least."

Once again, Hector tries to change the subject. "Are you going to answer my question or not?"

"What question?"

"Why the fib about where you lived when we first met?"

"Jesus, Hector, what does it flippin matter?"

"I guess it doesn't, but I am curious."

"Okay. I'll tell you if you promise to drop it."

"I just met you, and I didn't want you to know where I lived in case you turned out to be a jerk. Don't ask again." He knows it's time to leave well enough alone and answer her next question.

"Where do you stand on the sergeant's promotional list?"

"I'm third on a list of twenty. At least ten will be promoted by the first week of January; even though my official record is clear, the powers to be know what happened. I exercised poor judgment."

"Hector, that's bull shit. They can't pass you over like that. Aren't there civil service rules regarding promotions?"

If it weren't so serious, he'd laugh. Aside from the humiliation, Hector can't afford to ask Maria to marry him until he gets the pay raise that goes with the sergeant's stripes. "Yes, there are civil service rules, the rule of three. When there's a promotion, three names are submitted for consideration. They promote one of the three. Then they add the next name to the list. Those names are submitted for selection. That's the way it goes for each promotion."

"That seems reasonable enough. You should be promoted."

"Not if they don't want to promote me. Each group of three is considered new. My name could be submitted dozens of times and not be selected."

"It doesn't seem fair."

"Nobody ever said the process had to be fair. All they're required to do is submit three names."

"If they do that to you, it'll be wrong."

"No, Maria, it won't be wrong."

"Why not?"

"I don't deserve to be a sergeant."

34

"BJ HAS LEFT the room." *Deshawn Galloway reads the text with a rare smile. Time for a new burner, but I'll make one call first.* Tapping the callback button, he waits for two rings before disconnecting. Five minutes later, his burner rings.

He answers, "Any problems?"

"No."

"Can you get away for five or six days?" If not, Galloway will have to deal with the other problem himself.

"Yes." The assassin does not waste words.

"Don't contact me. I'll send a photo." That was all that was necessary—one more man will vanish.

It was time for Galloway to take a drive without his driver or bodyguard. Making sure he was not being followed, he drove through Phoenix to a Krispy Kreme shop. He waited until it was his turn to be served by a middle-aged Latina.

"Have you tried the jalapeño?"

"No, are they local?

"Yes."

"I think I'll stick with the chocolate with chocolate glaze."

"How many?"

Before answering, Galloway checked the time. It was two in the afternoon. "I think three would be perfect."

"You look like a man who could manage four of these beauties."

Galloway agreed that four worked better than three. He handed the woman a fifty-dollar bill and told her to keep the change.

"Thank you."

Leaving the bag of donuts untouched, Galloway took a leisurely drive arriving at South Mountain Park & Preserve at three-thirty. Stopping at the first public restroom, he tossed the unopened bag of donuts in a trash can before relieving himself. Double checking to make sure he wasn't followed; Galloway drove to Dobbins Lookout. It was ten minutes to four. He remained seated in his car and watched for five minutes before strolling to one of the benches overlooking the valley.

Precisely at four, a nondescript sedan parked, and one Hispanic-appearing man got out of the right rear passenger door, looked around, and then walked to Galloway's bench and sat down.

"Hey, blood, I hear you want to talk."

"Hey, *Ese*, I do."

This was an extraordinary meeting, hastily arranged, so they got right down to it. The two men had known each other their entire lives. One had gone into the 4-Aces; the other worked his way up in the cartel.

"I have some information that your people will find interesting in El Paso."

"Que Pasa?"

"The man with the keys at Rogelio Sanchez is dead, cirrhosis of the liver."

"Damn, Blood, that pruno will get you every time. Fucker, should have gone to AA."

"Yeah, *Ese*, there's a power struggle underway within the Whites for the shot-caller job."

"We know that."

"Do you know who else is in the game?"

"No, what's that got to do with my employer?"

"How would you like to take over? I can give you the names of the top three Whites."

"We can figure that out."

"What you don't know is that a group of brothers is banding together. They plan to take out the Whites and get control." Galloway says.

"No, we didn't know that."

Galloway gives his friend the names of the top three Whites and then hands over a list of five Black men he wants removed for one reason or another. Having them killed during the power struggle would lend credence to his story for sending Big Joe to El Paso. And, once the cartel was firmly in control, making peace would further solidify his position with the 4-Aces.

"These are the five brothers who will lead the takeover. If you can eliminate the three Whites and the brothers, your people will have the keys to Rogelio Sanchez."

"What's in it for you and the 4-Aces?"

"The cartel protects my people inside and keeps hands off the pussy traffic in El Paso."

"I'll pass it on to my employer."

"Good. We can make it official once your people have control." Galloway knew this was an opportunity the cartel would not pass up. The killings would add even more weight to Big Joe's story about a takeover in the El Paso prison and further distance Galloway from the man's disappearance.

"I got one more question, DeShawn."

"Yeah?"

"What'd you do with the donuts?"

35

AT THE AGE Office, New Liberty Police Department, Hector finds Steve Kowalski sitting behind what had been Bob Toliver's desk the last time Hector was in this office.

"Good morning, Hector. I'm glad you decided to come in today. Some thought you would quit. I'm not one of them."

His greeting pisses Hector off. He's never been a quitter, never. What does he mean? "Why would anyone think that? I'm no quitter."

"I know. Do you have any questions you need answered? This is your one opportunity to ask. You won't get another chance."

Kowalski's comments take Hector by surprise. He decides to begin with an easy one and then jump to the difficult one. "The lieutenant told me to report to Sergeant Kowalski. What's that about?

"I didn't tout it, but I was first on the Sergeant's list. My assignment here is temporary. Delacroix didn't want the position to go vacant, especially when the unit was in such disarray with the loss of half its members, including the sergeant. Once things have settled down, a permanent replacement will be selected, and I'll be assigned to either patrol or the jail."

"Congratulations."

"Oh yeah, congratulations. My best friend is killed, and I'm promoted to replace him. Yeah, God Damn wonderful. Do you have any other questions?"

Hector has many more questions, but before he goes on, he's struck by a thought, *Steve's got to be as screwed up over this as me.*

"Yes, I do. What was that about when Sergeant Collins interviewed me?"

"He had to take your statement as a witness to the shootings."

"Cut the bullshit. Will you answer my questions, or was that all a lie?"

"Be careful how you speak to me, Officer Navarro."

"Why? You told me I could ask anything. Is that the truth or not?" He adds a sarcastic, "Sergeant Kowalski."

"Alright, Hector. I had that coming. I'll tell you what I can. If you ask me something I can't answer, I'll tell you why—fair enough?"

"Yes. Tell me about Sergeant Collins."

"It's not a long story. You figure that it's your fault Bob Toliver was killed."

"It is. If I had told Bob, or you, that Davey had a drinking problem, Bob would be alive today."

"You may well believe that and blame yourself but throwing yourself on the sword won't bring Bob back."

"You don't know what I think or might do."

"Oh, but I do. You need to know that Toliver, Delacroix, and I knew all about Jones and his drinking. Why do you think Toliver put up with his shit and kept him on AGE?"

"What do you mean? Did you all know Davey was an alcoholic?"

"We did."

"Why didn't you do something?"

"You remember the Marines you talked to at Davey's funeral?"

"Yes. What does that have to do with it?"

"Did they tell you he saved their lives?"

"Something like that."

"Something like that? Are you that naïve? Jones should have been awarded the Medal of Honor. He was a true hero. He never recovered, and those Marines owe their lives to a man you thought a racist. Must I remind you that two of those men are Black and the third Hispanic?

"I don't understand."

"Remember the gunnery sergeant? I'm sure you do. When he showed up, Bob was on the verge of bouncing Jones from the unit and recommending termination. He told Bob about Davey's service. None of us knew what he'd been through in Iraq, let alone that he was highly decorated."

"I was surprised about his service, but what does that have to do with being a cop?"

"I'm getting there. Bob thanked the gunny and told him he would see what he could do. After the gunny left, Bob told the lieutenant what Jones had done in Iraq. Jack Delacroix's another decorated Marine. I bet you didn't know that either."

"No. I didn't."

"The three of us talked it over and decided to give Jones another chance. The department has a great Employee Assistance Program. It's anonymous. We gave Jones a choice, contact EAP and go into a rehab program or resign. He went into a program for ninety days and came out clean. He remained sober for a year before falling off the wagon."

"What caused that?"

"We're not sure, but we assumed his relapse was related to the death of one of his

Marine buddies. Jones went to a memorial service and likely suffered a flashback. He started drinking again several weeks before you transferred into the unit."

"So why didn't Toliver fire him?"

"This December thirty-first, Jones would have been eligible for retirement. Delacroix went to Captain Windsor and asked her to keep him on until then. The decision went all the way to the Chief. He gave the okay."

"So, let me get this straight. The brass knew Davey was a drunk and decided to hide it. Is that right?"

"That's a bit harsh, but we did hide it."

"None of you thought to tell me. You couldn't tell me that I was partnered with a drunk? No wonder you want to cover this up. Hell, I'm a victim. The only difference between Bob and me is that he knew—and he's dead."

Hector is positive; the whole situation will be swept under the rug—covered up.

He must have hit a sore spot because Kowalski explodes as he comes from behind his desk. "Who the hell you think you are? We're all suffering, from the Chief on down. We're second-guessing our decision to keep Jones. Every one of us has to live with the consequences of that choice. Do you think I'll ever get over the death of my best friend? Well, do you?"

Just as Hector thinks Steve will slug him, the wind goes out of Kowalski as he slumps back onto the desk. "I helped kill Bob. I helped kill three men, two of them brother officers, one of them, my best friend."

Hector knows better than to offer up a retort.

"Follow me." Kowalski stands and leaves the room.

"Lieutenant Delacroix, please excuse this unannounced visit. I have Officer Navarro here, and he has a few concerns you can help lessen."

"Come in, Steve, Hector, grab a seat." After they sit, the lieutenant says, "Steve, tell me what Hector knows and what he thinks he knows?"

"I've told him about the Marines, Jones's visit to rehab, and the decision to let him remain until the end of the year. Hector knows all that."

"What's he think he knows?"

"He hasn't said it, but I'm sure Hector thinks there's a cover-up that runs all the way to the Chief." Turning, Kowalski asks, "Isn't that true, Hector?"

He's right. Hector hadn't said it, but he sure as hell thought it. "Yes, Sergeant." The sarcasm has disappeared from his voice.

"Hector, let me begin by telling you that Steve wanted to tell you what was happening with Officer Jones. He felt you had the right to know, Bob Toliver, and I didn't. In hindsight, I see that Steve was right. We should have told you. I apologize for misjudging you. I was wrong."

"Thank you, sir, but I should have spoken up the minute I realized what was going on with Davey."

"That's true, but you weren't alone. Besides the three of us, two others participated in the decision-making process. I say two because Steve and Captain Windsor objected at every step. That's one of the reasons he's a sergeant."

"Who else knew?"

"At this point, does it matter?" Steve asks.

Lacing his fingers together, Delacroix takes a deep breath, bites his lower lip, and leans back in his chair. Staring at the faded yellow ceiling, he exhales, lowers his head, and drops his hands to his lap. "He deserves to know the whole story."

"You're the boss." Steve looks disappointed as he shakes his head.

Delacroix turns his head to his left and lets out another long breath, "Some days, I wish I wasn't." He looks back to Kowalski. "Steve, you've been through all this. You can leave if you wish."

"No, Lieutenant, I'm as much a part of this as you."

"Before Jones went into rehab, Bob came to me and told me the choice he wanted to offer Jones. I thought it was the right thing to do. I reported to Captain Windsor what we were doing. After the Chief weighed in, she consented, with the caveat that Jones stay sober and attend Alcoholics Anonymous meetings at least once a week when he returned to duty. Except for Steve, we all agreed with that, including the Chief. Jones returned sober and remained that way for a year. He was in Alcoholics Anonymous and attended meetings. I was his sponsor, and we were in the same AA group."

The surprise Hector feels is apparent because Delacroix answers his unasked question. "Yes, I'm an alcoholic, ten years sober. I knew I should have suspended him when he fell off the wagon. I didn't."

"Don't be so hard on yourself. We all knew, and we didn't do anything."

"Steve's trying to protect me. He wanted Jones off the street, as did Captain Windsor. Bob and I convinced the Chief that we could manage Davey until retirement. I promised to take him off the street if he started drinking. I failed to do my duty."

"I need to know if there's a cover-up. Is there?"

"Steve feels that you can handle the truth. I should tell you that I take your failure to report your observations as a lack of good judgment. Steve tells me that you have paid for your sins. In that Steve is one of the few of us who did the right thing, I will honor his request. There's no cover-up, and you'll not receive any punishment."

"So, what changes?"

"Disciplinary action is underway. The Chief will retire at the end of the year and be on vacation until then. He made the final decision, after all. Next to Bob, his punishment's the harshest of all. I'll never make captain. I'm being transferred to Property Control until I retire."

"What happens to Captain Windsor?"

"Mary fought the Chief, Toliver, and me all the way. She wanted Jones terminated, or at least disarmed, assigned to a desk job, and removed from all contact with the public. We should have listened to her. The Deputy Chief of Operations will assume the Acting Chief of Police position. Mary will be the Acting Deputy Chief of Operations. It's a foregone conclusion that their promotions will be permanent."

"Were the City Manager and council told the whole story?"

Delacroix takes another deep breath, exhales audibly, and pauses. Hector can see his lieutenant's body sag—shrinking before his eyes. The lieutenant is not a young man but looks as if he's aging even before Hector's eyes as he lifts his head and continues. "Yes, they know everything. Regardless of what you might think, the Chief is one of the most honorable men you'll ever meet." Hector nods, and Delacroix continues. "Once the funerals were over, the Chief called a meeting. Besides those already involved, he called in the Deputy Chief of Operations, Bill Fugett from Internal Affairs, and Jim Collins. Jim, because the killings were his responsibility to investigate. The Chief was all business, no-nonsense. He told us that we were there to address all, and he meant all, the issues surrounding the officer-involved shooting at Ernesto's that claimed the lives of Sergeant Toliver and Officer Jones."

Hector can't help thinking that must have been some meeting. *I wish I could have been a fly on the wall.*

"The meeting was brief. The Chief took full responsibility for the deaths. He announced that he'd be on vacation until December 31, when his retirement's effective. Before submitting his retirement papers, he cleared the appropriate personnel actions with the City Manager. The first action was promoting the Deputy Chief of Operations to Acting Chief, no surprise, and met with a round of applause. The man deserves the job."

"Once the Chief leaves, can't the Acting Chief rescind all the other orders?"

Delacroix says, "He could, but that would be political suicide. The Chief may be leaving, but he has almost as much political influence in this city as the mayor. The new Chief knows that, besides, he's a decent man. He'll do what's right. This is right."

"What are the other personnel changes?"

"Mary Windsor fought the Chief every step of the way. She wanted things dealt with properly. Her promotion becomes permanent on the first of the year. No one will object. She's the best person for the job." He stops; his face flushes as he bends forward and rubs the back of his neck. He's at a loss for words.

"The next in line's me. The Chief looked at me, turned, and stared out the window at the Estrella Mountains for the longest time. No one said a word." The lieutenant takes a deep breath and exhales before continuing. "'The silence was overwhelming. Finally, I spoke up. 'Where does that leave me?' The Chief was having a tough time. He's used to making tough decisions, but he was struggling.'"

Kowalski speaks up, "'The Chief said, 'Jack, we can do this in private.' The lieutenant said, 'no, let's get it over and done with.'"

"That's right, Hector. I knew what the Chief had to do. He was easier on me than I expected. I still have a job and won't lose my pension."

Steve continues, "Jack was slated for promotion to captain next month. The Chief removed him from the promotional list. He'll remain working in the property unit until eligible for retirement."

It seems harsh to Hector, who chimes in. "That doesn't seem fair. Why's he so hard on you?"

"He's not hard on me. He's hard on himself. By allowing me to keep my job, he'll face harsh criticism. His career and mine are over, but he's allowing me to keep my pension. I owe him a great deal. Had I done my job in the first place, none of us would be in this position."

Hector has to ask. Otherwise, he'll always wonder. "Why was Steve promoted? Why'd he get Bob Toliver's job?"

"Like Mary Windsor, Steve opposed the handling of Jones. He argued for a return to rehab and a desk job until Jones was eligible to retire. Steve was not a decision-maker, and except for Mary, everyone overruled him." Delacroix pauses long enough to shake his head. "Steve was number one on the sergeant's list. He knows AGE better than anyone else in the department. Once things are back to normal, a replacement will be brought in, and Steve will go into uniform as a patrol sergeant." Hector can see that what he says makes sense.

"Why were the Internal Affairs Lieutenant and Sergeant Collins at the meeting?"

Delacroix says, "'The Chief gave Bill Fugett a direct order. 'Bob, your IA investigation's over. You found no evidence of wrongdoing by Officer Navarro or any current department member. You'll have a report to that effect on my desk by eight a.m. tomorrow.'"

Wow, the Chief gave me a pass.

"What'd Lieutenant Fugett say?"

Kowalski says, "'Sometimes I have doubts about you, Navarro. Lieutenant Fugett said, and I quote, 'Yes, sir. The investigation is closed, Sir.' What else do you think the man would say?'"

"Does this have anything to do with how Sergeant Collins acted last week?"

"You gotta be shitting me? You'd better get your head on straight, or you'll wind up in parking enforcement. Jim and Bill Fugett worked out the questions, cleared you of any wrongdoing, and closed the homicide investigation. Mary Windsor and the new Chief signed off on it." Kowalski's face is red with anger.

"So, what happens? What about me?"

"I'll notify you on Friday of your new assignment. I can tell you today if you wish?"

"Please, lieutenant. I know. I'm no longer welcome in AGE."

"It's not so much that you're not welcome but that you'll be more comfortable working somewhere else."

"Where?"

"You'll be promoted, but not until just before the list expires. In the meantime, you leave AGE."

"Do I go back to patrol?"

"Steve, would you explain that to Hector?"

"Hector, you won't return to uniform until your promotion comes through. Homicide has an opening for an officer-level investigator. You have the rest of the week off with pay. Next Monday, you report to Jim Collins. He'll be your supervisor until you make sergeant."

"Is this a way to keep me quiet?" Hector expects one of them to blow up and is surprised when, instead, they smile. He thinks the lieutenant is giggling. "What's so funny?"

"Jack, how come I always have to do your dirty work?"

"Because you're the sergeant, and I'm your lieutenant."

"Jack, do you have anything to add?"

"Yes, I do, Hector. Let's get this finished. I have to be fitted for the uniform I'll be wearing. I'll be lucky if I'm not assigned to the graveyard shift." Delacroix continues, "The Chief asked if anyone had any questions or wished to say something before he finished."

"It seems to me he covered everything."

"'You're right. Almost everyone felt the same way. As we were getting up to leave, Jim Collins spoke up. 'What about the Navarro kid? Whatcha going to do with him?' The Chief said something to the effect that you'd go back to patrol until promoted. I thought that was appropriate and was ready to send you back. That's what I recommended. Collins didn't accept it and said, 'The kid's getting a raw deal. He has potential. We have a slot for an officer-level investigator in Homicide. Transfer Navarro there. He can work for me.'"

"What'd the Chief say?"

"Neither Windsor nor I agreed with Collins's suggestion. I started to voice my objections when the Chief spoke."

"What'd he say?"

"'He said, 'It's done. Have Navarro report to Homicide next week. Sergeant Collins, do you have any more comments?' Jim said, 'No sir.'"

36

WITH THE CARTEL firmly in command of Rogelio Sanchez Prison and the El Paso human trafficking in control of the 4-Aces, the disappearance of Big Joe faded into obscurity as collateral damage from the blood bath that took out close to a dozen inmates at the prison. The prison officials and the media attributed the riot to racial unrest between the White supremacist gang and Blacks.

Among the casualties were the top three members of the White supremacist gang and the five Blacks Galloway wanted dead. The cartel had the prison tightly in its grasp.

Galloway's assassin arrived in New Liberty a week after the El Paso blood bath. Hoody had the victim's name, address, and photo. After being watched for another week, the target was followed to Tucson, where he visited family overnight. The next afternoon he went to his nephew's soccer game, followed by a drunken barbeque. He slept for a couple of hours before heading back to New Liberty. Stopping in Chandler for a nightcap, he was approached by a slight figure in a dark hoody. "This seat taken?"

"No, make yourself at home. Can I get you a drink?"

"I'll have whatever you're having."

After placing the drink order, the target noticed the hood was pulled tight, exposing little of the dark face. The left arm was resting on the bar counter with the right hand supporting it. "You ever take that hood off?"

"Only at home or sometimes in a car."

"Excuse me, but I gotta drain the lizard."

While the target was gone, the assassin placed a hand over his glass and switched glasses."

After another drink and a few minutes of conversation, the assassin said, "You up for a bit of backseat fun? I might even take the hoody off."

Thinking he was in for a blowjob, at the least, the target said yes, and the pair went out to his car, a blue two-week-old Chevrolet Silverado Pickup.

An hour later, a blue Silverado Pickup missed a curve at high speed and crashed into and over a guard rail coming to rest at the bottom of a twenty-foot drop. When the highway patrol officers arrived, they found the driver, the sole occupant of the demolished sixty-five-thousand-dollar truck, dead of a broken neck, which was not a surprise considering the high-speed impact.

The officers reported it as a DUI accident because they smelled an alcoholic beverage on the body and found several open containers in the vehicle. A routine blood test came back with an alcohol level double the legal limit. After a perfunctory autopsy, the case was closed.

When the toxicology report came back some weeks later, no one seemed to notice or care there was a high level of Ambien in his blood, which caused the victim to be unable to stay awake.

The assassin flew home without notifying Galloway. After all, it was all over the local news.

Galloway expressed his profound sorrow over the candidate's death and delivered a warm eulogy at the funeral. The 4-Aces, to a man, wondered if Galloway had orchestrated the accident, but no one had the cajones to bring it up to the de facto president.

The timing, so soon after the disappearance of Big Joe, bothered some, but no one was concerned enough or possibly afraid to mention it. Galloway sent two of the 4-Aces to El Paso to search for him. They learned that he had been drinking heavily at the hotel pool before leaving around six in the evening. Hotel security cameras placed him poolside for most of the day, leaving the property at 8:01 p.m. Except for the Mustang being found destroyed in Juarez, the trail died there. When the two were in El Paso, a race riot erupted at Rogelio Sanchez. One of them had been in Ernesto's the night Big Joe and Galloway had met. Big Joe had bragged about the upcoming takeover of the prison and the part he would play in it. Because of that, they assumed that Big Joe's disappearance was connected to the murders and power struggle within the prison walls.

One month after Big Joe went to El Paso, Deshawn Galloway was unanimously elected president of the 4-Aces Social Club and its branches. Rogelio Sanchez State Jail went from a White-controlled prison to one firmly in the hands of the cartel.

37

MONDAY, HECTOR REPORTS to the Homicide Unit at 0823 hours. Detective Sergeant James "Jim" Collins is not happy. "You ever show up in the middle of the day again, and you'll be lucky to find a place to work in Animal Control."

Hector's day began at 0731 hours with a call from his new boss, Sergeant James Collins. Much later, when he tells the story to his parents, he explains that 0731 hours is 7:31 a.m. in civilian time.

He and Maria had been up late, making plans for the engagement party her parents were giving them on Christmas Eve. His parents will be there to share in their joy when they make the announcement to friends and families.

Maria had spent the night. "Hector, I can't be late for work. Would you fix me a bowl of instant oatmeal and put on the coffee?"

"If you moved in with me, you wouldn't have to rush like this."

"For the last time, my parents are old-fashioned and wouldn't understand. Ask again, and you won't get me here again until we're married."

Before Hector can answer, his cell phone rings, "Now what?"

"What'd you say, Hector?"

Not answering her, he sees the caller ID reads "James Collins." Muttering another "Shit," he answers, "Hector."

Before he can add Navarro, there's a shout. "Where the hell are you? I couldn't give a rats-ass when you assholes in AGE work. Here we start at seven-thirty."

Listening to a dial tone, Hector looks at the kitchen clock. It's seven-thirty-one—he is one minute late.

"You should have been here an hour ago. Unless I permit you to come in at a different time, I want you at your desk and ready to begin the day at zero-seven-thirty. Do you understand?"

"Yes." Hector tries to offer an excuse.

Sergeant Collins silences him with a glare that would wilt cactus. "Sorry."

"You better be sorry. Don't ever be late again. If you work for me, I expect you to be here on time and remain until I say you can go. If you have a problem with that, tell me. I can have you back in uniform by noon."

"Yes. I mean, no. I don't have a problem with that."

"Officer Navarro, I missed my morning coffee because of you." Sergeant Collins points to his office door. Hector's been dismissed. "Close the door on your way out." He has no idea what to do or where he is supposed to work. Several detectives glance his way, shake their heads, and grin. No one offers to help. They heard every word Sergeant Collins uttered and Hector's feeble responses.

Feeling lost, Hector sees movement at the far end of the homicide office. Looking closer, he sees an elderly Black woman with her arms crossed, standing behind a neat desk, shaking her head. She is not smiling. With her right hand, she signals him to come. She turns and walks out of the office as he starts her way. In the hallway, she gives him a terse, "Come with me." They take the elevator to the basement cafeteria. Hector follows her to a table in the corner.

"Yes, Ma'am?"

"I'm Mimi Contreras, the unit secretary. What's your first name, Officer Navarro?"

"Hector, I was assigned to Sergeant Collins as an investigator. No one told me what time to report for duty. I thought..."

"It doesn't matter what you thought. You should have called the office or Sergeant Collins and found out when to report. But that's water under the bridge. Jim Collins is the finest homicide investigator you'll ever meet. He asked for you, which means he thinks highly of you. Don't let him down."

"I'll do my best."

"You best not let him down. Let's see what we can do to get you a fresh start."

"How do I begin?"

"By calling me Mimi. Next, you get over to Dean's Beans across the street."

"Dean's Beans?"

"Yes, Dean's Beans. He missed his coffee because of you. Jim reviews files with his investigators at seven-thirty sharp. Once that's finished, he walks across the street and gets coffee before his daily meeting with the lieutenant.

"Okay."

"Another piece of information you should have found out last week. If you had, you wouldn't be in trouble today."

Hector's getting frustrated and angry, but before he can make a bigger fool of himself, Mimi says, "Extra-large, extra hot, with room for cream. Add a dollop of cream and one packet of pink sweetener. Get it to him while it's hot. I suggest you hurry."

"I didn't become a cop too . . .."

"Don't be an ass, and you'll never have to get coffee again. Give the sergeant his coffee, come back and see me. I have your desk, phone, and business cards ready. Don't expect him to thank you." Mimi leaves Hector sitting there.

A moment later, Hector realizes he had better hurry before he makes another major mistake.

Stopping at Mimi's desk, he asks, "Could you write that down?"

"Don't worry, ask for Cathy. She owns the place. Just tell her it's for Jim Collins.

Hector's hungry and ready to ask Mimi to take a meal break when his desk is half covered in shadow; he looks up and realizes Sergeant Collins has arrived. "What, if anything, can you tell me about a killing outside Ernesto's in July? The bodies of an elderly couple were found lying in the street."

"Not much. I heard mention at AGE. Why do you ask?"

Sergeant Collins hands Hector a USB Drive and drops a large expansion file folder on his desk. "This is the file on the Walter and

Eunice Jackson murders. Read it and the online file from cover to cover. After you finish, write an evaluation of the investigation. Point out anything you want answered. I want your recommendation on how to proceed. Can you do that?"

"I've never investigated a murder."

"I didn't ask you that, Navarro. Can you do what I ask?"

"Yes."

"You have three days. Email me your report."

Reading and comprehending the files takes a dozen cups of black coffee over a day and half a night. Finished, Hector knows several things and has even more questions. To begin with, he needs to talk to the Medical Examiner, Dr. Elizabeth Bannister, about the autopsy results. His first call will help him reach Dr. Bannister.

"Sergeant Kowalski here."

"Hi, Sarge. Hector Navarro."

"How's the newest homicide investigator doing?"

"I'm not sure. I'm afraid to ask Sergeant Collins. We started on the wrong foot. I imagine you heard."

"I did. Believe me, Hector, you're not the first to make a coffee run to atone for your sins. Mimi Contreras has saved many an unwary officer, even a few supervisors, from the well-known wrath of Jim Collins. Don't sell that woman short."

"I won't."

"Good. You're on the right track. What can I do for homicide?"

"Sergeant Collins gave me a murder file. I have to read it, learn everything about the murders, and write a case evaluation. I have until Thursday."

"Interesting, he doesn't usually start rookies out that way. What do you need from me? I've never worked in homicide. I'm not sure what I can do for you."

Hector explains that he's read the murder book and will review the entire file again. "In the meantime, there are a few issues that I'd like to clear up. The first is the autopsy report. I don't know enough to know what I don't know."

"Who's the Medical Examiner?"

"Doctor Bannister."

"I should have known."

"I understand that you and the doctor are, ah . . . close."

"That's one way of putting it. What do you want me to do, call her and convince her to take time out of her busy schedule to break in another new homicide investigator?"

"Yes, that's part of it. The other part's getting Dr. Bannister to allow me to witness an autopsy."

"And she's to do all this by Thursday?"

"Yes, as far as the Jackson murders, I'm afraid so."

"Geez, Hector, you don't ask much, do you?"

"It's a lot to ask, but she can call me anytime it works for her."

"I'm betting Mrs. Contreras told you never to use the word *can't* with Jim Collins. I'll call Liz as soon as we hang up. What else do you want?"

"AGE worked their informants hard after the murders but didn't come up with anything."

"What makes you say that? Is there something in the book?" Hector feels Kowalski's irritation coming through the phone.

"No, Sarge, there isn't anything in the file. If AGE had found anything usable, it would be there. With nothing noted in the book, it's obvious the snitches didn't have any useful information."

Kowalski's tone softens. "You're right."

"Three months have passed. Someone has to have heard something. If you go back to the well, it's a good chance something will have floated to the surface."

"Good thinking Hector. I'll see what I can find. Somebody will have slipped up and leaked something. Unless you have anything else you want us to do to solve your case, I have real police work to manage."

Tuesday, October 29, zero-eight-forty hours. Hector takes a call from Dr. Elizabeth Bannister of the Maricopa County Medical Examiner's Office. "Officer Navarro, I understand you are questioning my autopsy reports on the Walter and Eunice Jackson murders."

Taken by surprise, he doesn't have an immediate answer.

"Doctor Bannister?"

"Yes, I'm Doctor Bannister. Answer my question, do you have a problem with my work?"

"No, Ma'am. I've seen your autopsy reports, the ones you prepared for the Jacksons' murders. I'm having trouble understanding what I'm reading. I'm hoping you can walk me through the reports. I want to do a good job. That's why I asked Sergeant Kowalski to ask you to help me."

"Be in my office in one hour."

"Thanks, Ma'am..." He's wasting his breath; she is no longer on the line.

"If you call me Ma'am again, you can hit the road. The unburnt powder can cause tattooing or stippling. But the variations can be enormous."

"Doctor Bannister, your report describes the particulate residue as in a well-defined zone around the entry wound.' You also refer to tattooing and soot deposit."

"Yes, that's what I wrote. What's your question, Officer Navarro?"

"You state that, in your opinion, the shot was fired from a short distance. Can you tell me the exact distance?"

"I hate the word never, Officer Navarro, but you shouldn't expect to find that information in an autopsy report. The one time I've seen such an estimation, and I mean estimation, centered on an officer-involved shooting. While subduing a hostile suspect, the officer said the man somehow pulled his weapon from its holster. Struggling to regain the weapon, it fired, killing the suspect. A police-hating witness said the officer stood over the man and executed him. In that case, the medical examiner refused to testify about the distance."

"What happened to the officer?"

"He was lucky. The incident occurred in Oakland, California. Three professional law enforcement officers conducted a series of tests. They determined stippling patterns at different distances."

"What'd they learn?"

"After compiling the data, the District Attorney accepted their findings that the weapon was fired from a distance of six to twelve inches, not the three feet claimed by the witness."

"I have one other question. This one's personal."

"Go ahead. I'll answer if I can."

"You did the autopsy on Officer David Jones."

"What do you want to know?"

"With Mr. Jackson, the bullet went in but didn't come out. In Officer Jones's case, the bullet came out the back of his head along with all kinds of brain matter and blood. Why?"

"Many factors play into a shot to the head and the physical damage. The caliber of the weapon is one consideration. The shot that killed Mr. Jackson was fired from the side. The bullet penetrated the skull above the left ear, which absorbed a great deal of energy. After penetrating the cranium, the bullet passed through the brain, coming to rest against the right side of the skull."

"That was in your report for Mr. Jackson. I wasn't allowed to see your results for Davey Jones."

"If you want to see the file, I'll get you a copy. To be honest, you won't get much help. Let me explain the difference. To begin with,

Officer Jones used a three-eighty, which is larger and more powerful than a twenty-five. He placed the barrel inside his mouth and pointed the pistol up and to the back. When he fired, the slug passed through the soft brain tissue and the skull."

A cheeping sound interrupts their conversation. Pulling her iPhone from her lab coat pocket, Dr. Bannister raises her right index finger signaling Hector to wait. After a second or so, she keys in a response before turning back to Navarro. "I'm sorry, Hector. I have to cut this short. Phoenix P.D. has a murder-suicide. I'm the Duty M.E. I'm going to have to leave."

"Thanks, Doctor. I appreciate you taking the time to talk with me."

"I'm happy to help, Hector. In the future, call me direct. The next time I have a New Liberty shooting victim to autopsy, I'll call. Clear it ahead of time with Sergeant Collins. We wouldn't want you making any more coffee runs."

Her comment about coffee runs catches Hector off guard. "Geez, Doc, does everyone in Maricopa County know how I screwed up?"

"Nobody cares what you did to piss off Jim Collins. They all enjoy knowing the good sergeant has found a new coffee runner. Don't be angry. It means he sees something in you. Be happy. It's a good thing."

38

"MARIA, I'VE WRITTEN and revised my report for Sergeant Collins three times, but I'm nervous about sending it. Would you mind reading it over for content and grammar?"

"Hector, I'm no detective."

"*Mi Amor,* please humor me. I have to email this to him. I can't let him down."

Maria agrees to help. After Hector prints his five-page summary, she starts reading and making notes on the report. Hector tries to look over her shoulder. Not a good idea. "You want me to do this or not?"

"Yes."

"Then leave me alone. Get out. Go to the 7-11 and pick up a loaf of bread."

"I don't need bread."

"Then get something else. Get out and be

gone for at least an hour."

To be safe, Hector's gone well over an hour. Returning, he finds Maria watching the evening news. "Your report's on the kitchen table."

Maria found a few typos and wrote several questions in the margins. Hector asks her what else she noticed.

"You talk about two teenagers killed but don't say anything about who they were."

"That's because I don't know who they are."

"Are you going to recommend a way to find out who they are?"

How'd I miss that?

She has a few other questions and suggestions that enhance his report.

39

TO ANYONE ELSE, the text, the emoji image of three chocolate-glazed donuts with rainbow sprinkles, nothing else, would have seemed odd, but not to DeShawn Galloway. He had been expecting it since the riot and killings at the Rogelio Sanchez prison in El Paso. He knew that this day would come. The cartel and his friend had to know they had been played. He could expect a harsh response, but not enough to warrant fear of death. He would already be dead if the riot had turned out differently. Galloway had gambled, not much of a gamble, that the cartel would succeed—they rarely failed.

He did not respond to the text. The only time Galloway, or the man he referred to as *Ese*, responded was if it were impossible to meet. Neither had sent the response, a coffee cup, in at least five years. The donuts were only sent when a meeting was imperative.

Once again, Galloway took a roundabout route to the South Mountain Park & Preserve, where he used the restroom, made sure he was alone, and then drove to Dobbins Lookout. *Ese* was waiting.

"Hey, Blood, my employer is upset with you."

"I figured he would be. But the thing at Rogelio Sanchez worked out well for him."

"Yeah, but you worked us—those five you had us remove weren't part of a takeover. Like I said, you played us. The Whites wanted to settle the change peacefully."

"Look, *Ese*, instead of the Whites holding the keys, the place is firmly in your control. If it weren't, we wouldn't be here."

"Yeah, you would be one dead man. I have a message for you, Blood."

"I have a pretty good idea."

"It's simple. Pull any shit like this again, and you and those two people in Texas, the ones you care about, will be staked out and fed to the ants."

Galloway didn't respond. He had no qualms about death but had thought his Texas life secret—safe. He wanted to tell his friend; that he would kill *Ese* and his employer before ever letting harm come to those two. Galloway knew better than show any sign of concern. Besides, he never intended to abuse his friend or the cartel again. Instead, he changed the subject.

"Now that you have Rogelio Sanchez and El Paso, we need to solidify our agreement. The 4-Aces there are under the protection of the cartel. Agreed?"

"You ask a lot for someone who took advantage of my employer and me. But he has agreed to that. About the other thing you wanted."

"The prostitution business in El Paso was to belong to the 4-Aces, but because I overstepped things, I'll let that slide."

"That's mighty white of you, Blood."

"It's a sign of good faith."

"I doubt that. My employer has decided that your group will have the trade in El Paso—with conditions."

Galloway did not want the trade; it could make some of his people curious about his involvement in the prison takeover and the disappearance of Big Joe. Considering his current position with the cartel, he had to go along. His friend handed him a matchbook; inside were two numbers.

"Each month, you will pay the percentage of gross or the dollar amount, whichever is greater. You will buy all your stock from our representative, no one else. *Comprende.*"

"What if I don't agree?"

"Let me make this clear, my old friend. You don't get to agree or disagree. You do this, or you will visit the anthill with your friends, and every brother of yours visiting Rogelio Sanchez will die—one at a time."

40

MIMI TELLS HECTOR when he reports in at 0730 hours. "Sergeant Collins wants you to meet him at Dean's Beans,"

"I thought he had court in Phoenix this morning."

"So did I." she shrugs, "go figure."

"Okay."

Hector asks if she knows what it's about. She doesn't.

Hector started visiting Dean's Beans soon after his transfer to Anti-Gang Enforcement. It's always busy. Today, the high standing chairs for the counters that face against the front windows are packed elbow to elbow with folks working on laptops. As usual, a couple of fresh off-duty or soon-to-start officers are finishing up reports mixed in with the civilians. *If there weren't cops in here at all hours, the computer snatch-and-grab robbers would love this place.*

The din from a dozen or more conversations add to his trouble in spotting Sergeant Collins. Pursing his lips, Hector scans the crowd. *Where is he?* Jim Collins is a large man and hard to miss. Giving up his search, Hector gets in line for service. When he reaches the front, Cathy Dean is behind the counter. "I'm supposed to—"

"Here's your drink. Go on into the back office."

Hector stammers, "Uh?" and adds, "I gotta pay for the coffee."

"Past the bathroom, the door marked employees only. It's unlocked. Coffee's covered."

Hector knocks before opening the door. From inside, a voice, "Come."

That's not Jim Collins.

Inside is Lieutenant Bill Fugett of Internal Affairs. *What the hell's this about?*

"Good morning, Hector. Don't worry. Sergeant Collins knows I'm here and is okay with us talking. Come sit down and—"

"Why the ambush?"

"No ambush. I apologize if it looks that way. Tongues would wag if I called you up to

IA or visited your office."

"Why here?"

"Cathy's my cousin. She's let me use this room to write reports ever since I worked in this area as a patrol officer. I have a key and come through the back door."

"Okay, so what's this all about?"

"Do you know John Riley?"

"You know I do. He was recently promoted to sergeant and is working narcotics."

Fugett pushes a yellow legal pad across the table and says, "Do you know this guy?"

"I assume you've reviewed the Confidential Informant Registration File, so again, you know I do."

"Our conversation is not being recorded, but this is a criminal investigation. I will question you, and you will answer directly and to the best of your recollection."

"Uhm."

"Do I make myself clear, Officer Navarro?"

"Yes, sir." *Is he threatening me? I thought this was supposed to be informal.*

Fugget points to the pad, "You know this guy?"

"Yes, sir. He's a confidential informant I used a few times in Anti-Gang Enforcement."

Flipping up the page reveals another name. "What about this woman?"

"The same, a CI from AGE.?"

"You are not to discuss this meeting with anyone, that includes Sergeant Collins."

"Yes, sir. Can you tell me what this is all about.?"

"After a random audit, Sergeant Riley's confidential undercover fund records were short at least $5,000."

"How does that affect me?"

"Only indirectly. Let me continue. Riley wrote several search warrants using these two CIs as the source of information. His lieutenant saw how much he claimed to have paid these and other informants. It raised all kinds of red flags. In one case, the male informant was paid $500 for a warrant that resulted in the seizure of one gram of cocaine."

"Holy Shit. I never paid that CI more than $50, and that was for a half-pound of coke."

"In another case, the CI was supposedly paid $1,000. The recovery was a stolen assault rifle.

"The female CI was paid $2,250 for three search warrants."

"What did they recover when she snitched? I ask because all her information was sketchy when I used her."

"They didn't recover anything on those three cases."

"Shit."

"Yeah, shit."

"Well, lieutenant, whatcha you need from me?"

"Talk to the CIs and find out what Sergeant Riley paid them for the information he used to obtain the search warrants."

"I'm not thrilled, but I can do that."

"The search warrant locations, dates, and suspects' names are listed on the next page. Do you need their contact info?"

"Nah, I have it. Aren't you worried that when I ask the woman about Riley, she'll call him? If I tell him to, the male CI will keep his mouth shut."

"Riley knows the investigation is under-way and should expect calls to the informants.

"When can I expect an answer? I only need a verbal report for now."

"Have another cup of coffee. I'll take a walk, make the calls, and should be back in half an hour.

"I got the information. It's not good."

"I'm listening."

"The male CI was hesitant to discuss Sergeant Riley, but after a bit of persuasion, he opened up. He stated he did not receive a dime on the case where Riley says he paid the CI $500. On the one where Riley claims to have paid $1,000, the CI states he got $50."

"I was afraid that would be the case. What about the female?"

"It's even worse. According to her, Riley's been banging her since his time in AGE. Before you ask, I had no idea."

"Fuck."

"Yeah. According to the female CI, Riley gave her a quarter ounce of meth after one of the searches. She believes he found it and kept it for her. She states she did not receive any money from Riley for the information she provided him."

"If necessary, will they testify?

"I wouldn't think so. If they do, the world will know they are informants. I believe they would be dead within weeks, if not days."

41

AT 0729 HOURS, Hector walks into Sergeant Collins's office carrying two coffees. The sergeant looks at him with a questioning expression.

"Extra-large, extra hot, a dollop of cream, and one packet of pink sweetener?"

For an instant, a smile's beginnings are visible before his sergeant frowns and growls, "Have a seat." Hector sits as Collins tries the coffee; the sergeant seems satisfied, so he starts a conversation.

"Sergeant?"

He ignores Hector for several minutes. After a few swallows of the coffee, there is an almost inaudible "Thanks." It is all that Hector can expect.

"I gave you three days. Why didn't you

take it? You emailed your report in under forty-eight hours." A questioning—no, menacing—look as Collins pushes his smallish reading glasses down to the tip of his mammoth nose and looks Hector in the eye.

Hector is nervous and intimidated, but he'll be damned if he'll let it show. "My review's complete. I've given you some new information and made recommendations that require your authorization. If you approve, I can continue."

"Tell me about the two who killed the Jackson couple."

"All I have is that they were young Black teens. They probably lived somewhere in Maricopa County. When they went missing, I doubt there was much of an investigation." Hector pauses.

"Why not?" Sergeant Collins raises his hands, palm out, to stress the importance of his question.

Hector knows why, but he's unsure he should voice his opinion—Sergeant Collins is Black.

In a soft but firm tone, the sergeant says, "Look, Hector, unless you're honest with me, you're going back to patrol. I won't have an investigator working for me who won't call a spade a spade."

He's right; Hector has to be honest with

him regardless of the subject. This man has always treated him with respect. Jim Collins has never been anything but fair.

"They were young Blacks, punks, who dropped off the grid long before they were killed. The fathers were not in the picture, likely dead or in prison. Even if someone filed a missing person report for either of them, no one cared, not even their families. Their only value was as a basis for their baby mamas to get a little extra public assistance."

"Now we're getting somewhere. We have two forgotten Black teenagers killed by order of Geronimo Dixon, who, in turn, is killed by Officer Davey Jones. According to your report, Dixon had Galloway get rid of the boys.

"How do you propose to identify the two punks?"

"It's a long shot, but we should reach out to every police agency in Maricopa County." He pauses.

"I didn't say stop." Sergeant Collins's scowl and the tilt of his head show annoyance.

"We ask for a copy of every missing person's report filed between July first and today, listing Black males between the ages of twelve and seventeen."

"May I offer a few suggestions?"

"Please, Sergeant, go ahead. This is all new to me."

"Drop the humility thing. It doesn't work. You are here because you have talent. Limit your search to July and August. If that doesn't work, you can expand the parameters."

"Why not request all four months?"

"Once you start collecting reports of missing Black children, the sheer numbers will overwhelm you. Over 800,000 children of all races have been reported missing since 1999, and don't forget. Those are just the ones reported. These kids have been all but forgotten."

"I never realized how big a problem missing children was. We need a starting point and knowing who they are seems important. They were killers, but if we identify them, we can at least bring closure to their families."

"Closure? What kind of closure?"

"What are you getting at, Jim?"

"'Look at it this way, you find out that one of your young killers was reported missing by Ms. Baby Mama. You knock on her door with the news. 'Hi, Ms. Baby Mama, your son was murdered, and his body dumped in the desert. And, by the way, he was a stone-cold killer who murdered an elderly Black couple.' How do you think that will go over?'"

"Not well. Even so, we have a duty to

solve the boy's murder and that of the Jacksons. Right?"

"Yes, you're right, we do. There's a saying in television—hokey but true—*We speak for the dead*. Whether we like our victims or not, we have an obligation to them. So, get out there and find out who these kids were."

"What about my other suggestions, Sarge?"

"We'll solve these killings, all four of them, step-by-step."

Hector's quest begins with a visit to the Missing Person's Unit of the New Liberty P.D. Sergeant Collins gave him the name of a long-time unit member, Samuel Morgan, who agreed to meet Hector later that day. "Navarro, I have an hour, and then I'm off to my youngest daughter's soccer match. What can I do for you?"

Hector explains to Detective Morgan what he's learned about the Jackson killings and his belief that members of the 4-Aces gang then killed the two young Blacks.

"I can help you with your search, but it'll be difficult. What do you have for me?"

Hector tells the detective what little he knows about the two boys, including the weapons they used. "What kind of investigation do you conduct when one of these kids is reported missing? I don't recall any BOLOs."

"You ever take a missing person report?"

"Once, an eighty-five-year-old woman walked away from her home. She lived with her son and daughter-in-law."

"Dementia?"

"Yes, we found her sitting in a park a mile from her house and took her home."

"It's quite different with kids and youngsters," Detective Morgan said.

"We didn't have many lost or runaways out on The Island. We had training about dealing with kids ten and under and a different set of guidelines for those older."

"Hector, tell me if I'm wrong, but for kids under ten, everyone turns out and goes full speed, right?"

"Yes, Sir."

"Please, call me Sam."

"Okay, Sam."

"The search for the little ones lasts for days, sometimes longer. Older kids are lucky if the search lasts longer than one or two shifts. And don't forget the enormous socio-economic impact of the sizeable population of New Liberty.

"We take the reports and file them unless it's the child of a prominent person."

"How can you let that happen?" Hector asks incredulously.

"We're overwhelmed by the sheer numbers of missing kids. Answer me this, if you see a Black teenager on the streets, do you wonder if he's missing or in need of help? No, no one does. Most people, including you and me, a Mexican and a Black man, are suspicious of him. These kids wouldn't be on the streets if they had a father like the one James Avery played on *The Fresh Prince of Bel-Air*, a father who cares."

By the time Hector leaves, he has a list of eighty-three teenage Black males reported missing in New Liberty during July and August. The detective tells him to return in the morning, and he'll have the files ready. Then adding to Hector's dismay, "If you include Phoenix and the rest of Maricopa County, you'll have at least double that number of missing kids. Good Luck."

Hector arrives at Detective Morgan's office at zero-seven-thirty hours and hands him an extra-large Dean's Beans coffee and an apple fritter. Morgan grins, "Thanks. I see you work for Jim Collins. How'd you know what I take?"

"Easy, I asked your unit secretary yesterday. Something I learned from ours, Mimi Contreras."

An hour later, Hector is alone in an

interview room with sixty-eight files. Later, nearly halfway through the records, he takes a break and asks Morgan about fifteen closed files.

"They've all closed, one way or another."

"One way or another? What does that mean?"

"Most returned home, a few were in custody, and three were dead. You'll have to go through the files here. They don't leave the office."

Six hours later, Hector has eliminated all but ten of the missing boys. Three have no criminal record, and he puts them aside, rejected by profiling. After downloading the most recent photographs of the remaining seven to his iPhone, he calls Mimi Contreras. "Hi, Mimi. I have a favor to ask?"

Finished telling her what he needs, she says, "That's not a favor. I'm here to help."

"Thanks. I'll send you an email with what I want. I have to check with the Identification Bureau. I'll see you back at the office."

A call to the ID Bureau reaches a sympathetic clerk. She saves him a trip. "We can get those for you, but they won't be ready until late tonight. Stop by after seven a.m. tomorrow, and they'll be at the front counter."

It is close to five. Hector gives Mimi another call, explains what he has accomplished, and asks, "Do you think Jim will mind if I take off the rest of the day?"

"I'll tell him you called and are headed home. It'll be fine. Make sure that you're here by seven-thirty tomorrow."

42

"It's paid for. Why don't you drink it in the back office?"

It must be Fugett. What now?

Hector winds his way through the line of customers waiting to use one of the two all-gender toilets, his stomach full of knots. His heart beats faster. *What did I tell him last time? Is he going to want more from me than I want to give?*

"Good to see you, Hector."

"I'm not thrilled to be meeting like this. What gives?"

"Let me put your mind at ease. We don't need anything else from you. You might have heard that John Riley is no longer on administrative leave—gone for good."

"Yeah, I heard a rumor he had resigned.

Why wasn't he fired and prosecuted?"

"When I met with Riley's attorney, he told me his client would plead not guilty and demand a jury trial if prosecuted.

"That wasn't a big deal, but he said he would drag every CI Riley ever used into court and force them to testify."

"Shit."

"I agree. Before the chief made a final decision, I told him about the probability that the CIs would be murdered."

"What then?"

"The chief called the attorney and Riley in for a meeting. Personnel and I were present. The attorney started to speak, and the boss told him to shut up. Then he fired Riley and informed him that if any law enforcement officer ever contacted the NLPD about a background or criminal investigation regarding John Riley, he would personally share the entire IA file with them."

"That's great. How did Riley and the attorney react?"

"'That's the best part. The chief rarely swears, but he did then. He said, 'get out of my office, you filthy piece of shit.'"

43

ELROY "FROGGY" ROBINSON isn't happy
working for DeShawn "The Knife" Galloway.
Before Geronimo died, the gang's leader had
clearly understood the prostitution business.
Froggy discussed issues with his former
president and got approval if his proposals
were sound. What worked best was that
Geronimo never demanded an accounting as
long as there was a positive cash flow. With
Galloway, he has to explain everything in
detail. Even then, Galloway doesn't always
understand what Froggy's trying to achieve.

Shortly after, Galloway called for a
meeting of all the remaining lieutenants in
the 4-Aces. The gathering was to confirm
what everyone already knew, Galloway was
the boss, and if you didn't do things the way

he wanted, he demoted you—or worse. No one wanted worse.

Fortunately for most of the 4-Aces, things would continue as they had under Geronimo. The most significant change was Froggy's organization, whose territory was expanding into El Paso, Texas. This expansion came as a surprise. Robinson had neither sought nor wanted anything to do with moving into new territory, especially not in Texas.

Near the end of the meeting, Galloway announced, "We have some good news for Froggy and his business."

The assemblage was all ears. Robinson, taken off guard, stammered out, "What?"

Galloway told the lieutenants that the cartel had contacted him after the power shift at Rogelio Sanchez State. He said they had made an offer the 4-Aces couldn't refuse. "We have been granted two significant concessions. The first is especially important to our brothers doing time there."

"What's that? What are the spics going to do for us?"

"Things remain the same in New Liberty. It has nothing to do with the gangs here and throughout Arizona. The cartel has placed the 4-Aces in El Paso under their wing of protection, including all the brothers doing time at Rogelio Sanchez. In return, the brothers will stand with the cartel in all disputes." Arms crossed, holding his left elbow, Galloway looked around the room to measure the reaction from those there. None seemed upset over the arrangement; it was good for the brothers doing time in El Paso.

One foolish brother asked, "This got anything to do with Big Joe's disappearance?"

"I don't know. I was assured that the cartel had nothing to do with whatever happened to Big Joe. Any other questions?" Many went unasked. They would remain unasked for fear of what they could lead to. Many questions about the power shift and Galloway's part in it would never be asked. To a man, the 4-Aces feared DeShawn "The Knife" Galloway.

To move away from that subject, someone asked, "What's the other thing?"

"Froggy, the other thing is the rights to human trafficking in El Paso."

"What's that mean?"

"As of today, we, the 4-Aces, own the rights to El Paso County. The cartel is not interested in the prostitution trade and will support our movement to eliminate competition."

Froggy could visualize the effort this would take and was not thrilled. But he knew that any expansion would put more money in his pocket. He was also smart enough to know that when a done deal was thrust upon him, he wasn't going to buck the President. "That sounds good, DeShawn. What are the details?"

"You and I will sit down tomorrow and iron out whatever you need to start the new business. Do you want someone to step up and help with the current operation?"

Because of certain irregularities in his books, Robinson couldn't afford to have anyone look closely at his operation. "Nah, I can manage it."

Getting into his car, Froggy's burner rings. "Yeah?"

"Hi, Froggy. You alone?"

He knew the voice but asked, hoping he was wrong. "Who is this?"

"I don't have time to waste. I said, are you alone."

"I'm alone. How'd you get this number, Kowalski?"

"It doesn't matter."

"You want something. Otherwise, you wouldn't be calling."

"You remember the couple killed outside Ernesto's?"

"If you're talking about the old Black couple in July, I told you I was out of town."

"Look, Froggy. It went down months ago. You better not shit me; I know you've heard something. What is it?"

"I don't have much."

"I'm listening." Annoyance is evident in Kowalski's voice.

"The old couple stopped, and these two youngsters tried to jack the car and killed them."

"How were they killed?" Kowalski needs to know if he's lying or telling the truth. Homicide had kept the caliber of the murder weapon out of the news.

"The man was shot in the head with a twenty-five, and the woman had her throat cut. I heard it was messy."

"What else?"

"The punks didn't have Geronimo's permission to pull shit in 4-Aces territory. They must have pissed him off because he had Galloway kill them. I heard the car was an Infiniti or something like that."

"Go on."

"Galloway and two brothers took the punks out to the desert. He had the brothers kill 'em, pour gas over the bodies, lit 'em on fire, and pushed 'em and the car over a cliff."

"You know where they are?"

"Hell no. Somewhere in the desert."

"Froggy. Tell me. Who are the brothers who killed the kids?"

"I don't know."

"Find out."

Robinson doesn't see any reason to tell Kowalski about the new arrangement with the cartel.

Steve Kowalski gets back to Hector in less than twenty-four hours. "You were right about the Jackson homicides. My informant gave me enough to get you started." He continues, "How'd it go with Liz?"

"I bet you can answer that better than I can."

"You did well, Hector. With her and Jim Collins in your corner, you'll succeed in homicide. So, do you want to hear what I have or not?"

Hector almost says, "Shoot," but catches himself in time. "Please, go ahead."

44

SERGEANT COLLINS HAD one habit he found impossible to break: eating. Mrs. Collins allows him one over-the-top breakfast a month. He could not get what he wanted, neither in choice nor quantity of food at home; instead, he went to Halmo's Diner. Collins always invited his two detectives. He never needed to order; without asking, the sergeant was served a platter, not a plate, with what Matt Halmo called The Big Jim. Collins claimed it was the one meal each month that wasn't part of his diet. Hector found it hard to believe, especially when the big man put it away before the officer finished his oatmeal and fruit, no toast.

This monthly get-together was looked forward to by him and the detectives. In a less than formal meeting, the three enjoyed the opportunity to discuss cases, problems, issues within the department, and occasionally what was happening in their lives. A bear of a man, and a stern taskmaster, this was the chance for him to relax, let his hair down, and let his team broach any subject they wished.

Hector asked about going to the FBI's Homicide Course at Quantico. "Is there any chance I could go as an officer investigator?"

"We only have so many slots available and a training budget that remains static. We can barely send detective-level officers. Not even all the sergeants get that training. Sorry, Hector, you should make sergeant if you can learn to stay out of trouble."

The three discussed the latest homicide, a convenience store robbery gone wrong that left the store clerk dead, until Collins said, "Well, that's that." His signal that it was time to get back to the department. He got up and gave his check to Mrs. Halmo, paid in full, and strode out of the old-time diner. Hector and the detective finished their coffee, took their half-off checks to Mrs. Halmo, and paid her.

45

ANXIOUS TO RETALIATE for Chucho Montemayor's killing, Sanchez holds no sorrow for
the man. His sole desire is revenge. Revenge
for the protection of his reputation—*no one
kills one of mine without payback.*

Sanchez must act. He realizes *the
problem is the Blood that ordered the hit on
Chucho is dead. Shot by a crazy White cop. I
gotta come up with something, or I'll look
weak.* Calling his lieutenants together, he
tells them, "We have to show the 4-Aces they
can't kill one of ours without paying."

Sanchez knows what he'll do but asks his
lieutenants if they have any suggestions.
After allowing them time to raise and discuss
several ideas, he stops them. "That's enough.
I'll tell you what we're going to do." Once

finished, all agree that his plan is unique enough to send the message to the 4-Aces, and every other gang in Arizona. All the gangs will soon know the violence they can expect from Los Scorpios Locos.

"*Jefe*, this will start a war. Do you want that?"

"Are you afraid of war? Maybe you should join our enemies."

"No, *Jefe*. I don't fear war with the Blacks. I want to be ready to protect Los Scorpios Locos if we do this." The man is more afraid of Sanchez than the 4-Aces or war. He's clever enough to add, "*Por favor, Jefe*, let me carry this out for you."

Thursday, November 21, Twenty-three-forty hours. Hector is asleep when his iPhone begins its angry buzz. The sound it makes is almost as loud as the ringtone. He answers with a sleep muffled, "yeah."

"Hector, Teresa Ontiveros, Sanchez's planning something big to pay back the 4-Aces for Chucho Montemayor.

"I tried calling Katie, but all I got was her voicemail. I can't leave a message, and I won't talk to anyone else."

"I understand. What you got."

"I don't know what he's planned, but it'll be this week. Sanchez ordered us women out to his ranch this weekend to entertain him and the Vatos. Sunday afternoon, there will be a large gathering to celebrate payback for Chucho's murder. The *tenientes* aren't talking except to say it will be huge. I overheard a couple of them talking. It has something to do with kidnapping and killing a couple of 4-Aces."

"Jesus, Teresa, that's in three days. Can you find out anything else?"

"I'll try, but I have to be careful. If I ask too many questions, they'll kill me."

"Be careful. I don't want you getting hurt or worse."

"I will. I'm not ready to die. Do you know where Sanchez's ranch is?" After an audible sigh, she adds, "Hector, there's something else."

"What?"

"They're going to sell my baby."

"When?"

"They have a dealer coming next week. She'll examine Olivia and take pictures of her for potential buyers. If she finds one, she'll take my daughter away. They always take the babies within a week of picture taking. I can't lose her. You have to do something."

Hector knew this day was coming but wasn't prepared for it. *I wish Katie were here to take care of the problem—it's more than a problem—it's a baby's life. What can I do? I don't know how, but I'll find a way to save Olivia.*

"If you do anything, Sanchez will kill Olivia," Teresa's crying, "and me."

46

FRIDAY, 0735 HOURS, Hector is in Deputy Chief Mary Windsor's conference room. "Officer Navarro, you showed good sense in calling Sergeant Kowalski last night instead of waiting until this morning. No one wants to see a war between Los Scorpios Locos and the 4-Aces." Unlike her old conference room in the basement, this one is on the tenth floor. No fifty-year-old asbestos tiles will be found here. Next to her corner office, this room seats a dozen or more around a horseshoe-shaped table. In the center tabletop space in front of each chair are flip-up lids concealing power outlets and USB ports. In front of these pop-ups are miniature but powerful microphones. The off-and-on switches are fluorescent orange, bright enough for all but the dimmest guest to see. The chairs, not old wooden hand-me-downs, are all matching high back and easily hold a man the size of Jim Collins. Windsor sits at the head of the table. At the foot, the table opens to an unobstructed view of an eighty-inch flat screen. Ten other officers are spread out around the table. She brought Lieutenant Paul Morales, sitting to her right.

Deputy Chief Windsor grips the edge of the table, pressing what must be a hidden button, and curtains close, covering the windows. The view of the Sonoran Desert is beautiful; even so, Hector is glad the curtains obliterate the view. They're here to discuss an ugliness concealed within the desert. He glances at the four corner-mounted HD cameras, each sporting a solid green light. He relaxes for an instant before the lights begin flashing red prior to remaining static. He has never been in this room but knows it means that D.C. Windsor has activated the teleconferencing and event recording system. The ultra-compact microphone in front of each of the officers is live. The image of the Police Chief comes into focus on the flat screen.

"Good morning. Thank you all for coming. Deputy Chief Windsor and I appreciate that you're all here. If you had a late call and an especially early wakeup, blame Officer Navarro." After a pause for the obligatory laughs, he continues. "In all seriousness, Officer Navarro, we are grateful for bringing us this alarming news. Your information should save lives and prevent a vicious gang war."

Hector nods: he's merely the messenger.

The Chief continues. "Chief Windsor, I'll leave this with you. If this bloody congressional call I have to take ends sooner than expected, I'll return to the meeting. Thank you all." The screen goes blank, and the camera lights return to solid green. At least the meeting won't be documented. Somehow, he hopes the lack of a recording will create less danger for Teresa Ontiveros.

Everyone in the room is above his pay grade. His biggest fear was that Jim Collins would be angry; he called Kowalski first, but his sergeant hadn't been upset. It was close to midnight when Hector called him. Collins wasn't happy about being woken from a sound sleep. But, as soon as Hector gave him an overview, he agreed that Hector had done the right thing. As they talked, another call came in, and Hector put him on hold.

"Hector, Steve Kowalski. Intelligence picked up a rumble that the Los Scorpios Locos may be starting a war. This is heating up. I spoke by phone with Deputy Chief Windsor, and she's scheduled a meeting for seven-thirty tomorrow morning. Be there. Any questions?"

"I'll be there. Jim Collins..."

"Tell Jim to be there. Anything else?"

"Yes. What can we do for Teresa Ontiveros and her baby?"

"That's a tough one, Hector. We'll talk tomorrow." Hector switches back to Collins and tells him what Kowalski said.

"I'll be there. Do you have anything else?"

Hector doesn't.

47

SATURDAY, 0128 HOURS, Hector finds a text from Teresa Ontiveros, "BLACK ESCALADE," is the entire message. According to Hector's iPhone, the communication came at 2323 hours, 11:23 p.m. It had sat unread for two hours. *Oh God, how could I have missed it?* He had been making love with Maria. If he hadn't gotten up to pee, Hector wouldn't have seen the message until four-thirty, when his alarm was set.

"Hector, what is it? How come you turned on the light?"

"Sorry. I have a text message I'm sure is from Teresa Ontiveros. If so, she's taken a great risk. It's something she's always refused to do for fear of discovery."

"What do you mean?"

"She's not allowed to have a cell phone, but she managed to buy and conceal a burner she uses to call and send text messages. As dangerous as it is for her to call me, texting is doubly so. If she gets caught, they'll kill her."

"What are you going to do?"

"Call Sergeant Collins. He'll be mad I didn't pick up the message earlier."

"Sarge, Hector Navarro." Not completely surprised at this early-hour call; Collins isn't his usual gruff self.

"What's up?"

"I have a text message I'm sure is from Teresa Ontiveros." There's the sound of concern in Hector's voice.

"What's the message?"

"That's the strange thing, Sarge. It's two words in all caps, BLACK ESCALADE. The one thing I can think of is it's the vehicle the LSLs will use to kidnap the 4-Aces."

"That's a reasonable assumption. How long ago did Teresa send the text?"

Hector is positive his sergeant is going to explode. "It came in at eleven-twenty-three. I didn't notice it until one-twenty-eight."

Hector is surprised by Sergeant Collins's answer. "Shit happens."

48

"WHATCHA DOIN' BITCH?" The drunken pig of a man had fallen asleep after forcing me to blow him. I thought he would be out for hours.

A few hours earlier, I'd heard Sanchez give orders to one of his lieutenants about kidnapping 4-Aces. "Steal a black Escalade and make sure it has blacked-out windows." The lieutenant had made the mistake of asking why. After picking himself up off the floor, Sanchez told him, "Take three Vatos with you. Find two Aces working a corner. With the Escalade, you should get close." The lieutenant nodded as Sanchez continued. "Jump them, tie 'em up in the back, and bring 'em here."

Almost afraid to speak, "What if someone

sees us?" The man mumbles.

"It doesn't matter. After tomorrow's entertainment, everyone will know Los Scorpios Locos is at war."

What Sanchez bragged about is going to happen. I have no more love for Black gangbangers than the Los Scorpios Locos. But no one, gangster or not, should die in the pit for Sanchez's entertainment. I have to tell Hector. I can't call him. One of the LSLs or their women might hear me. As much as it scares me, I'll have to send a text, something I've never done before. I'm dead if I get caught or they find my phone. I must stop Sanchez—I'd never forgive myself if I didn't.

I look around as best I can without sitting up. People are sleeping all around me on the floor, most in a drunken stupor. I reach into my bra for the cell phone and take another quick look. Clicking on the message, I enter Hector's number, type BLACK ESCALADE, and hit send. The right side of my head feels like I've been hit with a baseball bat; the cell phone hits the ground. He kicks me again, this time in the stomach. Snatching the cell from the ground, he hollers, "Whatcha doing, puta?" He doesn't know what the message means, but he's smart enough to know to tell Sanchez. Grabbing me by my hair, he pulls me up and drags me to Sanchez's room. The same room where he raped me while laughing about the girl fed to Diablo—I'll be next. He bangs on the door until Sanchez opens it.

After looking at the text message, Sanchez knocks me to the ground. Screaming, he begins kicking me. I'm sure the man is going to beat me to death. He stops and stares at me, his rage under control. His face changes from a frenzy to a calm expression that is even more frightening. Sanchez begins to smile.

As I vomit, he orders a Vato, "Lock her up."

I know what is in store for me—Diablo.

49

SERGEANT COLLINS TELLS Officer Navarro to meet at the station in three hours. On the way, Hector tries calling Ontiveros. There's no response. Trying again ten minutes later, the answer tells him everything he needs to know. "Yo, pig, you lookin for the puta?" followed by profanity. Hector disconnects without a word.

Sergeant Collins is waiting in the lobby with coffees for each of them. "Come on, Queen Mary's waiting."

"Sarge, they have Teresa Ontiveros. They know she's an informant."

"I figured as much. Hold on until we see Chief Windsor."

Hector's not surprised that most of the people from the earlier meeting are here. The animal control officer and Homeland Security Agent Butch Kennemore are missing. After he updates the group, Deputy Chief Windsor has a question for the SWAT Commander.

"Claudia, do you have surveillance in place?"

Lieutenant Foss says, "Yes, Ma'am. After the meeting yesterday, I initiated round-the-clock surveillance of the Sanchez ranch. Want me to get a status report?"

"Use the phone in Paul's office."

The group waits silently for Lieutenant Foss to return until Paul Morales fills the void. "Excuse me, Chief, but I took the liberty of ordering breakfast. I figured we'd be in for a long day."

"Thanks, Paul, good idea."

"The food's here. I'll arrange things while Lieutenant Foss gets the observation update."

Up most of the night and running on adrenalin, Hector is almost overcome by exhaustion and hunger. The one thing keeping him going is his fear for Teresa Ontiveros. Hector cannot get out of his mind what O'Brien had told him the day he met Teresa—*They will kill her one day.*

Lieutenant Foss returns. Waiting for Morales and the food, they stay in Deputy Chief Windsor's office. She shakes her head as she leans against the closed door. "It doesn't look good. Several hours ago, my team spotted a dark Escalade turn down the private road leading to Sanchez's ranch. They can't be sure if it was black. My best guess— it was."

Deputy Chief Windsor nods. "We have to assume they have two members of the 4-Aces as well as Miss Ontiveros."

"Another thing, Chief, there has been a steady stream of vehicles arriving. My people say at least a dozen. With at least two per car, we can expect at least twenty-four gang members and associates by the time we move."

After the briefest pause, Deputy Chief Windsor addresses Sergeant Kowalski. "Steve, what do you think will happen? Can you give us a timeline?"

"I can give you my best guess of how and when Sanchez will begin the killing."

Turning to Hector, he says, "You know what's going on as well as anyone. Stop me if you disagree with anything I say." Hector nods assent. He's too tired to talk. "We can assume that Sanchez intends to kill one of the Black men and send the other back as a message." There's a round of concurrences.

The caterer has set up a breakfast buffet and coffee. Deputy Chief Windsor tells them to take a short break to get food and drink. Anticipating what Kowalski will say, most lose any appetite they may have had.

Hector's coffee long finished; he fills the large paper cup with fresh steaming coffee. Jim Collins does the same. The officers, full plates, settle around the conference table. Kowalski continues, "Sanchez is going to kill Ontiveros. My hunch is he'll feed her to the dog first, so the other victims get to see what's in store for them. Would you agree, Hector?"

"Yes. I'm sure the bastard plans to do it that way."

"What do you mean, feed her to the dog?" A shocked-sounding U.S. Marshal speaks for the first time. Several others voice similar questions.

Hector looks at Kowalski, who shakes his head and says, "Navarro."

Hector begins; it's difficult for him. He recaps what Teresa told him about the girl who ran away and what happened to her and her parents. As Hector finishes, a glance around the room tells him he is not the only one holding back rage. Suddenly it dawns on him, and he addresses Deputy Chief Windsor. "Ma'am, her mother, they'll kill her mother. We have to do something."

Deputy Chief Windsor says, "We're going to do all we can to save them." Within an instant, she adds, "and the Black men." Turning her attention to the SWAT

Commander, "Claudia, as soon Sergeant Kowalski finishes, I want you to prepare an operational plan designed to take down Sanchez and every other gangbanger at the ranch. You have one hour."

"Yes, Chief."

"Once it's written, have your team assembled and ready to go thirty minutes later. Can you get it done?"

"Yes, Ma'am. We'll be good to go."

"Steve, please continue."

"How this goes down is an assumption on my part, Ma'am.

"Lieutenant Foss's observations have confirmed it. Sanchez wants all his people there. He needs them to appreciate the message he's sending the 4-Aces. Even more, it will remind them Sanchez is the boss. Killing Miss Ontiveros will emphasize what happens to people who cross him—he will kill her first."

There's a quiet knock at the door, and it is slowly pushed open. It's Homeland Security Agent Kennemore. Deputy Chief Windsor waves him to a seat. Getting coffee, he apologizes for being late. Deputy Chief Windsor signals Kowalski to continue by asking, "What do you think the timeline will be?"

"Sanchez doesn't have enough room at the ranch for all the Los Scorpios Locos to spend the night. The way I see it, many of the members and a few associates will arrive before ten tomorrow morning. Sanchez might even invite a few members of other gangs, including the Vietnamese."

"Why the Vietnamese?" Someone asks.

Kowalski stalls for time by saying, "That's a good question." He takes a deep breath and exhales. "Los Scorpios Locos is the dominant Hispanic gang, and Sanchez needs to keep it that way. There's a fragile truce between the Hispanic and Asian gangs. The killings will allow Sanchez to demonstrate his power and the viciousness of the LSL. He cannot afford to have other gangs attacking them while LSL fights a war with the 4-Aces." All agree; Kowalski's reasoning makes sense.

With a trace of annoyance at the delay, Deputy Chief Windsor again asks for a timeline.

"With the majority arriving after ten, I expect Sanchez will host a large lunch for everyone there. They won't want to eat later. Lunch finished, he'll move the party to the barn, and the killing will begin. Afterward, he'll want everyone gone as soon as possible so he can get the place cleaned up. He has to know we'll eventually come looking for Ontiveros."

"If Sanchez knows we're coming, why not call it off?" Sergeant Collins asks.

Hector answers his question. "Sanchez can't stop. He's making his big play. If he backs off, even for a few days, he'll suffer a loss of face. He can't afford that, might even lose control of Los Scorpios Locos."

Deputy Chief Windsor says, "That doesn't give us much time. Paul, would you please set up the whiteboard and get the Chief on the line?"

"Yes, Ma'am."

While Lieutenant Morales arranges the whiteboard, Homeland Security Agent Kennemore says, "Excuse me, Chief Windsor, may I take this opportunity to explain my late arrival."

"None's necessary, but you may if you wish."

"Thanks. As you know, Homeland Security has access to a wide variety of resources. I was in Tucson, arranging for some unique assets. They should be here by zero-eight-hundred."

By zero-six hundred hours, Deputy Chief Windsor has approved an operational plan. Far from perfect and dangerously short-handed, it's the best she can hope for on such short notice. The Phoenix Gang Unit has promised to send seven officers by zero-seven-forty-five.

The Chief arrives as she finishes up.

Grabbing a plate full of cold bacon and eggs, he withdraws with Deputy Chief Windsor to her office. Emerging twenty minutes later, he announces he's satisfied with the plan. "I'll be in the mobile command post with Deputy Chief Windsor. She'll be in operational command." Turning to Agent Kennemore, the Chief says, "Where will you be?"

"My manager will be here shortly. He'll join you in the mobile command post. My instructions are to inform you we're here to assist. My mission is to accompany Lieutenant Foss and facilitate her orders to the Homeland Security assets in the field."

Agent Kennemore says to Lieutenant Foss, "If it's okay with you?"

Smiling, Lieutenant Foss says, "We should be able to accommodate you and the assets you bring to the party." Her comment brings a few grins to the otherwise somber assemblage.

The Chief ends the meeting, "It's all yours, Deputy Chief."

At seven, Deputy Chief Windsor addresses the group. "You all know the seriousness of the situation. I have nothing but the highest regard for you and your abilities. Each of you has much to accomplish in an impossible time frame. Be at the assembly point by eight."

50

Teresa Ontiveros Fights Back

THE BENEFIT OF being locked up and marked for death is I will no longer be forced to satisfy the sexual demands of the LSL pigs. This thought comes when I regain consciousness.

The room is dark; I can see a glimmer of light beneath the door. I'm lying naked on straw laced with decades of feces and urine; the stench is horrendous, a combination of straw soaked with urine and animal feces mixed with the dust that floats on the light rays. When I breathe the foul air, my stomach roils as if vomiting, and my mouth fills with bile. The walls are roughhewn wooden planks that scratch my hands and transplant slivers as I try to rise. Unable to stand, I slip down to a sitting position with my back against the wall—more splinters. Minor wounds are an acceptable alternative to remaining in the noxious hay. I recognize this room. Before feeding her to Diablo, they kept the girl from McAllen, Texas, here. The area had been a tack room for at least a hundred years, back when the place had been a working ranch. The rumor is it has been in Sanchez's family since the eighteen-hundreds, handed down from father to son. I remember the ranch's history when I add to the filth and smell as I urinate and suffer diarrhea. My thoughts verge on hysteria.

When I was Sanchez's woman, he said that growing up he hated the ranch and his father even more. He told me, "My mother died in a car wreck. My father was driving, loaded on heroin, so I killed the bastard and buried him in the desert."

I'll be a fine specimen when they come for me, so covered in filth, Diablo will turn his nose up at me. Aloud I say, "You know better." Sanchez ordered all food withheld from the filthy animal the minute he decided to kill one of the 4-Aces. *The dog's starving. He'll eat me no matter how bad I smell. Please kill me before you start eating me.*

The door opens, the bright light blinding me. Blinking, I see two women—the same ones who beat me down and inked me in when Sanchez first wanted me. I remember the beating and the tattoo. *How I hate you two monsters. I wish you could join Diablo in the pit.*

They're laughing. Both have something in their hands. Whatever it is, they're twirling them around in front of their bodies. The older one says, "Do you remember us?" I refuse to answer. "Cat got your tongue?" She laughs and says, "It won't be long until the dog has your ass." As my eyes adjust to the light, I see they're carrying whips from this tack room. The old hag holds one to my face, almost touching my nose. I can smell her foul breath. "You know what this is, what it's used for." I remain silent. My silence feeds the anger these horrible women carry. If I didn't hate them so intensely, I might feel sorry for them and the life they lead—my mind races. Maybe I can attack them and escape. I begin to move, knowing it is pointless. Even if I get by them, I'll never get out of the barn. As if in anticipation of an attack, they strike me with the whips. They raise the straps to strike again. Sanchez enters the room.

"Stop. Get out." The women hurry from the room. With a sneer, he says, "Soon, my dear Teresa, you'll have the opportunity to feel the work of the whips. But not yet. In an hour, the putas will return. Do you know why?"

How can it matter? I'm going to die and never hold Olivia again. Please, God, let a good family buy her.

I manage to spit. The harmless wad lands at Sanchez's feet.

He smiles. "I'm not going to kill you and deprive Diablo of his long-awaited feast."

I can't work up another wad. I glare at this evilest of men.

Almost as an afterthought, Sanchez says, "Did you notice each of the whips has a split end?" I can't suppress a look that tells him I don't understand. "I guess not. Yes, the ends are special. The putas will use the whips on you. Each strike will leave two small cuts. After they finish your back, they'll do the same to your tits. The cuts will bleed, not much but enough to raise Diablo's interest. By the time the dog gets to you, he'll be in a frenzy. His bloodlust will be fantastic."

Later, the women return with whips. The torture becomes a blur of pain, and I pray I pass out. Mercifully, I do.

"Wake up, puta." I hear the woman screaming, and a warm liquid—urine—is thrown in my face. "Sanchez is ready for you. Diablo waits."

Instantly alert, rough hands haul me to my feet. It's the same man who discovered my betrayal. How ironic, the last man to rape me and then inform on me is leading me to my death. I spit in his face. He slaps me so hard I fall to the floor. Grabbing my hair, he drags me through the urine and feces-laden hay—the whip cuts sting.

I scramble to my feet as he turns my back to him. The pig of a man pulls my right arm down and behind me, laughing at the scream it elicits. Handcuffs snap shut on my right wrist. Another vicious wrenching brings my left hand up, and he squeezes the restraint even tighter.

"Puta" is followed by the sound of spitting. I feel the gob sliding down my back.

Dragged into the barn, I see Sanchez has the rest of the enslaved women standing to one side of the pit. Their colorful clothes are in stark contrast to the thick gray dust filling the building. The LSLs look alike in their green plaid Pendleton shirts buttoned at the neck and pressed khakis. Thrown to the ground, I lay like a slave awaiting Cesar's decision to feed me to the lions or allow me to live. In my case—judgment has already been decided.

The first time I was in this place, I watched another girl killed by Diablo. This time every detail of the scene is seared into my mind. The roof is dark, with a few large pieces missing allowing me to see the sky. It's a shade of blue—is it cerulean? Will this be the last time I see the sky?

The hard-packed dirt has been turned a dull gray by years of shit and straw ground into it. The foul mixture rubs against my bleeding breasts. It's as hard as adobe. The air's filled with dust particles shining like miniature diamonds, the beauty of it fouled by the stink of dog and feral cat feces. If Diablo doesn't get me, I'll die from an infection. My breasts and back are alive with cuts from the quirt. Sanchez is in his glory. In moments, he'll announce his mastery over life and death. Sanchez is sitting on an oversized high-backed antique chair. It's as if constructed for a giant of a man—he is not even five-six. To add to his position of dominance, the tiny man has the chair on a raised platform.

"Puta, you'll be the first in the pit. Diablo's anxious to meet you."

I can see the glee on his face as Sanchez stands and faces the two 4-Aces men. "My Black brothers, this is a day you'll not live to regret. Your life will end long before the sun sets." He doesn't tell them one will live to spread his message of torture and murder. Sanchez is all smiles. "You should appreciate what's about to happen. Let me give you a tiny hint." Taking one of the many stray cats, he walks to the edge of the pit. Diablo barks and jumps at the small animal Sanchez dangles above him. Dropping the cat,

Sanchez steps back. Diablo grips the animal in his jaws and devours it even as it shrieks its death cry. I'm surprised at the amount of blood. As Diablo shakes his feline victim, blood flies from the pit, spraying me. For the first time, I notice the black spatter surrounding the hole. Soon the cat's blood will turn dark red and black as it dries. I gasp as I realize my blood will soon join that of the cat and who knows how many other victims of Sanchez.

The Black men grasp their fate. Fear shows on their faces. One, a light-skinned mulatto, begins to whimper. The other one remains stoic. I won't be here to see it, but Sanchez will choose the weaker man as an example. He'll provide a better show for the audience's enjoyment—or revulsion.

My fear is tempered by the knowledge my death will free me from these evil monsters and unite me with my Lord Jesus. Sanchez orders the handcuffs removed from my wrists. Diablo is in a frenzy. "The girl's the appetizer. You niggas will be the main course."

"Diablo's waiting for you, puta."

I will not give him the pleasure of seeing my fear, nor will I plead for my life. All eyes are on me.

WHOMP-WHOMP, WHOMP-WHOMP, WHOMP, -WHOMP.

The barn shakes. A hush settles over the gathering as Sanchez freezes. Several black-clad figures appear at the fringe of the crowd; their faces are concealed behind dark balaclavas. One throws an object in the direction of Sanchez. He steps back, almost to the pit's edge, while I shut my eyes as if by instinct. I hear a loud explosion followed by a flash of white visible behind the lids of my closed eyes. The screaming begins as I open my eyes. I join the screaming with "Damn you, damn you to hell," as I shove the off-balance Sanchez. He stumbles, shrieks, and falls into the pit—his cries lost in the din.

51

SUNDAY AFTERNOON, THE police officers and federal agents are back in Deputy Chief Windsor's conference room. The dust settled; for the time being. Deputy Chief Windsor has pulled the Task Force back together.

"Well, Officer Navarro, you seem to be the center of attention—again."

"Yes, Ma'am."

"This time, three lives were saved. I won't say innocent because two were far from innocent." After a pause to sip her coffee, she continues, "Sanchez's death will cause an upheaval in Los Scorpios Locos. I believe it has postponed war between them and the 4-Aces. I'm not naive enough to believe fighting won't come. Both gangs have suffered a void at the top. The process to replace the leaders will be violent."

She directs her following comment to the U.S. Marshal. "I have a rough idea of what happened, but please tell us how you managed to get the results you did?"

"It was a success for my agency. We arrested six federal fugitives. One had been running for seven years from charges in California including murder, murder for hire, kidnap, and torture." After a round of polite applause, she continues. "I joined the Task Force late in the game. Unfortunately, I wasn't able to find the time to notify our Mexican associates until the raid began."

The marshal is interrupted by several chuckles and an "oh, darn" from Kowalski.

"My manager was devastated by my failure to follow the proper protocol." She joins in the chuckles. "Our Mexico City office managed to have marshals available to liaison with the Mexican Federal Police. We picked up four of their escapees who had been serving long terms for murder and drug trafficking.

Following polite applause, Hector asks, "What about Teresa Ontiveros, her mother, and daughter? At the ranch, I covered her with a ratty blanket, took her outside, and we talked for a few minutes. Steve Kowalski called me aside. When I turned back, she had disappeared."

"After you told us what she had

experienced and known, I went to the U.S. Attorney before the raid." The U.S. Marshall answers. "The A.G. called the FBI. We agreed the FBI would open a racketeering investigation. As a vital witness, Ontiveros and her family are eligible for the Witness Protection Program. The second the raid began, three teams of marshals went into action, one for each member of the Ontiveros family. The team assigned to Teresa held back a few minutes, allowing you and her to talk."

"I'm glad they're safe, but why wasn't I told?"

"Officer Navarro, our mission is the protection of the witness. Once we accept responsibility, we tell no one until the witness is secure. Teresa and her family are safe. That's all I can tell you."

Deputy Chief Windsor thanks the marshal and points at her swat commander. "Claudia, I understand you were forced to put the dog down. What's the story?"

"Our animal control officers couldn't control or sedate the animal—I shot it."

"Way to go, lieutenant," was shouted and followed by applause. All agreed that the creature had to be put down.

Once Deputy Chief Windsor restored order, she addressed Homeland Security Agent Kennemore. "I have to admit the assets you brought to the table were amazing.

Wouldn't you agree, Claudia?"

Lieutenant Claudia Foss agrees. "Homeland Security asked me to ride with them. I accepted, not for an instant thinking we'd be in a Jayhawk helicopter."

"Neither did I." Deputy Chief Windsor's comment elicits a few "Amens" from around the table.

Agent Butch Kennemore says, "That's why I was late for the last meeting. I was trying to convince the Coast Guard this was an appropriate use of aerial resources. After all, the choppers are designated for law enforcement as part of their mission statement. The Squadron Commander lacked the authority to make the decision. The question wasn't answered until after our last meeting here. The request went all the way to the Secretary of Homeland Security."

Deputy Chief Windsor tilts her head as she says, "You achieved a great deal in a relatively short time."

"Yes, Ma'am. I didn't know at the time, but the Commandant of the Coast Guard ordered a joint Coast Guard, ICE, and local law enforcement "training exercise" mounted. The four choppers were almost to our staging area before the Secretary gave the green light."

"I have to commend you for the out-standing manner in which the training exercise was carried out."

"Thanks, Chief, but I can't take all the credit. Lieutenant Foss's assuming tactical command allowed us to coordinate the efforts, on the run, of several agencies."

Deputy Chief Windsor puts an end to the love fest. "There's enough credit to go around. The addition of helicopters allowed the rapid deployment of integrated swat teams. Their use at the four corners allowed for the containment of over fifty bad guys. No one escaped."

The meeting concludes with comments from Steve Kowalski. "Besides the federal arrests, we apprehended twenty-eight Los Scorpios Locos on various charges." After yet another round of applause, he continues. "We recovered fifty-eight firearms, including a fifty-caliber machine gun. Overall, it was a remarkably successful operation. The only law enforcement casualty was a broken ankle. A Maricopa County SWAT member fell getting out of a chopper. Oh, a bit of irony. We arrested both 4-Aces kidnap victims on warrants."

"Thanks, Steve, you've pretty much covered it. The Chief has something he wants to share with us. Everyone, please hang on for a moment. He's on his way."

With a few minutes to kill, a half dozen conversations break out. Hector is curious about the Jackson murders and his report to Sergeant Collins. "Sarge, have you had a chance to finish reviewing my report and recommendations?"

"I have. It's a good start. We'll talk at the office ..." Collins is interrupted by the arrival of the Chief.

The Chief waves everyone down, "Relax." There's a chorus of greetings as he takes an empty seat at the foot of the table. "I want to add my congratulations to those of Deputy Chief Windsor. We had a front-row seat to the action from the Mobile Command Post. I've never seen a more professional and well-orchestrated action of this size. With seven local, state, and federal agencies thrown together in a matter of hours, success was never certain. You folks beat the odds. You're all to be commended. Please give yourself a round of applause." Once the cheering settles down, the Chief continues. "I spoke to the Commandant of the Coast Guard an hour ago, and he shares my opinion.

"Those of you who know the Maricopa County Sheriff understand how sparse her praise tends to be."

"Stingy would be more like it," someone says.

Even the Chief laughs. "I was on the phone with the sheriff from the scene. She was effusive with her praise." Turning to D.C.

Windsor, "'She did have one complaint, 'Chief, how-in-hell am I supposed to house all those people you arrested?'"

As the meeting breaks up and people leave, D.C. Windsor asks, "Chief, did you have something else you wanted to mention this morning?"

"Yes, Mary, there is. Do you have the items I requested?"

Smiling, she says, "Yes, sir, I do."

The Chief moves to the front of the room and turns to face the group. He asks Sergeant Collins to join him. "Jim, there will be an official ceremony next week." Jim Collins looks confused as D.C. Windsor hands a jewel box to the Chief. "Lieutenant James Collins, you're not in uniform, but I want to pin these beat-up old lieutenant's bars on you. They were my first."

Jim Collins, the department's newest lieutenant, stammers, "Thank you, sir." Pandemonium breaks out as cheers ring out, and his fellow officers crowd around, congratulating Lieutenant Collins.

Once order is restored, the Chief announces, "Please take your seats. I'm not finished. Officer Navarro, step up here, please."

Hector doubts the Chief will transfer or punish him in this setting and does as he's told.

The door at the back of the room opens—

Lieutenant Morales ushers in a woman—
Maria. Hector is confused.

"Officer Navarro, this has been a rough
year for you. You overcame massive issues.
We're all proud of your growth. Sergeant
Kowalski, Lieutenant Collins, and Deputy
Chief Windsor have convinced me you have
earned these." D.C. Windsor opens an
envelope and removes a pair of Sergeant's
Stripes. "Deputy Chief Windsor, would you
care to do the honors?"

D.C. Windsor says, "Thank you, Chief. I
would." She says, "This was my first set of
stripes," as she pins one set on his shirt
sleeve, "Sergeant Navarro."

Once the congratulations are complete,
the Chief says, "Deputy Chief Windsor, do
you have assignments to announce?"

"I do. Lieutenant Collins and Sergeant
Navarro, Monday, you report to Patrol."

"Yes, Ma'am. Thank you." The always-
gruff Jim Collins has tears in his eyes. He'll
claim his eyeballs were sweating.

My God, he is human.

COMING SOON

NEW LIBERTY - *Unfinished Business*

A Hector Miguel Navarro Novel

CHAPTER 1

"TAKE CARE, BE safe, and make a difference." Sergeant Hector Miguel Navarro finished the line-up with his ritual caution. Navarro felt good; two years ago, he came to this patrol crew, a rookie sergeant with enough baggage to start a world cruise.

For Navarro, life was as good as it gets. He and his wife, Maria, had recently celebrated their anniversary with the news that they would be parents. His mother and father's wedding gift, along with the money he had saved for a new Harley-Davidson motorcycle, had been enough for a down payment. The couple bought a fifteen hundred square foot three-bedroom, one and a half bath tract home on Scottsdale's outskirts. It was a paint peeling as-is home but would serve them until the child was born. At the same time, Hector learned how to repair plumbing, remove wallpaper, and the myriad other tasks that fell upon a homeowner's shoulders.

Patrol supervision began a bit on the rough side for Hector. He had spent his first years as a patrol officer in the quietest division in the department. An upper-income area known as The Island is separated from the central part of New Liberty by a dry riverbed. The only way into the neighborhood was a quarter-mile-long two-lane bridge. Crime was rare; most of his calls had involved neighbor disputes and the occasional domestic violence complaint.

Hector placed high on the sergeant's promotional list and was transferred to Anti-Gang Enforcement. The department wanted him to have investigative experience before being promoted. It had been quite an experience. He partnered with David Jones, a Marine combat veteran who suffered from PTSD and alcoholism. Hector learned a great deal about the right and wrong ways of being a police officer and investigator.

Several actions and decisions led to an incident in which Hector's partner killed their sergeant, Bob Tolliver, while under the influence of alcohol. Hector suffers dreams and flashbacks to that tragedy. His dreams are as vivid as that night his fellow officers died. The first dream is for Toliver; he checks his sergeant for signs of life.

"He's gone. He's dead," Hector gasps. Holding Bob Toliver in his arms, his sergeant's bulletproof vest is on the inside of his raid jacket. Looking down, he sees blood on Bob's left side, but not much. There's a small amount on Hector's shirt. In his dreams, he can't wash away the blood that stains his shirt and chest. His thrashing wakes Maria: he's drenched in sweat. She holds him wrapped like a child in her arms until he falls back into a troubled sleep.

Moments after killing Sergeant Toliver, Jones murdered a Black gang leader. Other officers took his duty weapon and placed him in another detective's car. After a few minutes, Hector had gone to the vehicle where Jones was being watched—guarded. He had a nagging feeling that he was missing something.

"I want to talk to Davey."

"Go ahead." An officer says, "we're not stopping you."

"In private."

The officers exchanged glances, shrugged, and walked away.

"Hector, I killed him." Jones sobbed. "I killed him. I killed Bob. They're all saying I was the one who killed him. I fell. My gun went off. I'm so sorry." Jones was weeping and asked Hector for privacy. He stepped away. Within a minute, there's a gunshot—close. Hector spins around as Davey slumps forward—a small pistol falls to the car floor. Hector saw the back of Davey's head gaping open with blood, hair, and brain matter showing in the glare of the parking lot lights. The back window is dark with blood splatter.

Davey's drinking killed three men; I could have prevented it—It's my fault. Hector usually wakes from his dream at this point. After being rescued by Jim Collins with an assignment in homicide, Hector began to heal; occasional flashbacks continued after being promoted to sergeant.

"Maria, I'm not sure I'll be a good patrol sergeant. I've never supervised anyone and look at all the mistakes I made in the gang enforcement unit."

"Honey, you'll do fine. They wouldn't have promoted you if they didn't think you could do the job." Thanks to his wife, Hector regained his composure.

The transition wasn't as bad or as hard as Hector had imagined. For the first month, he was paired with a seasoned sergeant. After every situation they encountered, the two sergeants debriefed the incident. They talked about why decisions were made and alternatives. When Hector didn't know, they spent extra time debriefing the reason for the decision. It didn't take him long to realize he knew the old-timer's answers before the man opened his mouth.

"What happens when something new comes up?" Hector worried.

"You fake it based on your best judgment."

"How long did you fake it?"

"Look, Hector, I still fake it all the time. Our job is in constant flux. When I started here, some things, like missing persons, were so low on the priority list that we didn't always report them. They have become a high priority. You learn from the incidents. And, believe me, you will fuck up some of the calls you make."

"What happens when I fuck up?"

"It depends on how bad you fuck up and the results of your decision. With any luck, most of those wrong calls will be learning experiences."

"I've made bad decisions, and the bosses know that."

"Listen, Hector. We've all made decisions we regret. We can't take them back. I'm sure you've heard this before, but you wouldn't be here if the bosses didn't think you could do this job."

At the end of a month, Hector attended four weeks of Sergeant's Training hosted by the Phoenix Police Department. He was surprised that one speaker was his deputy chief, Mary Windsor. Her topic was incident management. During the presentation, she mentioned Hector's part in the takedown of the Los Scorpios Locos street gang. Hector took some good-natured ribbing from his classmates, like him, all rookie sergeants.

Sergeant training was followed by a few weeks of working with the patrol division's administrative sergeant learning the paperwork. At the next watch change, he met his crew. Hector expected to be with this group of officers for at least four years. After that, he would be moved to a different shift.

"Take care, be safe, and make a difference." Sergeant Hector Miguel Navarro said, finishing his first line-up. Hector knew some sergeants often admonished their teams at the end of the line-up. Hector had never heard these particular phrases strung together. He wrote them down and vowed to close every line-up with these words.

Hector's crew was eight officers, five men and three women. He was with them for two exhilarating years. He made many decisions; fewer were necessary as the officers learned to trust him and knew what his advice would be—Navarro felt good. The officers had been unsure about their new sergeant's credibility and leadership skills. Times change, and his officers are happy with him. They trust Navarro's judgment; he is fair, and he has their backs.

Pulling his rain poncho tight, Hector knew it was time to climb into the patrol sergeant's new Ford Explore. A shout stopped Navarro. "Hey, Hector, you got a visitor." Looking up, the watch commander stood under the porch roof, waving at him. "He's waiting in the breakroom."

"Okay, Boss."

Sitting there in uniform and nursing, a paper cup of lousy coffee, was Hector's mentor and former boss, Lieutenant James "Jim" Collins. Hector hadn't talked to him in months. *What's going on? Jim never visits me at work.*

"What brings you over from my old district for a visit?"

"It sure as hell wasn't this coffee."

After a couple of man hugs and well wishes, they sat and talked sports until, "Okay, Jim, what's going on?"

"Still as suspicious as ever." Both laugh. Neither is suspicious of the other. "You needn't worry. I'll get to the point. Last week Deputy Chief Mary Windsor called me up to the ivory tower. Anyway, the long and short of it is that some moves are happening. The Investigation Captain and the Homicide Lieutenant are retiring at the year's end. D.C. Windsor's former aide, Paul Morales, has been a captain for less than a year and has no investigative experience. He's an excellent administrator. The Chief picked Morales to head up the detective division. Mary wants him to succeed, and so do I. He's a good man. Paul asked me to head up Homicide. The man thinks somehow I'll make him look good."

"*RIGHT.*"

"Don't be a smartass. Remember, I'm a lieutenant, Sergeant Navarro." The friends share a laugh.

"What's that got to do with me?"

"I don't need anyone to make me look good. But I like Maria, and if you take the job, the overtime in Homicide will take care of your kitchen remodel and the nursery. You might even earn enough to start painting the ugliest house on your block—yours."

"How'd you know?"

"Dumbass, your wife, and mine talk a few times a month. If you can, please shut up for a minute. I'll explain why I'm here. One of the homicide sergeants is also retiring. I want you to take her place."

"Not interested. I like my job, and I've got the best crew in patrol."

"Vacancies abound. The homicide team is short a detective, and in my magnificent magnitude, I will allow you to name the replacement."

"My patrol team's not short, and I have eight great cops."

"Look, I need you."

"Sergeants with a lot more experience are available. And, if I say yes, you'll take heat for pulling me in ahead of those more qualified."

"I don't mind the heat, especially with the backing of Deputy Chief Windsor. She agrees you're the right choice."

"Why me?"

"Remember the murder case I gave you the first day in homicide? The old couple from Ernesto's."

"How could I ever forget it? Two youngsters murdered the old couple. The boys, in turn, were killed by DeShawn "The Knife" Galloway on the orders of Jerome "Geronimo" Jones."

"It was filed inactive the day you and I left the unit. Come back, and you and your people will solve it—you'll get all the assets you need. How's that for incentive?"

"I'll consider it, but only if you're right, and I get to pick the detective." Hector had decided to take the transfer. He loved investigations and could use the extra income but would play hard to get. He had two detectives in mind. One was in Missing Persons, and the other was in his old unit, Anti-Gang Enforcement. Neither would ever leave a stone unturned.

"You have someone in mind?"

"I do, but I need a guarantee that whoever I select will get the job. No half-ass promises. I know how that works."

Collins assured Hector the choice would be his, but the lieutenant would confirm it with Deputy Chief Windsor and call him the following day. Laughing, he couldn't help himself, "Well, Sergeant Navarro, I hope you enjoy waddling around town in your rain suit for the rest of your shift."

Hector didn't have to wait to decide— Jim's word was good.

About the Author

An enrolled descendant of the Karuk Tribe of California, George Cramer enjoyed forty-year investigative career in law enforcement and private and corporate investigations.

He attended the Institute of American Indian Arts, earning a Master of Fine Arts / Creative Writing – Fiction. A BA-History from California State University-Hayward preceded this graduate degree. After the MFA, he attended Las Positas College, earning an AA in English.

As a licensed Private Investigator, George conducted thousands of investigations throughout the Americas and Asia. He kept his investigative skills honed by volunteering as a Missing Person investigator with a Northern California police department.

George's debut novel, *The Mona Lisa Sisters*, was released in 2020, followed by, *Robbers and Cops in 2022*.

He lives in Northern California with his wife of forty years.

Thank you for reading my book!

Please don't forget to review it: http://www.Amazon.com/review/create-review?